P9-CLR-051

A few minutes later, the train halted

As the heavy door swung open, Cahill fumbled in his vest pocket for a card. "Thank you," he said. "Nice to have met you, Mr.—?"

"Belasko. Mike Belasko."

"Mr. Belasko. I gather from your accent that you are a transatlantic visitor. You must come to one of my séances while you are here. Take my card, this is the address where you will find me during my stay in this country."

Bolan took the card. Cahill smiled and stepped down to the platform. Bolan moved to hand him the remaining suitcase. At the rear of the train a whistle sounded.

Suddenly in midstep, Cahill's knees buckled and he dropped to the ground. Before anyone could get to him, he rolled over, his back arched, and his body started to shudder.

At first Bolan suspected an extreme form of Cahill's trance routine. Then, as the convulsions eased and the face went slack, he saw that the guy was dead.

Bolan bent over him, and bit back an exclamation of astonishment. In the center of the medium's forehead, surrounded by an area of skin that was already turning blue, a tiny feathered dart was lodged.

Accolades for America's greatest hero Mack Bolan

"Very, very action-oriented.... Highly successful, today's hottest books for men."
—*The New York Times*

"Anyone who stands against the civilized forces of truth and justice will sooner or later have to face the piercing blue eyes and cold Beretta steel of Mack Bolan, the lean, mean nightstalker, civilization's avenging angel."
—*San Francisco Examiner*

"Mack Bolan is a star. The Executioner is a beacon of hope for people with a sense of American justice."
—*Las Vegas Review Journal*

"In the beginning there was the Executioner—a publishing phenomenon. Mack Bolan remains a spiritual godfather to those who have followed."
—*San Jose Mercury News*

"Mack Bolan stabs right through the heart of the frustration and hopelessness the average person feels about crime running rampant in the streets."
—*Dallas Times Herald*

DON PENDLETON's
MACK BOLAN.

HARDLINE

A GOLD EAGLE BOOK FROM
W●RLDWIDE.

TORONTO • NEW YORK • LONDON • PARIS
AMSTERDAM • STOCKHOLM • HAMBURG
ATHENS • MILAN • TOKYO • SYDNEY

First edition December 1991

ISBN 0-373-61425-X

Special thanks and acknowledgment to
Peter Leslie for his contribution to this work.

HARDLINE

Copyright © 1991 by Worldwide Library.
Philippine copyright 1991. Australian copyright 1991.

All rights reserved. Except for use in any review, the
reproduction or utilization of this work in whole or in part
in any form by any electronic, mechanical or other means,
now known or hereafter invented, including xerography,
photocopying and recording, or in any information storage
or retrieval system, is forbidden without the permission
of the publisher, Worldwide Library, 225 Duncan Mill Road,
Don Mills, Ontario, Canada M3B 3K9.

All the characters in this book have no existence outside the
imagination of the author and have no relation whatsoever to
anyone bearing the same name or names. They are not even
distantly inspired by any individual known or unknown to the
author, and all the incidents are pure invention.

® and TM are trademarks of the publisher. MACK BOLAN,
GOLD EAGLE, WORLDWIDE LIBRARY and the GLOBE DESIGN
are registered in the United States Patent and Trademark Office and
in other countries.

Printed in U.S.A.

We have unmistakable proof that throughout all past time, there has been a ceaseless devouring of the weak by the strong.

—Hubert Spencer
1820–1903

It has never ceased to amaze me the measures some men will take to exploit the weaknesses of their fellow man. A day of reckoning is coming. Believe it.

—Mack Bolan

PROLOGUE

The man with the long-barreled sniping rifle shaded his eyes against the sun's glare as the giant aircraft touched down and slid to a halt at the end of the desert runway. He raised his head to stare out over the rock at a collection of concrete huts that flanked a wide apron halfway along the runway. Three civilians stood among the group of high-ranking Army officers waiting beside an armored command car parked outside the largest hut. The range, the rifleman estimated, was a shade over five hundred yards—well within the gun's capability but tough enough for a dead-accurate grouping under noonday desert conditions. The whole operation depended on split-second timing.

The huge jet was a B-2 Stealth bomber, the doomsday ship designed to pulverize command centers after an initial nuclear exchange and smash any second-strike missiles before they could be launched.

The marksman knew all about the B-2. He knew its forty-thousand-pound payload could blast bunkers buried too deep to be damaged by missile-based warheads. He knew the ship could fly unchallenged through the world's most sophisticated radar defenses because its "signature," or radar cross-section, was no bigger than that formed by a large bird.

But he wasn't concerned with the B-2 itself. Not this time. He had no interest in the pilot or copilot. His concentration centered on the civilians standing with the Pentagon top brass.

One of them was tied in with design modifications to the two hundred onboard computers that were alerted by airborne enemy radar and automatically plotted a course that steered the plane clear of them. The other two were the gunman's targets.

The Stealth bomber had taxied as far as the apron. The enormously wide wafer wings swung through ninety degrees, the eight wheels of the low-slung undercart stopped rolling, and a crewman flagged the bomber to a dead stop facing the huts.

Lying flat along an upward-slanting outlier, the gunner rested his elbows on the scorching rock slope and raised the rifle until the butt plate tucked into his left shoulder. He extended his right arm to steady the barrel, the fingers of his left hand placed alongside the trigger guard. The modifications to sniperscope and safety demanded by his southpaw stance had been carried out in his own workshop.

He lowered his head, tilting it sideways so that he could squint through the scope's rubber eyepiece. A lens hood on the far end of the sight hid the curved glass from the rays of the sun and minimized the risk of a giveaway reflection.

His targets were partly obscured by the military, but he reckoned they'd be vulnerable when the officers walked out to greet the bomber crew as they disembarked from the jeep that had rushed out to get them.

Shifting the rifle so that it rested more comfortably in his grip, he checked the target duo—a slightly over-weight man wearing a rumpled brown suit and a tough-looking guy, as tall as the rifleman himself, dressed in jeans and a black roll-neck sweater.

The pilot and copilot were climbing out of the jeep. The group of watchers eddied and split as several officers strode forward. For a moment the three civilians were on their own.

The sniper held his breath; it was now or never.

The report from the center-fire Magnum cartridge was colossal, slamming the eight-pound rifle back against the assassin's shoulder with a breech pressure of twenty tons to the square inch. A thin film of oil coating the exquisitely machined breech mechanism gleamed momentarily as he worked the bolt to slide in a second round. Easing his position, he fired again.

The tall man in the black sweater plummeted to the ground as abruptly as a puppet whose strings had been cut. The guy in the rumpled suit stumbled, hugging himself with both arms, fell onto one knee, then rolled over and lay still.

A sudden gust of hot wind stirred the hairs on the back of the killer's head. Tumbleweed, somersaulting along the desert floor, rose over the edge of the out-cropping and briefly obscured his vision as he squeezed the trigger a third time.

He cursed. The telescopic sight showed him a scene of confusion on the apron—like a disturbed anthill, the circle of asphalt framed by the scope was filled with figures rushing in every direction. In the distance a siren wailed. One of the soldiers was on the ground now, and the man in the rumpled suit, supported on both sides, was clambering to his feet.

But the assassin's schedule allowed no reload, no second kick at the can. Crouching, he slung the gun across his back. Covered by the rock, he dropped onto his hands and knees and started the four-hundred-yard crawl to the perimeter.

The sun beat down on his back; sweat collected between his shoulder blades and trickled down his ribs; grains of sand worked their way into his pants and tennis shoes, chafing the skin. His left shoulder was already sore and stiff from the rifle's mule-kick recoil.

He'd made no more than half the distance when he heard the shouts—a stentorian voice through a bullhorn several hundred yards to his left; a much fainter reply, away on the other side. Somewhere an engine was gunned; the wind carried the scrabble of heavy-duty tires over the stony surface of the desert.

Panting, the killer increased his pace. Once over the wire it should be plain sailing. The Jeep Cherokee hidden in the arroyo was fitted with Nevada plates; the gun would be buried; the chopper was less than ten miles away.

Once over the wire... But he had to be there at exactly the right moment. Two minutes had been allowed for the crossing, and the patrol wasn't going to wait.

The whine of gears was suddenly close. A jeep bearing armed military personnel skidded to a halt between him and the perimeter.

Shooting a glance at his wristwatch, the hunted man stifled a groan. Eighty, ninety yards to go, and only three minutes to make it. Out beyond the fence he could already hear the engine of the approaching patrol truck.

He lay flat on his face beneath the sagebrush, his cheek pressed into the hot sand, willing the jeep to disappear.

CHAPTER ONE

Mack Bolan recovered consciousness thirty minutes after the shots were fired. It had been a narrow escape—the 150-grain hollowpoint had barely grazed his temple, but he'd been felled as if he'd been struck by a sledgehammer.

Now, lying on a gurney in the base's emergency first-aid station, he opened his eyes and stared at the face of the uniformed doctor who was leaning over him.

"Who fired on us?"

"Terrorist."

"I thought security was pretty tight on this base."

"A hitter with a high-powered rifle was staked out among the rocks at the far end of the runway. You were lucky. He only creased you."

"And the other two?"

"Colonel Anscombe is dead. He was hit between the eyes and died instantly. Your colleague—"

"Brognola. He was hit, too?"

"He'll be okay. The bullet passed between his arm and his body. He got a grazed rib and a flesh wound in the biceps. Painful, and he lost some blood, but there's nothing a shot of rye and a couple of days rest won't cure."

"Where is he?"

"In the next room."

Mack Bolan, a.k.a. the Executioner, sat up and swung his feet to the floor, suppressing a grunt of pain as the throbbing in his head crescendoed. "Did they get the guy?"

The doctor nodded. "Picked him up by the perimeter fence. But the son of a bitch bit on a cyanide pill before they could bring him in."

Bolan raised an eyebrow, involuntarily lifting a hand to touch the bandage taped to his forehead as the pain flamed through his temple once more. "Very professional," he commented as he opened the door and strode into the next room.

Hal Brognola's features were creased into a ferocious scowl. He was sitting cross-legged on a bed, wearing a white hospital gown and chewing on an unlit cigar. His left arm was in a sling.

"When we came out to this little shindig, the last thing I expected was to come under fire," the big Fed complained. "Who'd send a hit man a million miles from nowhere when everything happening out here is strictly routine?"

"You tell me," the Executioner replied. "This place was supposed to be secure." The base—little more than a strip used by the Air Force for top-secret test flights—in fact, had a priority rating. The two men, part of a group evaluating modifications to the B-2 Stealth's onboard computer system, were there on a watching brief. "You figure the hitter was gunning for us?"

"Yeah, I do. Like you said, the guy was a pro. And we *were* hit. An inch or two either way, and it'd have been my heart and your head. I don't read that as an accident. Colonel Anscombe was head of security here. That *could* have been a mistake. What would be the point in wasting the man when the gunman was already inside the perimeter?''

"What would be the point in wasting us? At this time, in this place?"

Brognola sighed. He was head of the Administration's Sensitive Operations Group, working out of Justice, and had the ear of the President. He'd been the Executioner's sole link with the Oval Office, back in the days when Bolan himself directed an antiterrorist operation secretly funded by Uncle Sam. Now the big guy was out on his own, a solo campaigner battling the dark forces that threatened to cripple the world. But Brognola could rely on him, if the cause was just, for covert assistance in those cases too hot for the regular intelligence agencies to handle. "Face it," Brognola said with a wry grin. "Some people would pay well to have us eliminated anytime, anyplace."

"You answered your own question, Hal. For my money, just the same, there has to be a link."

"You figure the attempt for some kind of a block relating to the Stealth?"

"Believe it. Look, if it was just us, period, they could set it up easier in a dozen places. If someone goes to the trouble of sending an assassin all the way out here, there's got to be a connection."

"We're here checking out the new hardware on the B-2. Someone thinks we're checking too hard. Is that what you're telling me?"

"That's exactly what I'm telling you."

The big Fed removed the cigar from his mouth, inspected the chewed end, then placed the stogie carefully in an ashtray. Checking the hardware was perhaps putting it too strongly. There had been a whisper, no more than the vaguest hint from Her Gracious Majesty's intelligence services, that all might not be well with the British company manufacturing and supplying the Mark II Stealth bomber's modified equipment. Bolan and Brognola had been roped in as unofficial observers while it was tested.

"The stuff works well, and it's an all-round improvement," Brognola said thoughtfully. "Hanson and the ship's captain both confirm that. Right across the board."

Hugh Hanson was the third civilian on the base. He was an engineer, an electronics wizard who represented the manufacturers. He knew nothing of the reasons behind Brognola's presence on the base.

"There was no attempt to hit him," Bolan mused. "The way I see that, someone's trying to stop us from finding out something—but it's not concerned with the functioning of the new hardware. Otherwise they'd have dusted him, too."

He stared out the window. In back of the concrete huts stood a prototype of HOTOL—a revolutionary horizontal takeoff and landing satellite launcher. The vehicle, which looked like a huge slug with embryo wings, was a reusable shuttle that could fly off an ordinary runway like a conventional plane. Components of its single-stage propulsion system, which used oxygen from the air as fuel in the initial stages of blast-off, had also been designed by the British. Preliminary tests had shown the installation to be faultless.

"Which makes me think," Bolan said, "that the problem lies with the manufacturing company itself and not the hardware it delivers."

"I'll buy that," Brognola said. "Whoever 'they' are."

"No lead from the hitter?"

"Uh-uh. There was nothing on the body. No papers, no name tags, no maker's labels, nothing."

"And the gun?"

"That's something else. A Model 561 Husqvarna Magnum. Handcrafted, a real beaut. There should be records, but it'll take time. And who's to say how many times it's changed hands illegally?"

"A real pro."

"You can say that again. So...big-time material, which means we have to return to the source if we want to hit pay dirt."

"You had something in mind?"

Brognola leaned forward to pick up his cigar, wincing as the movement disturbed his wounded arm. He cursed, then suddenly grinned. "Striker, it's time you took a vacation. They tell me the west of England's just lovely this time of year. You want to head across the big pond?"

"I'll take a look at the body first," the Executioner said. "Just in case it's someone I know."

CHAPTER TWO

The man in the corner seat began to behave strangely as soon as the train emerged from the tunnel beyond Kembleford railroad station. His head sank back against the seat, and his eyes rolled up so that only two slits of grayish-white showed between his half-closed lids. At the same time his breathing became deep and erratic, and his fingers started to scrabble at the knees of the fawn twill pants he wore.

Mack Bolan dragged his gaze from the passing scenery and stared. The man had seemed normal a few minutes earlier. There was nobody else in the compartment, and they'd been talking in a desultory way as chance acquaintances often did. As the conversation had waned, the stranger had taken refuge behind a newspaper and the Executioner had turned to admire the landscape. Now, like it or not, he was becoming involved again.

The man's seamed brown face had paled to an unhealthy gray. It looked as if he'd become ill.

Abruptly the stranger sat bolt upright, small wheezing sounds emerging from between his tightly stretched lips. Bolan figured he'd have to call for help.

He half rose from his seat, intent on pulling the emergency cord before going to the man's aid. It was then that the voice materialized.

Instead of the reedy tenor in which the stranger had been speaking, a deep, resonant bass issued from his mouth.

And the words were in German.

Bolan sank back into his seat, perplexed. He decided to wait it out.

After several minutes the voice stopped, the man's breathing became more regular and his hands ceased to flutter. He finally opened his eyes.

"Are you okay?" Bolan asked.

"Okay? Why wouldn't I be? Of course I'm okay." The man sounded almost aggrieved.

"I thought you were having some sort of attack."

"Attack? You mean when I dozed off just now?"

"Yeah."

"Head back against the seat? Was that it? Fingers drumming? Eyes turned up, that sort of thing?"

Bolan nodded. "That and the voice."

"Voice? What voice? What do you mean?"

"A very deep voice, speaking in German."

"Ah!" The puzzlement faded from the stranger's face. He nodded briskly, a man whose suspicions were confirmed. "That would have been the Herr Doktor Frodenborg."

"Doktor Frodenborg?"

"One of my guides. He died in 1872. A very sound diagnostician. Must have gone into a trance without realizing it. Damn awkward for other folks if they're not expecting it. I'm very sorry, sir.''

"No problem," Bolan said. "Would you describe yourself as a medium?''

"Not *a* medium. I'm Hanslip Cahill. You have perhaps heard of me?''

Bolan shook his head. "Afraid not.''

"Never mind," Cahill said tolerantly. "I've worked mostly in Australia and South America. Understandable, I suppose. Although I should have thought that a newspaperman...''

Bolan narrowed his eyes. He was using his Mike Belasko alias while he was in Britain, and his ID described him as a foreign correspondent. "How did you know I was a writer?''

"Did I say that?" Cahill chuckled. "The good *doktor* must still be around!''

"What brings *you* around, Cahill?" Bolan asked. "Why are you in England if you customarily work on the other side of the world?''

"There's a world congress of spiritualists in Exeter next week, but right now I'm on my way to see Sir Simon Joliffe.''

"The plastics tycoon?" Bolan hid his surprise. The baronet was boss of Universal Plastics International, the synthetics giant that manufactured everything from fiberglass powerboat hulls to rubber ducks, from astronauts' space suits to artificial flowers—and certain kinds of electronic hardware for advanced aviation projects, such as the B-2 Stealth bomber and the

HOTOL prototype being evaluated by the U.S. Air Force.

UPI, in fact, was the electronics corporation that the Executioner was in Britain to check out. Coincidence? Probably. But Bolan decided to take a little more interest in his fellow traveler.

"That's him," the self-styled medium was saying. "My word, he's a real enthusiast, that one! A man with a truly passionate interest in the other side."

"Really. You know him well?" Bolan *was* interested. Joliffe was known as the most difficult industrialist in Europe to interview. He was old, he was shy and he hated publicity. As one of the richest businessmen in the world, he was the despair of the media.

"Know him well?" Cahill echoed. "Never set eyes on the fellow. But he's having a weekend party at his country estate, and he asked me to come down and take part in some series of experimental séances he's organized."

"Yeah, I once read about the place," Bolan said truthfully. "At Peverill-St. Mary, isn't it? One of those ultramodern steel-and-glass palaces with lily ponds in the parlor, right?"

"It was designed by Oskar Mikkonen, yes. The old man manages to mention the fact in every letter. Must be a dreadfully vain old bird."

"Could be. Maybe with all that money you have to keep reassuring yourself you're getting good value."

A few minutes later the train slowed. Cahill rose to his feet and lifted down from the rack a pair of matched hide suitcases initialed in gold. The coach halted at a country station flanked by grassy slopes on which the name Peverill was spelled out in white-washed stones.

Bolan leaned over to thumb back the sliding door catch while the medium edged between the seats with his cases. As the heavy door swung open, Cahill lowered one and fumbled in his vest pocket for a card. "Thank you," he said. "Nice to have met you, Mr.....?"

"Belasko. Mike Belasko."

"Mr. Belasko. I gather from your accent that you're a transatlantic visitor. You must come to one of my séances while you're here. Take my card. The address will find me throughout my own stay in this country."

Bolan took the card. Doors were slamming down the length of the train. "Thanks."

Cahill smiled and stepped down to the footboard, flicking his free hand at his face as if he were brushing away a fly. Bolan moved to hand him the remaining case.

All at once the medium wasn't there.

In midstep he buckled at the knee and dropped like a stone to the rainswept platform. With frightening clarity, like an engineer editing tapes in a recording studio, Bolan heard each separate sound as the man fell—the clatter of his feet, the dull thump of the suitcase hitting the wet asphalt, a smothered exclamation from a woman outside. And then the scene shifted into top gear—suddenly people were running up from all sides.

The train jerked into motion. The motorman, unaware of the drama, was moving off in obedience to the conductor's whistle.

Bolan grabbed his own small overnight case and Cahill's second bag, and jumped down to the platform. The medium was sprawled on his face. Before anyone could get to him he rolled over, his lips snarled back in a hideous grimace, arching his back until only his head and his heels were on the ground. Then he subsided, his body quivering, his heels drumming.

At first Bolan suspected some more extreme manifestation of Cahill's trance routine. Then, as the convulsions eased and the face went slack, he saw that the man was dead.

Baffled, Bolan bent over him. In the center of the medium's forehead, surrounded by an area of puffy skin that was already cyanosed, was a tiny feathered dart.

CHAPTER THREE

The murder weapon was only a quarter of an inch long. The tuft of green, black and electric-blue feathers could have come from a miniature tropical bird. To Bolan that could only mean one thing, especially since the dead man had said he worked in South America— Cahill had been killed by a poisoned dart puffed from a blowpipe.

But poisoned darts and blowpipes belonged in kids' storybooks, in the cartoon-strip world. Had a killer from South America stalked his victim all the way to England? Who would want to kill a man who seemed no more than a harmless crank? And how would they have known the medium would be on this particular train, heading for this particular station? Most puzzling of all was why someone would kill him in such a bizarre way.

Bolan glanced rapidly around him. There were a dozen places from which the killer could have sent the tiny missile on its deadly journey unobserved. The deserted waiting room, the baggage check, the window of the washroom, a space in back of a stack of livestock crates, an empty compartment in a local railcar waiting in a bay on the far side of the platform—from any of them he could have drifted safely back among the

crowd, or even been halfway out of the station, before
Cahill hit the ground. A blowpipe didn't have to be five
feet long. An expert could be lethally accurate over
twenty or thirty feet with a tube no bigger than a child's
peashooter.

The rain had stopped, and the railroad station was
in chaos. The train, ignoring further blasts from the
conductor's whistle, had pulled away without him. As
the untenanted caboose vanished around a curve in the
track, passengers swarmed out of the railcar and
crowded excitedly around the dead man. The body had
already been moved—three men and two women who
had just left the train carried it to a wooden seat before the conductor ran up to say it had better be left
where it was until the police had been called. Several
others loosened Cahill's collar, felt his wrist and listened at his chest.

Bolan stood on the fringe of the crowd, waiting for
someone to ask for names and addresses. Nobody on
the platform seemed to realize that he had shared a
compartment with the dead man.

"Very rum, as the Brits might say, don't you think?"

The drawled voice, behind the Executioner and a
little to his right, belonged to an American. Bolan
turned slowly, knowing that he'd know the speaker.

Check. A lean-faced man in his forties, as tall as the
Executioner but thinner, with shrewd gray eyes. A cigarette drooped from one corner of his mouth.

It was Jason Mettner II, onetime crime reporter, now
ace foreign correspondent for the Chicago *Globe*.
Chance had thrown him and Bolan together in several

of the warrior's riskier exploits. In one or two the newspaperman had been an unwilling accomplice—on the promise of an exclusive story when the curtain rang down.

"Mettner! What are you doing here? As far as I know, there's nothing very newsworthy going on at Peverill-St. Mary."

"No, but there's terrorism, right?" Mettner jerked his head toward the crowd around Cahill's body.

"You're not telling me you got a tip-off, are you?"

"Uh-uh. Like you, I just got off the train. Also, like you, I guess I'm on the trail of old man Joliffe."

"How do you know that?" Bolan demanded. "Nobody even knows I'm in the country."

The newspaperman shrugged. "We have our sources. In any case, there's speculation over UPI's plans in, quote, financial circles. End of quote."

Bolan was about to reply when he heard another voice behind him.

"Mr. Cahill?"

The name was repeated twice before he realized it was addressed to him. He swung around. A chauffeur in a maroon-colored uniform was standing at his elbow.

"Mr. Cahill?" the man said for the fourth time. "Sir Simon instructed me to meet you and convey you to the manor, sir."

Following the direction of the man's glance, Bolan saw that he was still holding the suitcase he'd grabbed as the train had left—the hide suitcase stamped with the initials H.C. Because he was holding it, the chauffeur had assumed he owned it.

"Allow me, sir." The man took the bag from him and walked over to the platform edge to pick up its mate. Bolan opened his mouth to correct the mistake, then hesitated.

The uniformed driver hadn't deigned to look at the body stretched out on the bench. It was clear from the haughty expression on his face that he considered folks who had the vulgarity to be taken ill in public beneath contempt. In any case, he'd have no idea what Hanslip Cahill looked like—nor, according to the medium himself, could Joliffe or his houseguests, since Cahill had always worked on the other side of the world.

Bolan was toying with an idea. What if he allowed the mistake to remain uncorrected, just long enough to check out Joliffe from the inside? If he went to the mansion as Cahill, direct contact with the UPI boss would give him a far better lead than any painstaking legwork.

"If you're ready, Mr. Cahill," the chauffeur murmured politely.

The warrior made a snap decision. "Why, certainly," he said, tucking his own overnight case more firmly under his arm. "How far do we have to drive?"

Squinting one eye to keep out the smoke spiraling from the tip of his cigarette, Jason Mettner watched them go with a quizzical smile.

CHAPTER FOUR

Peverill-St. Mary was a single street of thatched cottages with a small Norman church at one end and a village green, complete with pub and duckpond, at the other. The village was more than one mile from the station, halfway between the railroad and Sir Simon Joliffe's mansion.

Once a Tudor manor house, Joliffe Hall had been torn apart and remodeled in the most severe Finnish fashion behind its ancient stone facade. The huge entrance gates stood at the head of a steep wooded valley; beyond them a driveway curled through plantations of beech and birch before crossing a stretch of parkland bordered by white fencing. The house was built on a knoll beyond this, and Mack Bolan took in flowered formal gardens and a balustrade decorated with classical figures before the silver Rolls-Royce glided through an archway into old-fashioned stables surmounted by a clock tower.

In the back of the hall he saw a pastoral landscape at whose horizon hills swelled against the evening sky. It was a very English scene—about as far from poisoned darts and postdoomsday bombers as you could get, he thought as he followed the chauffeur inside.

The old manor house was a protected building, so Joliffe had been unable to alter the massive, crenellated outer walls, but once past the heavy oak and wrought-iron doors the interior opened out like the departure lounge of an airline terminal. A gray-haired butler took the baggage from the chauffeur and led Bolan up a spiral stainless-steel staircase to the third floor. "The valet will be with you in just a moment, sir, to assist with the unpacking," he intoned as he placed the two cases and Bolan's own carryall on a stand inside the bedroom door.

"Thanks."

"Thank you, sir. Dinner will be informal tonight, and Sir Simon will be receiving guests over sherry in thirty minutes' time. That will be in the library, sir. To your right at the foot of the stairway."

Bolan turned to Cahill's suitcases as soon as the butler had shut the door. He had to check before the valet appeared. The dead medium had been almost his own height but much plumper, and he thought Cahill's clothes would be conspicuously different from the casual gear in his own case.

He raised the lid of the unlocked case and began sorting through the contents. Most of the stuff would pass, although it was very different from the Executioner's ready-to-wear threads. But it was a small mercy that dinner wasn't formal—Cahill's voluminous evening clothes would have hung absurdly on the Executioner's leaner, muscled frame.

He closed the cases and double-locked his carryall. There were things below the false bottom that he didn't want anyone messing with—such as a compact Beretta 93-R automatic with spare ammunition and a quick-draw shoulder rig, a leather ankle sheath carrying a short-bladed throwing knife and a wire garrote, among other tools of his clandestine trade. He walked into the bathroom and turned on the shower.

When he emerged, briskly towelling his battle-scarred torso fifteen minutes later, the valet had been there, and Cahill's clothes were neatly stowed on the sliding trays and hangers incorporated in the Scandi-navian-style closets lining one wall. Bolan donned his clothes and prepared to meet his host.

Musing about the situation, he almost collided with a heavyset man coming out of the adjoining suite.

"Oh, excuse me, please!" The guy had crimped sil-ver hair, a fringe beard and tiny red veins webbing his blade of a nose. "You must be Dr. Cahill from South America," he said. "Permit me to introduce myself. Konrad Vanderlee, from Heemstede, Holland."

Bolan shook hands. "Are you, too, a medium?"

"I'm not a practitioner, no." The Dutchman's voice was guttural, but his English was accentless. "I be-lieve I'm what the newspapers term an industrialist ty-coon. Joliffe and I have business interests in common, but we also share an amateur's enthusiasm for the oc-cult. We look forward with excitement to your dem-onstration tomorrow."

Bolan cleared his throat. "I hope you won't be dis-appointed."

He was in deep water here. What could he be sched-uled to come up with the following day? Cahill had mentioned experimental séances. Was he slated to kick off the series?

Whatever, the Executioner would be long gone before then. He just hoped he could evade questions enough to fake his way through dinner. But it would have been a help if he could have made it to a library first and looked up some kind of reference book on Cahill and his scene.

Twenty people stood chattering among the book-filled cubes of Joliffe's own ultramodern library. There would be plenty of stuff there, Bolan was sure. He wished he could have made it for another hour solo before the party. Right now it was essential to check out anyone who might have known the real Hanslip Cahill.

Bolan recognized the host at once—a skinny old man with fierce blue eyes beneath craggy brows. He was holding court in a far corner of the big low-ceilinged room. Bolan plucked a glass of sherry from a tray carried by a passing waiter and prowled warily on the outskirts of the gathering.

He'd rarely felt less at home. About one-third of the guests were women, mostly middle-aged, wearing expensive, jeweled designer clothes and styled blue-rinse hair. On average the men were older, with the groomed, pink-faced look that testified to the daily application of hot towels and a private barber.

"My dear fellow!" Vanderlee was at his side. "You met our host already? No? Then you must allow me to repair the omission!" Seizing the Executioner's arm,

Vanderlee piloted him toward the select group in the corner.

"Cahill?" Joliffe exclaimed, grasping Bolan's hand in both his own withered claws. "My goodness, I'm so happy you made it. I have followed your splendid career in Bahia and São Paulo with great interest. We're all looking forward to your manifestation tomorrow night. I'm sure it will be fascinating." The man's voice was as dry as the rustle of wind over dead leaves, but there was a life, a fire, a fanaticism almost, in his eyes, which spoke of huge inner reserves of energy. Bolan could sense at once the dynamism that had boosted Joliffe to the top of the industrialist charts.

"You're younger than I expected," Joliffe said. "And somehow more...well, vital. But then, why should I expect anything when you, like myself, have rigorously refused press interviews and photographers all your professional life?"

A younger, slack-mouthed man with smooth dark hair sidled up to the Executioner. "One does so hope," he said, "that you'll find everything you need in one's little lecture room below stairs. One would so appreciate any requests for special equipment in plenty of time."

"This is Rick Salter," Joliffe explained. "He's organizing our séances in a special info theater we have next to the ballroom, down in the basement. Rick will lay on anything you want in the way of, well, props and so on. What exactly do you need for your demonstration?"

"Er, a carafe of plain water," Bolan improvised wildly. "Three note pads with soft lead pencils. And ordinary chairs around a heavy table—oak, if possible."

"One does so sense the professional touch," Salter said.

"But surely you *expect* Dr. Cahill to be professional?" a thin man with a blond crew cut asked. "I thought everyone knew that only these amateur mediums have to have accessories to bolster them up—toy trumpets, Ouija boards and all that paraphernalia." He turned toward Bolan, a German accent becoming more noticeable as he grew excited. "Tell me, Doctor, which of the famous guides do you think we'll meet tomorrow? The Navaho Indian? The nineteeth-century scientist? Or that old Burmese priest who sometimes speaks through you?"

"I'd put my money on the Herr Doktor Frodenborg," Bolan replied, recalling the conversation in the train. He was spared the necessity of further comment because Joliffe seized his arm.

"By George, Cahill," he exclaimed, "here's a piece of luck for you! Nothing like a friend far from home, eh? I didn't know for sure if she'd make it, but there's Cleo Duhamel!" He piloted the Executioner toward a tall, fleshy woman with a slender waist and generous breasts, who was standing with a group of male admirers near the door. Bolan had time to register hooded eyes, a sensual mouth and cleavage bulging from a midnight-blue velvet dress before his host enthused, "You know Cleo, of course. As one of your foremost disciples back in Brazil, it would be rum if you didn't, eh? She's been to dozens of your meetings, but she's here this week as the founder of her own Bahia circle." He raised his voice. "Cleo! Spare me a moment. I want you to meet an old friend."

Bolan froze.

"You remember Dr. Hanslip Cahill, of course?"

Cleo Duhamel turned, her eyes fixed on his face. "But, naturally I remember him. What a pleasure to see you again, Dr. Cahill."

CHAPTER FIVE

Half the houseguests at Joliffe Hall looked more like socialites out for a good time than serious researchers into the occult. Bolan, himself no reader of the gossip columns, nevertheless recognized two jet-set couples whose private lives made international headlines. Among the fun-seekers and academics, Joliffe's own intimates stood out as doubly bizarre. They included Vanderlee, Rick Salter, a huge Oriental with a completely bald head, two women wearing black leather trouser suits and the crew-cut German, whose name, Bolan learned, was Wolfgang Kleist.

The Executioner was seated between a sociology professor and an elderly woman with pale eyes and wispy hair who was apparently a clairvoyant from Scotland. But while he exchanged meaningless small talk with them, his eyes wandered constantly to the top of the long refectory table, where Cleo Duhamel was placed at the host's right hand.

The butler had announced dinner immediately after her startling confirmation of Bolan's fake identity, and he'd been looking for reasons ever since. For starters, it didn't seem to make sense. Because if she really had been a member of Cahill's home circle or whatever it was in Brazil, then she must have known the Executioner was a phony.

So why not say so?

Was it because she didn't, in fact, have any previous knowledge of the medium, that she was an impostor herself and couldn't know Bolan wasn't the genuine article?

Negative.

Cleo Duhamel was clearly well-known to most of the other guests.

Okay, so she *was* Cleo Duhamel—but a Cleo Duhamel who had never been to South America and therefore never seen Cahill in the flesh? Was she simply claiming an experience she'd never had?

Unlikely. The real Cahill would have easily caught on once they started talking. Also, most of the guests were familiar themselves with her South American experiences, and it was too much to imagine that half the house party would be part of a conspiracy to underwrite one impostor in front of another.

No, only one explanation held water. Cleo Duhamel knew damn well he wasn't Hanslip Cahill, but for reasons of her own she'd decided not to denounce him.

Why? The answer would have to come later. Right now Bolan's original hunch, fueled by natural curiosity, was telling him loud and clear to stick around and disinter at least one of the secrets of Joliffe Hall.

"Miss Duhamel certainly is beautiful," he said to the clairvoyant, watching covertly to see if any spark of feminine jealousy illuminated her dreamy eyes.

"Who? Cleo?" The woman seemed surprised to hear any reference to looks at all, but there was no trace of resentment in her voice. "Well, yes, I suppose she is, when you come to think of it."

Was it his imagination, or did Bolan detect a trace of "if you like that kind of thing" in the reply?

"Our host seems most impressed, anyway."

"Simon? Oh, but he would be, in the circumstances, wouldn't he?"

"In the circumstances?" Bolan was puzzled.

"I mean, in view of his passion—I could almost say his *mania*—for those two cults. And, of course, her own background. Well, naturally he's interested."

"You mean his passion for the occult in general?" Bolan had no idea how much he was supposed to know about the old man's private life. So it was impossible to gauge what questions would be acceptable from him—and what would be a tip-off that he wasn't Cahill.

"Yes, yes, of course," the woman said irritably. "But we all have that, don't we? Otherwise we wouldn't be here. I mean, in particular the way he engrosses himself in Candomblé and Umbanda. And the fact that Cleo is one of the few Kardecist mediums prepared to accept those two cults as equally valid."

Candomblé? Umbanda? Kardecism? What the hell was he getting into here?

"I mean, if it's true about his own calling," the woman pursued, "Simon would naturally want to know everything there was to know about it, wouldn't he?"

"Naturally."

"And a Kardecist broad-minded enough to reconcile her homeopathic beliefs with rituals descended from the ancient Yoruba theogony in Africa... Well, you could hardly expect him to pass that one up, could you?"

"You took the words out of my mouth."

"How nice to find oneself seated next to someone so intelligent!" the clairvoyant exclaimed, a faint tinge of warmth enlivening her wan face for the first time.

"My own feeling exactly."

"As a convinced Kardecist yourself," the woman began.

But Bolan was no longer listening. Glancing toward Joliffe and Cleo Duhamel, he'd seen through an open doorway a man crossing a lobby beyond. He was tall and white-haired, with craggy features, and, presumably, was one of Joliffe's below-stairs servants, for he wore a sleeved vest and a leather apron over his corduroy pants.

He'd seen the guy before—wearing mud-colored camous splashed with green and ocher, lying blue-faced and very dead on a stretcher in the sick bay of the Air Force testing base in Nevada.

"Of course—" the clairvoyant lady's voice intruded once more "—we aren't all as eclectic in our beliefs as Cleo. Just the same—"

How could a dead sniper from Nevada turn up as a servant in a country house in the west of England? Could the suicide have been faked?

No way, Bolan thought. Yet here the killer was, alive and kicking. He would have dismissed it as a freak of nature, a one-off coincidence with geography playing the joker, if it hadn't been for the one undeniable fact—there was, after all, a link.

The rifleman had been gunning for people checking out UPI components on the Stealth bomber. And his double was working, half a world away, at the home of the UPI boss, where one of his targets had unexpectedly shown.

He was aware that the woman next to him had stopped talking. To keep her on the boil while he searched his own mind, he said, "You were talking about Sir Simon's 'calling' back there. I'm not sure that I understand what you meant by that."

She stared at him, clearly astonished. "But didn't you know? You, of all people, I should have thought—"

"I never met him before. We've corresponded, but that's all." At least that, he knew, was the truth.

"Oh, I see. Well, the fact is he's deeply psychic. Deeply." The woman leaned toward him conspiratorially. "I don't mind telling you, in the short time since he learned he had the gift, he's achieved the most remarkable results. Remarkable. Without in any sense being practiced, he has actually achieved—" she lowered her voice still further "—materializations. Now, what do you think of that?"

"Remarkable," the Executioner replied. It seemed to be expected of him.

"Don't you think? And there are hints—we're all pretty excited about it—that when he's in a trance, somebody is trying to get through who's tremendously important. Tremendously."

"You don't say?" Bolan tried to sound excited and as though he knew what she was talking about.

The woman nodded vigorously. "You know what a powerful medium Cleo is, of course?"

"Of course." That was safe enough, anyway.

"Well, Cleo herself told me she believes the spirit entity trying to speak through Sir Simon is no less than one of the major Umbanda divinities!"

"Really."

He was familiar with most of the words, but the sentences might as well have been in medieval Danish for all they meant to him. He'd discovered a little about his host, a little about Cleo Duhamel, and nothing at all about Cahill. Could this mumbo jumbo really have anything to do with desert snipers and the hardware installed in the B-2 bomber?

Rick Salter was on his feet at the head of the table, one hand grasping his chair back, the other resting casually on his hip. He tossed back a lock of hair that had fallen forward over one eye and he began to speak.

"Well, people, you know why we're here—followers of Candomblé, Umbanda, Kardecism and the European spiritualist cults, all eager to try something that's never been tried before. We're going to make an attempt to cross-penetrate, as it were—to persuade the spirit guides normally speaking or appearing through one medium to reveal themselves via another!"

He paused, running a calculating eye over the expectant faces ranged on each side of the long table. Bolan was reminded of a conjuror, surveying his audience before he proved the rabbit was in the hat, after all.

Salter continued. "In different ways, of course, this has been done before. Allan Kardec visited all manner of séances before he wrote his famous *Book of Spirits* more than a hundred years ago. But we pride ourselves on a different approach. One has arranged that representatives of each spiritualist discipline shall have the opportunity of summoning his or her familiars at a normal séance before one essays this experimental approach. Tomorrow night, therefore, Mrs. Haytor—" he inclined his head toward the woman sitting next to Bolan "—will start her first session in the salon downstairs. After that European opener Madame Duhamel, as a believer in Kardec's doctrine, and then Dr. Cahill, will take the stand, as it were. The Candomblé people and the Umbandistas will officiate on the following day."

From the far side of Sir Simon Joliffe, Cleo Duhamel raised her head and caught the Executioner's eye. Her lips parted, and a corner of her mouth twitched into a smile that was loaded with complicity.

"Next week," Salter was saying, "one does so hope successfully to intermix, to synthesize in some way, these beliefs. But before we go into detail one can no longer put off the announcement of one's little surprise—and that, people, is for tonight!"

Bolan was aware of a stir of excitement around him.

"Knowing the newfound gifts of our host," Salter continued, "one is trying, so to speak, to set the scene, to promote the right atmosphere. And in the hope that certain promises suggested by his very special powers might be realized, one has organized—yes, here at Joliffe Hall—a *tenda* of initiate priestesses from Brazil!"

He paused for murmurs of astonishment and gratification from the guests.

"Since their arrival three days ago, a high priestess has been conducting preliminary rites in purpose-built suites behind the stables. Before they leave, one hopes to have witnessed the Orunkó, the great day when they are finally visited by the controlling spirits who have chosen them as their human mouthpieces. But tonight at midnight we have the privilege of taking part in an interim ceremony at which these spirits—or saints as they are called in Candomblé—for the first time 'lower themselves upon,' or take possession of the girls." Salter smiled briefly and sat down.

There was an outburst of applause. "Well," Mrs. Haytor exclaimed, "Brazilian priestesses! That *is* a surprise, I must say. How very, very interesting, don't you think, Dr. Cahill? But then, of course, as you come from Brazil, you must be more than familiar with the Candomblé rituals, even if the cult runs counter to your own."

"Familiar would be an exaggeration," Bolan replied.

"Indeed, yes," Wolfgang Kleist said. "Before the Orunkó, before even the interim ceremonies, the rites

Salter quotes are most complex. Purifying baths, ritual depilations, group meditations, fasts and many other traditions. These young women will doubtless have been led through these by the high priestess, the so-called 'Mother of Saint' who accompanies them.''

"You're very well informed, Herr Kleist," Bolan commented.

"It is to be expected, even of a businessman! None of us would be here if we didn't share at least a part of our host's enthusiasm, isn't that right?"

As soon as it was socially acceptable, Bolan left the gathering and returned to his room. There, he leafed quickly through the local telephone directory. He needed help, fast. If Jason Mettner was sticking around in the hope of contacting Joliffe, it was a fair bet that he'd be holed up in Peverill-St. Mary's only pub. He found the listing easily enough—the Red Lion, a seventeenth-century coaching inn. He punched out the number and was in luck.

"What's up?" the newspaperman asked after Bolan identified himself.

"Plenty. You carry a morgue in your specialist's head?"

"Depends who wants in and why."

"I'm knocking," Bolan said. "You have any background material on spiritualist cults in South America, specifically Brazil?"

"Some. I did a background piece for the Sunday supplement a couple of years back. Spiritist, they call it there."

"Whatever. I'm strictly in a need-to-know situation."

"Oh, yeah?" Mettner sounded amused.

Bolan filled him in. "You know my status here. Already I have a hunch that something smells. I don't know what, but I plan to hang in here until I do. To make it, though, I have to have informed Intel. You read me?"

"Loud and clear. What did you have in mind?"

"I'm going to take a walk down Joliffe's long driveway. If you start around the same time and walk up toward the head of the valley, we should RDV someplace near the entrance gates."

"It's a dark night for a city boy. How will I know it's you?"

Bolan grinned. "In the middle of all the heavy traffic? I'll whistle the first three bars of Old Glory."

IT WAS DARK AT TIMES and quite cold. A breeze had sprung up, sweeping the low, dark rain clouds away to the east. In the gaps between them a late-rising moon spilled shadows across the white driveway, racing a long-legged Bolan shape ahead of the big man's stride.

The Executioner passed beneath the creaking branches of the trees and made the stone gateway as Mettner was laboring up the final section of the grade.

"The information that follows," Mettner panted, "comes to you not only as a trade-off against exclusive rights but also on the strict understanding that Mrs. Mettner's favorite son will be kept in the picture all along the line, right?"

"Deal. For starters, what are Umbanda, Candomblé and Kardecism? What is a *tenda?* An Orunkó? And what are they all about?"

"They all share a belief in spirits and an afterlife," Mettner told him. "They all believe in magic. They are all—this is one hell of a simplification—basically Christian. But in Candomblé the Church's beliefs are mixed in with rituals derived from the pagan gods brought from Africa by black slaves. In Umbanda the original gods of the South American Indians are involved. In each case these gods are supposed to 'speak' through priests and priestesses, specialized mediums, if you like, when they're in a state of trance or literally possessed."

"And Kardecism?"

"More for the intellectuals. Kardec was a French psychic researcher, a serious guy. The others are for simple folks. You know."

"Okay, but what do they do?"

"Spread the word, I guess. And help folks who are sick by a kind of faith healing, surgical operations without instruments, you must have heard. In the case of Kardecism, through homeopathic medicine."

"You must have researched all this yourself," Bolan said. "How do you rate all this stuff?"

"No comment."

"One word I did know, I haven't heard at all," Bolan said.

"For instance?"

"Macumba. I thought that was the great South American cult."

Mettner was pacing up and down. He lit a cigarette, then shook out the match. "Everyone gets that wrong," he said, blowing out smoke. "These cults, whatever you think, aim to do good. Like white magic. Macumba's the other side of the coin. Witchcraft, sorcery, casting spells. So-called black magic. It's the equivalent of voodoo in the West Indies."

Bolan filled him in with a story-so-far routine, and then asked, "What would you say if you heard these people at the hall were figuring to pull off some kind of 'cross-pollination' between these cults?"

"I'd say that was a load of horseshit," Mettner replied.

Bolan nodded. "What I thought."

"Any more questions?"

"Keep listening. Remember a guy named Hal Brognola who you ran across a couple of times when you talked yourself into my business?"

"Sure," Mettner said. "I know Brognola. Works out of Justice and runs some kind of spook operation, right?"

"So they tell me. I want you to use your press facility to get a message to him fast."

"No problem. What's the message?"

"I'll give you a number that will get straight through to him. Tell him to run a trace, top priority, through Bear. I want all the Intel there is on three guys and a woman—a Dutchman who calls himself Konrad Vanderlee, Wolfgang Kleist, who's German, and a Briton named Rick Salter. The woman's South American, and her name is Cleo Duhamel. Here, I've written them down for you."

"I can tell you something about Salter," Mettner said, pocketing the slip of paper Bolan handed over. "He's a high-powered PR consultant, one of the smartest around, they say—but more unscrupulous than most, full of stunts that the British call dubious."

"That figures," Bolan commented. If that kind of guy was masterminding Joliffe's psychic "experiments," his hunch that there was something bogus about the whole deal could be right.

On the way back to the big house he ran over what he knew and what he would like to know.

The jackpot question was who had killed Hanslip Cahill and why?

One of Sir Simon Joliffe's guests? To stop the medium taking part in the old man's experiments?

If so, what could he have pulled that was worth taking a chance on a murder charge? Was someone else scared they could be exposed as a charlatan, a fake, a crook? Or was it something Cahill might *do* that frightened the killer?

Whatever, he or she would know Bolan was a fake. Would his presence among the guests be as dangerous to the killer as Cahill's would have been? Or would it be welcome because it would put off, at least temporarily, the discovery that the real man was dead? Would the murderer now be gunning for Bolan?

Three facts stood out among the questions. Poisoned darts and blowpipes were strictly South American material; Cleo Duhamel came from South America; Cleo Duhamel knew Bolan was an impostor.

Did she know why?

Mulling things over, he walked in through the hall's rear entrance and met the old man himself, treading down the spiral staircase.

"My dear fellow!" He hurried forward and put an arm around Bolan's shoulders. "I'm so terribly glad you were able to come, Cahill," he said warmly. "I appreciate the gesture more than I can say."

Bolan brushed aside the man's gratitude.

"No, no, I mean it," Joliffe protested. "I really do. Not everybody is so quick to humor an old man. I know how little time you have over here, and, well, let me say I'm most grateful." He chuckled. "And I'll tell you one thing, that suggestion you made in your last letter—in the end we had to do it, anyway!" He slapped Bolan on the back and moved away, still laughing.

Bolan went up to his room. There was still a half hour before the guests were to assemble and follow Salter to the ceremony. Turning a corner in the passageway, he came face-to-face with Cleo Duhamel.

She stopped and stared at him, her heavy-lidded eyes half-closed, her sensual mouth twisted again into a faint smile. "Well, Dr. Cahill," she said huskily, "I see we take consecutive places on tomorrow night's program."

Bolan stared back. "Why haven't you given me away?"

She smiled more broadly. "I have my reasons. Maybe I want to see how you make out at the séance tomorrow."

"You expect me to believe that?"

Cleo Duhamel lifted a bare arm and pushed a curl of black hair from her forehead. The movement raised the soft flesh of one breast until it was almost free of the swathes of velvet sculpting the top of her dress. "Very well," she drawled. "Let's say, then, that I just want to see how you make out."

Bolan cleared his throat. Such a bold and direct approach from a woman exuding such animal sexuality was something he wasn't used to.

"If you know Dr. Cahill," he began, "I can't understand why you aren't interested in knowing how I came to be here in his place. If you know him well, that is."

Duhamel's hands smoothed the dress material over her tightly sheathed hips. "Know him well?" she repeated in a voice tinged with scorn. "Know him *well?* I lived with the son of a bitch for seven years. Maybe that's why I'm happy to see someone with a bit more muscle on him."

CHAPTER SIX

Bolan found out about the mercenaries on his way to the initiation ceremony. Before that there was another surprise.

He'd allowed the members of the house party to go ahead, knowing that the ceremony was to take place on a lake island beyond the woods in back of the house. If he could contrive twenty minutes or a half hour alone, he'd decided on impulse, he could make a swift search, check out the rooms of the four guests whose names he'd given to Mettner. Cahill would be familiar with the preiiminary rituals, anyway.

His first target was Vanderlee in the suite next to his own. He stole out into the softly carpeted hallway and turned the handle of the door. He frowned, twisting the handle the other way.

The door was locked. Guests who locked their bedroom doors in private homes customarily had something to hide. He returned to his own room, operated the catch that opened the secret compartment at the bottom of his carryall and took out a ring of small stainless-steel instruments. Ninety seconds later Vanderlee's door was open.

The room was larger than his own, more richly furnished in the Scandinavian style. It smelled of cigar smoke and cologne. Bolan saw silk pajamas laid out on a bed with the covers turned down, street clothes folded over a chair back, a dressing table with silver hairbrushes and a manicure set in a leather case. Among the suits hanging in the closet was a wash-leather shoulder holster.

He whistled softly to himself. Contact points on the rig were shiny with use. Clearly this was a guy accustomed to carrying a gun—a heavy-caliber automatic pistol, Bolan guessed, looking at the rectangular indentation worn into the wash-leather by the barrel.

He replaced the rig and searched the dressing table drawers. In the lowest one he found a sheet of paper inserted between two freshly pressed shirts.

It was a photocopy of a memorandum from an undercover section of the British Ministry of Defense, with Secret slanted across the top left-hand corner. The memo was handwritten in a sloping script. It read:

UPI and the TASM
As you know the Tactical Air-Launched Strategic Missile, designed to counter Russia's AS-11 and the Mach 3.5 plane that launches it, is of enormous importance to NATO and the U.S. The UPI research program perfecting this stand-off weapon's guidance systems has thus to be monitored with special care. For the moment forget the space vehicle electronics, therefore, and concentrate on possible TASM leaks.

Two initials that meant nothing to Bolan completed the message. It was addressed to someone identified only by the code AX-12, clearly a government spook infiltrated into Universal Plastics with, literally, a watching brief. Along the bottom of the page, three lines in red marker had been scrawled—not part of the original message but added later.

As you see, we have competition. Whoever AX-12 is, presumably someone on the UPI payroll, he or she must be identified at once and eliminated. Too much is at stake to risk a cock-up now. RS.

Bolan replaced the paper. His face was thoughtful as he left the room and relocked the door. If RS was Rick Salter, there definitely was a link between the spiritist house party and the Stealth affair. A sinister link.

Salter's room was on an upper floor next to the glass-walled sanctum where Joliffe customarily ate, slept and attended to his business. The door was unlocked. Bolan turned up nothing inside that threw any more light on the mysterious memo.

He didn't know where Cleo Duhamel slept, and he was checking out the rooms along his own corridor in the hope of finding Kleist's when an electrician appeared with a toolbox at the far end of the passage and started tinkering with a fuse box high up on the wall. The lights dimmed, blacked out, then brightened again. Bolan decided to call it a day. He returned the skeleton keys to his carryall, strapped on his Beretta in its quick-draw rig and headed for the lake.

Looking for the kitchen wing and a quick way to the stables, he took a wrong turn behind the staircase and found himself in an unlit hallway with a gun room at the far end. Halfway there, a door opened on a narrow stairway leading below. This must be the way to the ballroom and the "info theater" Joliffe had mentioned. He decided to take a look.

The ballroom was simple and quite small, with a bandstand at one end and tables and chairs on a carpeted strip surrounding the sprung pine dance floor. The lecture hall next door was equally conventional. He was about to return to the staircase when a chink of light ahead attracted his attention.

He saw a two-inch crack between the paneled wall and a door that was ajar. He stared into the small room beyond, surprised.

Most of the space was occupied by a complex installation of ultramodern recording equipment. Four outsize decks stretched from floor to ceiling, each housing three vertically placed pairs of tape spools.

Two editing desks with inclined faces stood in front of a padded swivel chair, and at one side of these a control console bristled with rheostat levers, switches, wheels and colored indicator lights. From what he could see Bolan guessed there had to be a dozen input channels feeding the console, each identified by a coded letter and number. And these, since there was no viewing window and no studio visible, presumably represented twelve separate installations.

Where?

The close-fitting outside door was clearly designed to keep the room secret, so there could be only one answer—the whole building was wired for sound. Unknown to the guests the mansion was bugged.

A spiral staircase led to a smaller room on a lower level. Here, Bolan saw a video camera on a tripod, a small VTR screen, a moviola editor and shelves full of circular film cans behind a 16 mm movie camera.

He frowned. It was a strange setup, but he'd leave it, since it was evident that whoever was using the room would be back at any minute. He returned to the central hallway and left the house by the main entrance.

He heard the drums as soon as he was in the open air—a distant, insistent sound that rose and fell, now louder, now fainter, above the sound of wind in the trees. Following the direction from which the rhythmic pulse seemed to emanate, he passed half a dozen wooden shacks that housed, he supposed, the visitors from Brazil. Some of the lower trees surrounding them were hung with scraps of bright cloth, and he could see in a sudden shaft of moonlight that between the two largest cabins there was a wooden structure about the size of a doghouse. Dishes of food lay scattered around it. They were—Bolan guessed, remembering voodoo rituals witnessed on a visit to Haiti—an offering to the gods believed to inhabit the miniature building.

A footpath led toward the lake. Fifty yards into the woods it was crossed by a narrower path, and there was a ring of candles at the intersection in whose flickering illumination cigars and glasses of liquor had been arranged inside a circle traced in the dust.

The gods, he mused, were being well looked after.

Farther up the trail a shadowy shape flitting swiftly through a patch of moonlight filtered through the branches overhead. Bolan had stopped to look at the votive offering, but froze now until the figure was out of sight.

He was looking at the ringer he'd seen behind Jo-liffe at dinner—only now the guy was wearing ca-mous, exactly like the unknown rifleman who'd killed himself in Nevada.

The warrior gave chase, treading warily in case a snapping twig alerted his quarry. But the heavy rain earlier had waterlogged the undergrowth and the squelching of mud as the path emerged from the wood was more likely to be a giveaway. In any event, the man in camous was making no attempt at concealment—the noise of his own passage would drown any small sounds Bolan made.

The track crossed a meadow and skirted one arm of the star-shaped lake. The drummers' jungle syncopa-tion was much louder here. Across the dark water pin-points of flame charted the course of a torchlight procession moving among the island trees.

Bolan stayed fifty yards behind his quarry, follow-ing the man down a brush-covered slope to a beech-wood on the far edge of the estate. The moon was fully out now, and it was tougher to stay hidden. Near the priestesses' cabins pine needles deadened the sound of footsteps, but some of the leaves had already fallen in this belt of trees, and despite the wet ground they rustled. The Executioner was forced to drop back and move more slowly.

It was where the forest floor dropped away into a hollow and the trail divided that he lost the man. The hollow was moonlit, and black shadows blanketed each path on the far side of the glade. Bolan paused. By some trick of acoustics the drumming was louder than ever now. He could hear the swishing of undergrowth, but he couldn't tell which path it came from. Mentally he flipped a coin and chose the left-hand trail.

He'd traveled perhaps thirty yards when a dark figure materialized from behind a tree, a tall man, his seamed features etched from the night by the wan light. Blocking the pathway, he held a mini-Uzi machine pistol, the stubby barrel pointed at the Executioner's chest. Camouflage markings splashed the combat fatigues that he wore, but it wasn't the same guy Bolan had been following.

"Who the hell are you? What are you doing here?" Bolan demanded angrily. "Don't you know this is private property?"

"Damn right. One of the things we have to do, bud, is to keep it that way. Private."

"I'll ask one more time. Who are you, and why are you here?" Bolan asked. "I'm a houseguest here. I'm taking a walk and I want out."

"Securicare Incorporated," the man replied, his tone slightly less hostile. "Employed by Sir Simon Joliffe to guard the property. You can, of course, leave if you wish, but we can't allow you back in without a written pass signed by Mr. Salter. Like I say, our main job is to keep people out—especially journalists, television crews and the like.''

''Bullshit. I walked out the main gates less than one hour ago. Nobody stopped me coming back in.''

''You were lucky. Must have been during the swing shift changeover,'' the security man said. ''Here around the perimeter our orders are strict. Take my advice. Go back to the gates and try there again.''

''I'll do that,'' Bolan said.

''In any case,'' the guard called after him as he turned away, ''you got a twelve-foot wall with broken glass on top to get over here.''

The Executioner didn't reply. He didn't believe the story.

Sure, the estate was being guarded all right. He'd seen other figures in combat gear lurking in the shadows. And the moonlight had gleamed dully on the wire mesh protecting the windows of an armored truck half hidden in the bushes. But he didn't believe Sir Simon knew anything about it, however involved Rick Salter was.

For one thing, private security firms of the kind an industrialist might hire weren't allowed to carry automatic weapons, especially of the deadly type favored by army penetration units and terrorists. For another, their uniforms customarily resembled those worn by the police, rather than a full combat rig including concussion grenades slung from a battle harness. Lastly, he was sure the old man wouldn't knowingly tolerate the installation of the trip wires, sensors and video cameras he'd glimpsed behind the guy who had stopped him.

The clincher, for Bolan, was the fact that the man's face was known to him. The lined, rakish features were unmistakable. They'd fought on opposite sides once in a failed military coup in central Africa—Reagan O'Hara, onetime major in the Irish army, cashiered for misuse of mess funds and the supply of matériel to the outlawed IRA.

Whatever their reasons, Salter and confederates unknown had hired a group of professional mercenaries to seal off the Joliffe estate during the spiritist ceremonies.

Other than the fact that he was clearly a member of the group, the Executioner didn't know any more about the Nevada sniper's double. But it made the link stronger.

Once out of the beechwood he headed for the lake. Would the rituals there hand him a clue? He doubted it, but it was possible that the comportment of the principals might at least supply some kind of pointer.

A stone wall enclosed the meadow at the top of the slope. If a gate in the wall hadn't been fitted with iron hinges, Bolan would never have made the island.

The first bullet narrowly missed his left side, glanced off the metal and ricocheted into the night with a shrill scream. Before the second and third thunked into the woodwork he'd vaulted over and was lying flat in the long grass beside the path, the Beretta in his right hand.

He'd heard no shots. The gunman was firing subsonic rounds from a silenced weapon.

Bolan strained every nerve, listening with total concentration. All he knew was that the shots had come from behind him. The killer must have stalked him up the slope and opened fire from among the bushes when he was silhouetted against the moonlight sky at the top.

The wind carried the sound of male voices chanting from the lake. A groundswell of drums still throbbed below it. Above his head the grass rustled.

It was impossible to hear movement on the far side of the wall, harder still to identify the strangled thump of a silenced weapon. Wood splintered from the gate's lowest bar as a fourth round was fired. The fifth hummed uncomfortably close to the warrior's shoulder.

Then abruptly there was a lull in the singing and he heard distinctly two thumps overlapping, too close together to be from the same weapon. The slugs plowed into the earth in front of his face.

Two gunners, then. They must have closed right up before they opened fire, or they could never have gauged so accurately where he was lying.

Were they after him because Reagan O'Hara had recognized him? Or was the situation so delicate that *any* guest discovering there were mercenaries on guard had to be eliminated before he could talk?

He'd check that one out later. The priority now was to stay alive.

So far the gunners had been firing from the top of the slope, aiming through the gate. The obvious play now would be to spread out, one on either side, then run for the stone wall. Once he was enfiladed, once they had the wall for protection, Bolan was through. As soon as he fired at one to make him keep his head down, he'd be a sitting duck for the other. He'd have to act, then, before they reached the wall.

Very carefully, on elbows and knees, he edged back and to one side of the path. The moon slid behind a bank of dark clouds blowing up from the west. And in the moment that the light dimmed, Bolan clearly heard the squelch of footsteps, the rush of legs through damp grass. They were heading for the wall.

He was on his feet and running, away to the right where a furze bush grew twenty feet from the wall.

The gunner on the left of the gate was the first to hoist himself above the stonework. He fired twice at Bolan's dim shape, the muzzle-flashes momentarily printing the wall against the night. One slug nicked the heel of Bolan's boot, throwing him off balance so that he tripped and plunged behind the furze before the second came his way.

There was a sudden triumphant shout from the direction of the lake. A starshell arched lazily into the sky, towing a trail of sparks. It burst with a hollow thud, drifting down to flood the whole countryside with a livid green brilliance as the head and shoulders of the second killer rose above the wall on the far side of the furze bush.

Bolan was there in a combat crouch, both arms extended, the Beretta firm in his two-handed grip. With the gun in 3-shot mode he pumped a deadly burst at the killer before the man had time to turn his way. The 9 mm deathstream slammed into his chest, hurling him back and out of sight before his lips could choke out a cry.

Bolan saw more flashes from the far side of the gate. Bullets zipped through the spiny interwoven branches of the furze, but he was already facedown beneath the lowest.

The next move was his. No question of an enfilade now: the combat was strictly man-to-man. But the move depended on the surviving gunman and when he needed to reload.

Eleven shots had been fired before Bolan blew away the guy nearest to him. The survivor had choked out several more.

How many slugs had the dead man fired?

Bolan did a rough count. Handgun magazines varied from six shots in the big Smith & Wesson and seven for the Walther PPK to fourteen for a Model 59 and fifteen for the .45 Colt and his own 93-R. There was also a 20-round clip available for the Beretta, but it was too cumbersome for use in a shoulder rig.

From the muzzle-flashes the warrior guessed the killers were using something smaller than .45-caliber rounds. More like .38 or even a .32. He had to allow, therefore, for a 15-shot firepower on the other side of the wall. If the first eleven rounds had been roughly shared, that still left the guy four, five, maybe even six in hand.

Bolan pushed himself onto his hands and knees, stood and erupted from behind the bush, firing a second burst on the run. He sprinted halfway across the twenty yards separating him from the wall, dropped, rolled and came up again with a third trio burst.

The ruse worked. Flame flickered across the dry stones as the gunman emptied his magazine. But Bolan was already down below the wall. He waited almost ten seconds, then leaped over it, ducked down again and ran for the bush-covered slope.

He could see the guy as a dark blur, crouched in a shallow cut that followed the lip. Six rounds remained in the Beretta's magazine. He squeezed one out, and then another, watching the blur fade and almost disappear as the green light guttered and died.

There was no answering fire, but he could hear the man moving, racing for the slope, snapping twigs as he rushed through the bushes.

Bolan himself half rose, then caught on—the killer wasn't making an attack; he wasn't heading his way. He was getting out, fast.

No spare ammunition. Bolan guessed the mercenary leader who had sent him hadn't reckoned on his target being armed, hadn't known he'd fire back. So maybe he hadn't recognized the Executioner.

The warrior took off in pursuit. The moon sailed out into a space of open sky. He could see the killer, running, stumbling, leaping over the lower shrubs. He could have shot him down; he was no more than thirty yards away. But he preferred to jump the guy and put the arm on him. There were questions he wanted to ask.

In top shape, Bolan was gaining fast. He launched himself out from the edge of a small sandpit as the mercenary scrambled down in a shower of earth and stones.

Bolan landed on top of his back, knocking him flat. The impact drove the breath from both their bodies, but the gunman was quicker—and tougher—than the Executioner had bargained for. He was tall, wiry and strong. Uncoiling like a steel spring, he twisted out from under a tenth of a second before Bolan recovered. He clubbed viciously down with both hands, kneed the Executioner in the belly and butted him ferociously on the bridge of the nose before he was on his feet and running.

Bolan let the guy go. He was already crashing through the undergrowth way down the slope.

He started the climb back to the meadow. It would be interesting to see if any reference to the dead man by the wall was made at the party tomorrow.

More interesting still, he reflected as he headed for the lake and the throb of drums, was the fact that he was ninety percent sure that the guy who fought him in the sandpit was the Nevada sniper's double.

CHAPTER SEVEN

There was a small stony beach on the side of the island away from the house. Joliffe and his guests were installed on a grassy bank above it. Below the trunks of birch, beech and elm leaning over the shore, a miniature waterfall had hollowed a natural chalice from the rock. It was around this that the people taking part in the ceremony were grouped.

Bolan saw an outer ring of young women in white robes jumping down from the bank, their flaming torches scattering to rain toward the water like falling stars. An inner circle of black-robed initiates surrounded the pool, and on a flat-topped rock in the center of this stood the knot of priests and priestesses running the show.

Hurrying along the pathway that led from the footbridge linking the island and the lakeshore, the Executioner took in the scene with one penetrating glance. He lowered himself at the top of the bank, sitting where the light from the torches was dimmest. In such circumstances Cahill's ripped and mud-covered suit would be too difficult to explain.

The glade had been silent except for the splashing of the waterfall, but now the drums started again—softly, insistently, the rhythmic pulse compelling attention, stirring the blood. Several of the guests seated below Bolan started to sway and jerk. Around the pool the circle of white-robed young women shivered like corn in a gust of wind.

The drums grew louder. They were played, Bolan saw, by three impassive Africans squatting on a flat-topped rock among the trees.

The torchbearers began to sing. Their voices rose in a high, keening wail that climbed the scale in semi-tones, an eerie descant that had Bolan's scalp tingling.

He saw a sudden billowing of draperies among the initiates nearest the pool, a rising and falling of bare arms as the hammering of the drums rose to a crescendo and the singing grew more frenzied. Then twelve black robes fell to the stones and a dozen girls in bright dresses and bizarre regalia formed a line to pace in ritual measure around the chalice.

Shaven-headed and daubed with white paint, these were the novice priestesses, the Iaós to whom the evening was consecrated. The climax of the ceremony would be when the divinities worshiped by the sect—most of them of African origin—"descended" to possess their chosen votaries.

Back and forth, in and out, in circles and figures of eight the girls stamped in their gaudy robes of satin, silk and taffeta, their polished skulls gleaming darkly in the light of the flares. Voices and drums rose now to a shattering peak of noise...and suddenly stopped.

In the silence that followed, Bolan heard an abrupt intake of breath from among the houseguests ranked below him. Then three older women in multicolored robes moved slowly to the center of the circle. These were the Iyalorixá, the so-called Mother-of-Saint or high priestess directing this particular group, and her two assistants.

The Iyalorixá threw back a yellow satin hood that had been hiding her features and stared upward, above the heads of the worshipers and into the trees. She flung out her right arm and cried, "Let the Dagã and the Sidagã offer the *padê* of Exú!"

Two girls in white swooped down to pick up a bottle of palm oil, a bowl of toasted manioc flour and a beaker of sugarcane brandy that stood on the lip of the rock basin. As the drums started softly to beat again, the torchbearers started a question-and-answer chant and the girls burst through the circle to career wildly around the glade, scattering the flour and sprinkling the liquids to appease the god Exú, the capricious, all-powerful spirit on whose good graces the success of the ceremony was supposed to depend.

The novices were dancing again, swirls of violet and white, yellow and black, green and chestnut, each wearing the color particular to her chosen god or Orixá. At the same time the massed voices altered in pitch, gained in intensity, repeating the special chants of each spirit—Xangô, Ogun, Oxóssi, Omulu, Elegbara, Nanãburucu—calling them down to take possession, each of his own initiate.

The throbbing of the drums accelerated, grew louder; the chants were hoarse with anticipation. Beads, charms, shells, fetishes sewn or hung on the silk and satin gowns dipped and glittered. Sweat ran down the novices' faces and dewed their bare shoulders as they danced. In a gap opened between the clouds, the stars scythed about their heads. The wind howled in the trees.

And then each girl started to shiver uncontrollably, quivering, shuddering as she slewed from side to side. Powered by a fury of percussion, they lurched and swayed ever faster, the shaking of their limbs reaching a climax when the eyes closed, the mouths flew open, and each in turn fell prostrate to the ground, shouting in a great voice the name of her particular spirit.

The Orixás had "seated" themselves on their chosen; the Iaós had duly become possessed.

At the climax of the ceremony, Bolan stood and stole off through the trees. It was heavy going in the dark. The moon was still hidden, and once out of range of the torches it was difficult to tell the difference between thickets and shadows in the starlit gloom.

Unseen brambles tore at the legs of Cahill's suit; branches whipped unexpectedly across Bolan's face; the ground fell away before his feet. But finally the pewter surface of the lake gleamed dully between the tree trunks and he was approaching the bridge.

Behind him a fallen branch snapped suddenly. He whirled around, unleathering the Beretta.

He was facing the dim figure of a naked woman.

At first he figured it for some offshoot of the ceremony. Would they insist that the audience remain in place until it was through, send someone to lure back a fugitive? Then he saw, in the radiance reflected from the lake, that it was Cleo Duhamel.

"Well, Dr. Cahill," she said throatily.

"Very well, thank you."

"Still wondering if I'm going to unmask you?"

"I was wondering if it helps you to commune with your spirits when you yourself are...unmasked."

She laughed, a soft, intimate sound in the dark. "When the flesh is willing, the spirits are weak!" she murmured.

She moved toward him, and the next moment she was in his arms. She pressed against him, her knee forcing apart his thighs. Two sinewy hands cupped the back of his head, and her tongue flickered lasciviously between his lips. The Executioner was all man. Reluctantly he felt himself respond.

Soon she leaned away from him, the columns of muscle on her nude back firm against his left hand. "You can put that away. I don't have to be forced," she whispered, her voice tinged with amusement.

Bolan realized he was still clutching the Beretta. He drew back and releathered the gun.

"Come," she said. "I know a place just beyond that stand of birch. There's a folly—"

"A folly?"

"The kind you take shelter in, not the kind you commit."

"I wouldn't bet on it," he said dryly.

CHAPTER EIGHT

"It sounds phony," Jason Mettner said, "all along the line."

"That's what I thought," the Executioner replied. "But it's not my scene. Do you have a contact over here who could tell us how phony?"

"Give me a minute." Mettner took a small notebook from an inside pocket and began leafing through the pages.

It was 12:30 p.m., and the two men were at the Red Lion pub.

Nobody had challenged Bolan as he'd walked out the main gates of Joliffe Hall and taken the country road that led down the valley to the village—several members of the house party had already announced their intentions of taking a walk. But the Executioner was well aware of stealthy footsteps among the trees, of half-seen figures flitting through the woods as he'd strode down the leafy grade. Once in the distance he'd heard the unmistakable rasp of an order relayed through a transceiver, but he'd had no way of knowing whether the other houseguests were under similar surveillance.

Provided O'Hara's mercenaries weren't wise to the situation, he reckoned he was safe in the role of Cahill until the following morning. The murder at the railroad station had been too late to make the country editions of the Sunday newspapers, the national television newscasts had ignored it, and BBC radio hadn't considered it important enough to cover. But if no big story broke over the weekend, it could well be splashed on Monday—by which time, armed with whatever Intel he could glean, the Executioner would be long gone.

Meanwhile there remained the problem of the Cahill séance.

"There's only one person who might possibly fit," Jason Mettner said, "and that's no more than a guess. But fortunately she's based in Exeter, only a half hour's drive away."

"She?"

"Felicity Freeman." The newspaperman was holding his notebook with a forefinger inserted between the pages to mark the place. "She's a stage illusionist who used to work with one of the big European vaudeville names, but now she has her own show—mostly night spots, clubs, that kind of thing."

"Sounds promising."

"It could be. She doesn't do TV. With all the video tricks available now, she says Joe Public's going to write off all the clever sleight-of-hand material as fakery, anyway."

Mettner continued. "I was thinking, even though she doesn't use it herself, she knows all about the fakery scene. She mightn't be able to solve your occult weekend problem, but she should sure as hell know how to set up a phony séance."

"How do we contact her?"

Mettner removed his finger and opened the notebook. "I have her agent's number here and her unlisted phone number in Exeter. Maybe we should blow a couple of Her Gracious Majesty's silver coins in the pay phone outside."

"Do it."

FELICITY FREEMAN WAS the kind of small, dark, curvy woman usually described as "petite." When Jason Mettner's call came through that Sunday, she was sitting on the floor of her small apartment with the color supplements spread around her. "Why, Jay," she said, "how nice! I didn't even know you were in the country. What can I do for you this time?"

"Those aren't the words of the generous-hearted girl I know and love," Mettner replied. "You can do me a favor, honey. Will you?"

"That," the woman said cautiously, "depends. The last time you asked me to do you a favor I almost ended up in the slammer, and—"

"It's nothing like that. I'm not asking you to smuggle me into any confidential government committee meeting. It's just a small favor—not even for me, as it happens. It's for a friend."

"I said it depends."

"On what?"

"On whether it's going to cost me anything, for starters."

"It won't. Well, except for the gasoline, that is."

"So we know already that I have to go someplace. It depends, then, on how far, how fast, how long I have to stay wherever it is, and what I have to do when I get there."

"Just help this buddy who's in a bit of a jam."

"Explain."

Mettner cleared his throat. "You won't laugh?"

"I'll try not to."

"Well, this friend—another hack from home— seems to have gotten himself into a position where he's supposed to be some kind of psychic medium, and the poor guy is expected to perform, if that's what they call it, at a séance tonight!"

Felicity laughed.

"I knew you would."

"Jay, darling, I'm sorry. Really. But you have to admit it's not the kind of problem that arises every day. Tell me all about it."

"It began with this murder, you see. A guy was killed with a poisoned dart here in England. And as my buddy had been in the same compartment and he was holding the dead guy's baggage when the chauffeur showed, the chauffeur naturally figured him for the guy. Well, as nobody at Joliffe's place knew him, my buddy reckoned he could—"

"Jay!" the girl interrupted sharply. "Remember you're a journalist! Tell it the way it happened from the top!"

Mettner sighed. Why was it always such a hassle with women? He detailed everything Bolan had told him, from the killing to the ceremony on the lake.

"Jay," Freeman said when he finished, "you got me hooked. This is one hell of a strange setup. Particularly this gang of oddballs invited for this kind of weekend by a man who's boss of UPI."

"That's what Mike and I think. There's a story here for sure. You'll string along then and help out?"

"If I can. What do you want me to do? Don't tell me—you want me to help your friend fake his way through some kind of occult act."

"Hole in one," Mettner said. "As you're in another branch of the trade, so to speak, I reckoned you'd be familiar with the tricks. Am I right?"

"I've a pretty good idea how most of them work, sure," she admitted.

"So you'll drive down and bring the stuff with you?"

"Hold it, Jay. I didn't say that. I said I knew how the tricks were worked. I didn't say I was going to set up your friend. I happen to take the investigation of genuine psychic phenomena rather seriously. So before I start meddling I want to know why. Why does your friend want so much to fake a séance? After all, he could just leave. What's the end product if he does make it and stick around? If this is in aid of some sensational news story in the yellow press—"

"It isn't," Mettner cut in. "It's because we think something crooked is going on in there. Don't ask me what. Don't ask against whom it's directed. But I'm one hundred percent sure something's brewing, and it's connected in some way with this occult jazz. I have a nose for skulduggery—hell, I didn't fill the *Globe*'s chief crime reporter slot all those years for nothing!''

"Okay," Freeman said. "I guess that kind of sixth-sense hunch is acceptable enough as a motivation—for me, anyway."

"Great. Any other questions?"

"Yes, one. What kind of stunts do you need? I mean, if your friend is thinking of ghosts made from rolls of cheesecloth, or Ouija boards revealing folks' birthdates, then the deal's off."

Mettner laughed. She heard him strike a match and suck in smoke. "Nothing so elaborate. The simplest possible. He saw the real guy in a trance. I guess he'll fake the condition. All he needs then is a few phrases in a different voice and maybe a foreign language. We'll supply the script if you can handle the mechanics. It won't need too much gear, will it?"

The woman shook her head, remembered she was on the phone and said, "Not at all. Two small throat mikes, a miniature transistor speaker, a couple of matchbox-size transceivers with signal buttons, copper wire, aerials, batteries and a few other items. It'll fit into a regular briefcase."

"That's my girl. Can you make it by four-thirty? We'll need time to set it up and check that it works."

"Can do. Rendezvous where?"

"There's a small parking lot behind the village church," Mettner said. He coughed. "Nobody will notice us there because it's Norman, and folks come to see it on Sundays.''

''You smoke too much,'' the woman said as she hung up.

CHAPTER NINE

Jason Mettner would have been surprised if he could have monitored Felicity Freeman's activity immediately after their conversation.

She left her apartment and walked two blocks to a bank of phone booths. She entered one, fed coins into the telephone and punched out an area code and a London number. The phone at the other end rang once, then the receiver was lifted, although no voice spoke.

"Double F for AX-2," Felicity said quietly.

"Yes, Miss Freeman," said a man's voice, brisk and impersonal. "The colonel's number for today is 437-96000. Let it ring five times, replace your receiver, then call again at once." He hung up before she could reply.

She went into the next booth and followed the instructions she'd been given. On the second call the number answered at once. "Williams," a deep voice announced.

"Colonel, it's Felicity. I have to report an odd coincidence."

"I'm listening, Felicity."

"It's connected with AX-12's brief. It seems the subject is having some kind of occult house party this weekend, and—"

"Yes, we know about the party," Williams cut in. "Though we haven't had the details yet. What's your coincidence?"

"Well, I'm familiar with AX-12's interest in UPI, of course. And I know the reservations we have. But now there's another kind of interest, from outside. In fact, from an American."

For a moment there was silence. Then Williams said, "Odd, as you say. What kind of American?"

"Someone I know slightly. A newspaperman. Two, in fact. One of them has talked his way into the house party. And the extraordinary thing is, they've asked me to go down there and help them fake some kind of spiritualist séance."

"This man you know, what's his name?"

"Mettner. Jason Mettner. He's quite respectable—I mean, this isn't some kind of front-page exposé or anything like that."

"I don't understand. Why should they want to fake a séance if it isn't to show up some kind of chicanery?"

"They think there's something fishy going on. They want to find out what. And why. Because, you see, it's all tied in with that murder yesterday at Peverill-St. Mary. The dead man was on his way to the party, and the American on the inside has taken his place."

"His name?"

"I don't know. Mettner just referred to him as Mike."

"You'd better tell me everything you do know," Williams said, "and you must help them all you can with this trickery—on condition that you keep me informed every step of the way. Understood?"

"Yes, sir," Freeman replied. And she passed on all the Intel Jason Mettner had given her a half hour earlier.

"Although it's not really our territory, you're quite right to report this," Williams said when she finished. "AX-12 will doubtless confirm when something breaks. But he's in an awkward position there on the inside. Meanwhile, I agree. There's something damn fishy going, what with the house being bugged and this private army careering about the grounds."

"Do you want me to contact AX-12 while I'm there?" the woman asked. "We've never met, but I could probably—"

"No," Williams broke in. "Best keep it that way. Then if one of you is blown, the other can carry on regardless."

He sat drumming his fingers on the arm of his chair for several minutes after she hung up. "Private armies in Devonshire," he snorted. "Whatever next."

Finally he called a number in Whitehall, waiting a long time for the connection to be made. "Minister," he said at last, "it seems we may have been right about the Universal Plastics situation."

CHAPTER TEN

Felicity Freeman wasn't a full-time member of the British security services. But in her own profession she was in great demand at society functions. Because she was beautiful as well as talented, she was able to get close to a large number of people, some of them very important, some of them shady and some merely odd. Through her, therefore, there was the possibility of peering occasionally into the minds of those who might be enemies, and keeping a friendly eye on the equilibrium of those supposed to be friends.

Because of this—and because her father had been a cadet at Sandhurst with Colonel Williams—Felicity had joined that secret army of screened part-timers who could be called on if necessary to broaden the work of the professionals. In her case it was for the "AX" section of the Defense Ministry's counterintelligence service, which investigated the possibility of sedition among those in influential positions.

Jason Mettner, of course, knew nothing of this. To him, Freeman was an attractive contact he'd sweet-talked several times into special favors—notably introductions to places where journalists weren't normally welcomed.

Bolan saw a pretty woman in black ski pants, sneakers and a black roll-neck sweater. "In case we have to dodge around unseen while we're doing a dry run for the performance," she explained. "Right now I suggest we read through the part and get to know the equipment."

The afternoon was sunny. The rain clouds had blown away. Peverill-St. Mary, picturesque and as English as any village could be, had attracted a full ration of sightseers, and nobody paid them any mind as they sat in the woman's Mercedes, manipulating electronic instruments and reading through three pages of typescript the newspaperman had produced. "And the gear," Freeman announced with a sly smile, "was all made by the UPI high-tech subsidiary outside Exeter. How's that for dramatic irony?"

Later they drove to a stretch of moorland and tried out the mikes and speakers live over various distances. Then it was time to drop the Executioner within walking distance of Joliffe Hall.

Bolan managed to get out of wearing Cahill's voluminous dinner clothes on the grounds that he found it essential to stay relaxed and casual for some hours before he performed. He wore dark gray pants, and a fawn suede jacket he found among the medium's suits over a white shirt and a cravat. Behind the cravat were certain pieces of equipment supplied by Freeman. The patch pockets of Cahill's expensive jacket held several more.

Before dinner, over drinks in the modernistic library, Bolan faced the toughest test he'd come up against so far. Buttonholed by Vanderlee and the old man, with Kleist and the huge bald Oriental hovering nearby, he found himself questioned on life back in Brazil.

"As a European living in the country," Vanderlee asked at one point, "can you give us an objective view on the effect of religious syncretism there?"

"Not really," Bolan parried. "Any point of view is subjective when it relates to the place the viewer lives, isn't it?"

"Of course. As a Kardecist you must deplore the ritual and magic associated with the Umbanda associations of which Madame Duhamel is so charmingly a champion. But do you really believe, as so many of your colleagues do, that there can be no correspondence between them?"

"I try to keep an open mind on the subject," Bolan said evasively. He was finding it increasingly difficult to shape his dialogue the way he figured Cahill might have spoken.

"Surely," Sir Simon interposed, "however intelligent the mediums are, there has to be room for less brainy folks among their followers? I mean, personally I can't see why Kardecism and Umbanda couldn't be equally valid—but perhaps for different types of people."

"The Umbandistas say that Kardecism is Jesus Christ teaching, but their own cult is Christ actually working," said the Oriental, speaking for the first time. He had a high, rather fluting tenor voice, unexpected in a man of his size. "The fact remains that Umbanda designed to satisfy superstitious and illiterate natives, while we appeal to the thinking man."

Bolan made a mental note. The "we" signified that the guy was a Kardecist, a member of the same group as Bolan-Cahill, which meant that the Executioner had to watch what he said when the man was around.

"I don't see why they need be mutually exclusive," Joliffe was arguing. "What if an intelligent man, for example—a man intellectually suited for Kardecism— should find that the voices of spirits from the other levels, Umbanda or Candomblé spirits, were using him as a vehicle?"

Bolan was aware that they were looking to him for an answer. "You know of such a man?" he asked.

Vanderlee appeared to be trying to attract somebody's attention over Joliffe's head, but the old man ignored him and continued excitedly. "Know of one? Well, more than that, if you see what I mean."

"You left me behind."

"You probably heard that I am psychic." There was no stopping Joliffe now. "Well, it seems I've developed mediumistic powers late in life. But because of that, perhaps as a compensation, they're developing very rapidly. Unusually so, I'm told. A trance medium has no idea, of course, of the use spirits make of him while he's withdrawn. But I'm given to believe that I've been honored with manifestations, and spirit messages of the most advanced kind. I believe—"

"Our host is a remarkable man," the Dutchman cut in smoothly. "Ah, I think I see Salter coming this way.

I wonder if he's completed the arrangements for tonight?''

"What's so strange, so encouraging," Joliffe said, "is that although I am myself so much in sympathy with Kardec's teaching, the spirits choosing to speak through me have all been from the Seven Lines of Umbanda, gods from a primitive religion originating among Yoruba tribesmen in Africa. Now you see what I mean?''

"One does so hope this particular anomaly will prove fruitful," Rick Salter's soft voice murmured by Bolan's ear. "Meanwhile, one does have one's duties. If you would care to accompany me to the lower floor, Dr. Cahill..."

Deftly, no doubt in answer to Vanderlee's appeal, he steered Bolan away as Wolfgang Kleist joined the group. "Most interesting, Sir Simon," the Executioner heard as he moved toward the door. "And if your own analysis of the situation we have observed while you were in a trance is correct, it *may* be the beginning of the kind of breakthrough we hope for. But perhaps it's better not to take too many into your confidence until it's proved, yes?''

In the special lecture theater beside Joliffe's small but beautifully built ballroom, Bolan checked over with the PR man the simple arrangements he'd asked for. Soon afterward, guests began to trickle down the marble staircase and file into the semicircle of seats surrounding the rostrum.

Sir Simon Joliffe sat in the middle of the front row, with Salter and Vanderlee on one side and Kleist on the

other. The bald Oriental, whose name Bolan had
learned was Ley Phuong, was in the chair immediately
behind the old man. This group of intimates, Bolan
reflected, seemed determined at all costs to distance
Joliffe as far as possible from the rest of the house
party.

Interesting.

The remainder of the guests sorted themselves out in
pairs and fours around the crescent. And behind them
all, like some dark angel guarding the courtroom door
on the Day of Judgment, stood the high priestess,
glaring around with implacable eyes.

Finally Mrs. Haytor entered through a side door. A
servant sitting in a cubbyhole equipped with a very up-
to-date lighting control board dimmed the lights, and
a rustle of excitement stirred the guests.

The woman seated herself behind a desk on the rostrum, leaned her forehead on one hand and appeared
to go to sleep. After some time her free hand reached
for a pad of paper. She picked up a pencil and began
to write.

From what Bolan had been told, he was watching a
simple example of automatic writing in a trance—genuine, he assumed, since he couldn't believe anyone
could write so fast or so clearly unless they were in an
abnormal state. As the muttering among the guests
dwindled and died, the pencil flew across the paper
faster and faster. Sheet after sheet, covered in small
copperplate script, was discarded and fluttered to the
floor. When Rick Salter crept from his seat and began
gathering them up, the Executioner stole through a

pass door beside the lighting box and climbed a service stairway that led to the kitchen wing. He went out
into the garden.

The moon rode in a clear sky, flattening the angles
of the stable block in its milky light, hollowing the pale
shapes of bushes from the dark mass of the wood. Behind the stables, chinks of light outlined the blinded
windows of the huts where the novice priestesses were
housed. Bolan heard a shriek of female laughter as he
hurried down a rose walk and climbed the steps of a
small, rustic pavilion facing the lake. Felicity Freeman, who was to use this summerhouse as a transmitting and receiving station during his act, had urged a
last-minute get-together in case there were unforeseen
problems to iron out.

"I read through Jay's stuff again," she said, holding up the typescript, "and I think I'll add in a bit of
the real thing here and there. It'll make your performance more convincing, okay?"

"You reckon you'll be patched in so you can provide the answers to audience questions?"

"Oh, sure. That throat mike under your cravat will
pick up well over a radius of thirty to forty feet. And
the little speaker I have is a knockout. It's twinned with
the one you're wearing that'll carry my voice to the
faithful."

"Fine. We'll keep the code in, then. One for stop and
two for start. RDV back here at eleven-thirty, so I can
smuggle you out past the mercs."

"Good luck, Mike."

Bolan nodded and left.

Back in the small lecture hall Cleo Duhamel was on the rostrum. She wore a diaphanous crimson robe that hugged her figure, and leaned back in the chair with her heavy lids closed. Her hands toyed with a silver amulet on a chain, and the desk was littered with seashells, semitransparent stones and sheets of paper on which cabalistic signs had been scrawled. Her sensual lips were drawn back from her teeth, her nostrils were dilated, and from the back of her throat a deep voice was speaking. The spirit—if that was what it was—seemed to be answering a question from the floor.

Bolan stopped listening. The material was a little too close to his own script to be comfortable.

"Dr. Cahill?"

Salter was at his side. This was the moment of truth. To be more precise, he reflected wryly as he was led to the dais, it was, in fact, the moment of untruth.

Lowering himself into the chair, he heard a patter of applause—and was irritated to see that the backs of his hands were covered in sweat. He twisted his head to one side and leaned forward so that his eyes were shielded by the palm of his right hand, with his right elbow resting on the desk. The other hand was in the left-hand pocket of his suede jacket.

After a while he relaxed, breathing as deeply as he could and closing his eyes to slits... through which he was conscious of the many pairs of eyes concentrating on him, and above all of the glittering, apparently hostile pair burning in the skull-like face of the high priestess at the back of the room.

Finally, making his voice as sepulchral as he could, he said, "There is a spirit... one of the followers of Kardec and an adept of the way, who wishes to speak. A spirit recently discarnated who wishes to be heard." A pause, and then, "Let her speak. Let the spirit speak now."

With his left hand he thumbed the send button on the tiny transceiver in his pocket, then pressed the bar at the top twice for blast-off.

Abruptly, from the level of his own throat, the voice of Felicity Freeman said clearly, in a slightly French accent, "In our world every spirit is responsible for its own actions. And for each action there must be a reaction. We call this the Law of Karma, and it is exercised through the function of reincarnation. Through the use of their free will, spirits evolve progressively, by incarnating and discarnating successively until perfection is attained and further incarnations are no longer necessary."

Bolan pressed the bar once to halt the woman while he looked around the room. He wasn't giving them anything they didn't know—or hadn't already heard from Cleo Duhamel earlier—but the buildup was necessary as a prelude to the punch lines to come later. In any case, he still seemed to have them hooked. He depressed the bar twice.

"In each incarnation," Freeman's voice resumed, "experience is gained—in different environments, circumstances, ages, even at times planets. But in this there is an order, a rhythm, which must never be tampered with. The forces of nature are not to be bent to the will of mortals. To attempt to pervert the Law of Karma, even with the excuse of advancing knowledge, is to disrupt the equipoise of the infinite.''

Bolan thumbed the bar. This was strong stuff the woman was putting forth. In the silence that followed, he looked through half-closed eyes at the group around Joliffe. Were they aware that the message was aimed directly at them?

It sure looked that way. Salter was whispering to Vanderlee, his expression angry. Kleist had twisted around in his chair. He appeared to be trying to catch the eye of the old priestess in back. Bolan pressed the bar twice.

''To those of you who would meddle—''

Without warning the words slurred into an abrasive screech, a high-pitched howl that soared up the scale and then plunged.

Bolan sat bolt upright, and a moment passed before he caught on. The eldrich screams shrieking from the speaker hanging around his neck were simply violent oscillations of the kind once common in the tuning of radio receivers.

The hesitation cost him.

As the oscillations settled into a continuous ear-splitting whine, Vanderlee, Salter and Kleist charged the rostrum, leaping for him in a concerted rush.

Bolan sprang to his feet. His chair crashed over backward. The carafe of water tipped over the edge of the desk and shattered on the floor.

But such was the impetus of the three men's furious advance that the big man was hurled bodily across the platform and hustled through a doorway into the passage beyond before he had the chance to recover from his surprise and brace himself to meet them.

Salter kicked the door shut, and the three of them fell on him with flailing fists and feet.

If he hadn't been caught totally unawares, Bolan would have been a match for them. But this time the odds were against him. He slammed Salter against the wall with a powerful right, then crossed swiftly with his left to land a stunning blow high up on the German's cheek. Vanderlee meanwhile had landed a shrewd kick in the Executioner's crotch, momentarily doubling him up.

As Bolan straightened, gasping, he felt a cold ring of steel pressed to his neck. "All right," Kleist's voice grated, "stay exactly where you are, or your brains end up splashed against the wall."

Bolan froze. Experience had taught him the difference between a bluff and a threat that would be carried out.

He saw Salter sidle around behind him, his lip already puffed where the Executioner's fist had caught him. The PR man carried a leather-covered blackjack, and a sadistic glint gleamed in his eye.

For one hundredth of a second Bolan sensed a rush of air. Then a weight descended on his head and he felt himself falling into the dark.

CHAPTER ELEVEN

Bolan was in a mess. His pants were dusty and blood-stained, the suede jacket was ripped across the shoulders and his shoes were gone. Struggling back to awareness through waves of nausea, he realized that the conspirators must, in their fury, have continued to rain kicks and blows on his inert body after he lost consciousness. One of his eyes was puffy. Pain flamed through his left kidney, his nose was swollen and bleeding, and his groin ached more than a single kick would account for.

Vanderlee, standing in front of him, was still shaking with rage. "Perhaps now," he said harshly, "you would be prepared to explain the meaning of this...this *outrage?*"

"You stole my line," Bolan grated through clenched teeth. He was sitting in a ladderback chair, with his ankles roped to the front legs. His arms had been forced behind the chair back, the wrists lashed together with plastic-covered wire and attached to one of the rungs.

The room was small, furnished as an office, and lit by a single bright desk lamp angled on Bolan's face. Behind it he could see the scowling face of Kleist. Salter lolled negligently against the door with his arms folded.

As soon as the Executioner spoke, Vanderlee stepped forward and slapped him viciously four times across the face, backhand and forehand, at the full stretch of his arm. A trickle of blood seeped from Bolan's nose. "We don't want any smart answers, Cahill," the Dutchman shouted. "Come on, what the hell's the point of you, a genuine medium, insulting everybody with this cheap trick?"

"Maybe the spirits wouldn't say what had to be said," Bolan replied.

Salter had pushed himself upright and walked around behind him. Tensing his muscles in anticipation of another blow from the blackjack, Bolan felt the man's soft hands explore the ruined clothing. He produced the transceiver and then the throat mike and speaker from behind Bolan's blood-soaked cravat.

"*Scheisse!*" Kleist spit. "I thought the bastard might have been fooling with preset tapes, but this transmitter, the mike—"

"The voice must have been live!" Vanderlee broke in angrily. "That means an accomplice. All right, Cahill, where is she?"

"Who?"

Kleist came into the light, drew back his fist and slammed it into the pit of the Executioner's stomach. The chair crashed over backward, and Bolan groaned involuntarily as the wooden back carrying the full weight of his bound body mashed his wrists against the stone floor. Grimacing with distaste, Salter helped the Dutchman haul the chair upright. Kleist twined his fingers in Bolan's hair and dragged his head back.

"You're going to talk," he raged, "if he have to kill you!"

With his free hand he grasped the speaker and twisted it until the cord from which it hung bit deeply into the Executioner's neck. Bolan's body arched away from the chair. His chest labored as his lungs tried desperately to drag air through his constricted windpipe.

Vanderlee watched the congested flesh bloat beneath Bolan's eyes. When the skin turned a mottled purple, he leaned down to the suffocating man's ear and said quietly, "Come now, Cahill, this is your last chance. Kleist means what he says. Who is the woman, and where is she?"

The door opened.

The high priestess walked into the room. From behind her the sound of Sir Simon Joliffe's distressed voice echoed faintly, "Most truly sorry, my dear friends, for this unexpected and appalling..."

The woman closed the door. "I don't know about any female," she said, "but this man's not Cahill."

She held up a copy of a Sunday tabloid newspaper. "One of the servants just arrived from London with a late edition," she explained.

The second lead story on the front page, beside the photo of a busty girl in a swimsuit, carried the headline: VOODOO MAN SLAIN BY BLOWPIPE DART. Beneath it, in smaller type, was the legend: Jungle Poison Strikes in Devon.

Kleist released Bolan's hair and let the speaker fall. With Salter and the Dutchman he crowded around the old woman. Then Vanderlee turned slowly around.

"This makes a difference," he said harshly. "It explains the hoax, but it poses two more questions. Who the hell are you, and why did you kill Cahill?"

"I didn't kill him."

"Of course you killed him," Kleist raged. "You murdered him so you could take his place here, knowing that nobody here had ever met him. But why? Why this attempt to fool us all? What good would it have done you if you had made it? And who is the woman helping you?"

"I'm a newspaperman. Joliffe is difficult to interview. I figured on getting an exclusive story..." A possible murder charge was something the Executioner hadn't reckoned on.

"Do you expect us to believe that?" Vanderlee cried, drawing back to punch Bolan's bloodied face again.

The priestess caught his arm. "There are better ways," she said. "There are few questions that can't be answered by a needle or the point of a knife."

"Now that one knows this man to be an impostor, doesn't the problem rather solve itself?" Salter suggested nervously.

"What do you mean?" Vanderlee asked.

"I mean, now that one knows he's a murderer, why not simply hand him over to the police? Wouldn't that rather simplify matters?"

"Too much," the German objected. "The police won't tell us all they find out. And we *must* know why this man is here." He glanced at Bolan, who was slumped forward in the chair, his chin sunk on his chest. "Forget the murder. We have to remember this intrusion is directed against *us*. It's vital that we know why. The police will interest themselves only in what happened at the railroad station."

"I agree," Vanderlee said. "Also, we have much better methods of finding out than a country copper. I think we should certainly hand him over, but not before the morning."

"The police wouldn't want to drive all the way out here at this time of night on a Sunday," Kleist persuaded. "Think of the fuss it would make. No, I think we should use the rest of the night to find out all he knows, then turn him in tomorrow. That way, if we're lucky, we can handle the whole thing discreetly without the old man or the others knowing."

"Yes, Wolf, but look at the state he'll be in!" Salter argued.

"You worry too much, my friend," the German said. "We'll first clean him up. Have no fear."

Salter looked with distaste at Bolan's unconscious figure. "Suppose he tells them everything that we—"

"Who's going to believe a murderer? There was a struggle when we unmasked him as an impostor. He was...damaged before we could subdue him. All right?"

"I guess so." The PR man was doubtful. "But look at him now!" He gestured toward the chair. Below his battered face Bolan's clothes were soaked in blood. Behind him his wrists had turned blue. "I hate to think how he might look after another six or seven hours. I really do!''

The priestess showed her yellow teeth in a grin. ''We'll clean him up now, if you like,'' she said. ''You'll be surprised. Apart from a black eye and a few bruises, he won't look too bad once the blood's been washed away.''

''Yes, all right. But if—''

''As for finding out what he knows—'' she flexed her bony fingers ''—believe me, it won't take anything like six hours.''

CHAPTER TWELVE

Waves of pain washed Bolan back to the shore of consciousness. What the torturers hadn't bargained for was the soldier's iron will, that inflexible determination and dedication that permitted him to be agonized into oblivion before the painmakers were wise to the fact and interrupted their evil practices.

It couldn't go on forever, of course. They'd already dragged him back three times and then allowed the witch to resume. But each reawakening, each successive blackout was time gained...and time was what he was playing for.

Pain wasn't of itself debilitating; the physical battering he'd received before the arrival of the old woman was. And it was to restore the normal steel-spring shape of muscles, nerves and sinews that he needed the time. After that—he'd been covertly wrestling with the plastic-covered wire binding his hands—he would make his play.

Finally, in the hope that he'd be left alone while they checked out the confession, he faked a break. His real name, he told them was Jason Mettner....

They could check that: there *was* a Jason Mettner, he *was* a newspaperman and he *was* in England. The

genuine article, sound asleep in his bedroom at the Red
Lion, would be in no danger.

Yes, he told them, his aim was to write a sensational
disclosure, a revelation of how easy it was to hood-
wink the gullible. His accomplice—he invented a
name—was a lady columnist from the *Globe*'s London bureau. Her part of the phony "séance" had been
transmitted from a cabin where she was holed up with
one of the Brazilian initiates.

"It won't take long to verify that," Vanderlee said.
"Meanwhile—" he looked at the priestess "—you
better keep him quiet."

Bolan felt the flesh above his elbow being pinched,
then the prick of a needle. Very soon the room and
everything in it floated away.

AS SOON AS SHE REALIZED the system had gone ape,
Freeman switched off. She knew how easy it was to locate a transmitter if you had the right equipment. Bolan's throat mike relayed the next stage of the drama,
but that, too, went dead after the priestess's surprise
entry. She hesitated. Until she found out where he was
held there was nothing she could do. She carried no
gun, she had no burglar's tools and she had no experience in rescue operations—her work for Williams had
never involved anything more than the passing on of
information she'd gathered.

Whatever, she had to pack up the electronics and get
out of the pavilion fast. Because, as far as she knew,
Bolan was just a journalist and there was no telling how
soon he could crack and spill the whole scenario.

Should she go back to the village, rouse Mettner and ask his help?

No way. Bolan had told her about the mercenaries. An intruder not on the guest list, trying to leave the property at this time of night, wouldn't get very far. She'd get to Bolan, all right, that way—but as a fellow prisoner.

She stowed the equipment and got out of there. At the far end of the rose walk, she waited for five minutes in the shadow of a tall yew hedge. She heard no sound from the house and saw no movement. She crossed a sunken Dutch garden and approached the stables from the rear.

The arched entrance to the yard would be too risky, she decided. Half the bedroom windows looked over it, and it was too near the priestesses' cabins. But there was a high wall separating one side of the yard from a vegetable garden, and a pass door was cut into it. Freeman dodged through bean rows and raspberry canes, approaching the door across a bed of large-leaved, waist-high plants. The pathway was graveled and could be too much of a giveaway. She pressed lightly on the iron latch. The door was unlocked and swung open with a slight squeak.

She held her breath. No footsteps, no challenge. Okay—no mercs this near the house. She slipped through the doorway.

Mike, she imagined, would still be held in the basement—they'd hardly risk dragging him upstairs in front of the other guests. But, although the onetime manor house boasted this lower floor, probably cellars at one time, there was no area surrounding it. The ballroom, the lecture hall and the other rooms down there were all artificially lit and there were no windows to raise surprised eyebrows just above ground level. That was probably a plus for the Finnish modernist doing the conversion, but a pain for a trespasser vainly trying to locate from outside a room where a friend was being kept prisoner....

No, there was no alternative. She'd have to penetrate the hall at ground level if she was to make it.

She had a rough idea of the layout from Mike, but it would be strictly off-the-cuff material once she was inside.

She hid the equipment behind a row of garbage cans and was about to step into the arcade when she heard a door bang. Hastily she drew back into the shadows. A moment later a tall, white-haired man with craggy features, wearing a striped, long-sleeved vest, walked past, pushing a rubber-tired buggy full of empty bottles. He crossed the yard and went through the doorway into the vegetable garden.

Freeman nodded with satisfaction. That was good—it meant there would be an unlocked door in there for sure. She decided to go through it before the guy returned. Seconds later, breathing a sigh of relief, she was in a brightly lit butler's pantry. She crept through and found herself in a long corridor that led toward the front of the house. Halfway along this she heard approaching footsteps. More than one set.

Biting her lip, she backed through a doorway into a small closet. She left the door open a crack and peered through as the footsteps drew near.

A heavily built man with crimped silver hair and a fringe beard was walking with a young man whose hair flopped over one eye. Vanderlee, she guessed, remembering Mike's description, and the guy masterminding the occult side of the party.

"In the second of the huts, he told us," Vanderlee was saying. "But I wouldn't think she'll still be there. In any case, those little bitches would probably hide her, say they didn't know what we were talking about. You know these checkbook journalists—they'll buy anyone."

"We have clout," Salter said venomously. "I'll arrange beaters to cover the whole damn estate later. For the moment I'd rather one kept a low profile. One would so hate to alert the other guests that something was seriously wrong. They've had enough of a shock already with this ghastly trickster."

"You might be right," Vanderlee agreed. "Now that he's been injected by that old woman, he'll be out of harm's way until the morning, anyway, I imagine."

"Of course he will. She knows what she's doing. And Wolf will keep him under wraps in the loft over Joliffe's garage until the police come."

"Excellent. We'd better check out the huts just the same."

"I'd rather do that than watch that female's gruesome tricks!" The PR man shuddered and they passed out of earshot.

Freeman gave a sigh of relief. The problem had been settled for her. It seemed that Mike had cracked. But at least he would be spared further torture. There was no point in her trying to rescue him while he was drugged and unconscious. She'd wait until the morning and do her best to spirit him away before the police got their hands on him.

She could, of course, allow the police to take him away. But since he'd actually shared the murdered man's compartment—by his own admission without any other witnesses—it seemed they might not be prepared to free him before an investigation was completed. And apart from that, the fact that he'd incontestably impersonated the dead man for two days after gaining admission to Joliffe Hall on false pretenses . . . No, a police presence was definitely out.

So, what to do? Stick around until such time as Belasko recovered consciousness and was strong enough to help in his own escape.

In the loft above Joliffe's garage, they'd said. Maybe a brief recon was in order before they set the mercs on her trail. She was about to move out of the closet when she heard more footsteps, slow and shuffling this time. Staring through the crack between the half-shut door and its frame, she saw why.

A man wearing a chauffeur's uniform and a middle-aged Nordic type were carrying between them the limp body of the man she knew as Mike Belasko. His face was no longer bloody, but he was pale and his breathing was uneven. "I'll tell you one thing," the chauffeur growled, lifting an arm that was trailing the floor and placing it across his burden's naked chest. "It's going to be one hell of a job gettin' him up that bleedin' ladder in there!"

"No sweat," said the Nordic, who she knew must be Wolfgang Kleist. "We'll hoist him over your shoulder and you can make like a fire fighter."

The woman watched them go. Garage and loft had to be somewhere near the stables. She'd check them out once the two men dumped Mike and returned to the house. When they made it to the far end of the hallway, she left the closet and slipped out of the building as unobtrusively as she'd entered.

Fifteen minutes later she was hoisting herself into the branches of a lime tree that overlooked the priestesses' huts, wasn't too far from the stables and gave her a good view of the footpath that led through the woods to the lower part of the estate where the mercenaries were based.

And in the shrubbery bordering a sunken garden, a second intruder, dressed entirely in black—a short, lean shadow that had stayed close behind her all evening— watched her activity with a puzzled frown.

CHAPTER THIRTEEN

For Bolan there were two priorities. After those, he'd be content to handle things as they came. Whatever way events arranged themselves, in whatever order they came, he'd be ready. But first...

Number one, free his hands; number two, immobilize Wolfgang Kleist.

He was lying on a bed in some kind of utility room above one of the garages in the stable area. Dust motes swam in the shafts of moonlight penetrating the grimy cobwebbed windows, and the sweetish aromatic odor of gasoline rose from somewhere below. His hands had been bound again, but with the same plastic-covered wire that had lashed them to the chair in the house.

Covertly maneuvering his hands while he was roped to the chair, he'd picked at the plastic with his nails until he'd sliced through in a couple of places. The two-inch section of plastic thus isolated had been easy enough to remove once it was slit down the middle. The copper wire beneath was unplaited—twelve straight strands, only filament-thick, in each half of the duplex insulation.

Whole, the stuff was impossible to snap, stretch or break. With the insulation removed, the twelve-strand core was tough enough to cut through skin and flesh.

But each single filament, no thicker than a human hair, was easy enough to gouge through once it had been separated from the rest.

Bolan was halfway through the first half of the duplex when he was injected. The problem now, with his hands still behind his back and provided his captors hadn't paid any attention to the break in the plastic casing, was to locate the section he'd been working on. He eventually found it in an awkward position between his two wrists and started to pick at the remaining strands.

It was taxing work, tricky and agonizingly slow. The smallest movement was hampered by the weight of his body pressing down on his arms. And beyond an occasional twitch or jerk, he couldn't afford to show any movement at all. It was vital that Kleist, sitting in a broken-down rocking chair near the trapdoor, had no idea he'd recovered from the drug earlier than expected.

The conspirators, he reckoned, were experienced enough in whatever kind of crookery and double-dealing they were into, but inexperienced in the more physical side of wrongdoing. They weren't wise to the fact that the time a knockout drug was effective related to the age, weight and condition of the victim; they thought that by tying a man's hands behind his back they were rendering him harmless; and they were certainly ignorant about guns. Kleist held a Browning automatic loosely in his lap, but the slide hadn't been pulled back to lodge a round in the breech.

Several hours passed before Bolan felt the last filament in the second half of the duplex part. He flexed his raw wrists experimentally. The insulated wire shifted, easing the pressure clamping his wrists together. Once he was upright and the weight was off his arms, he could slip one hand out of the severed noose and unwind the wire on the other.

A few minutes later he contrived a realistic groan and twisted his body on the bed. Kleist turned his head, his fist closing around the gun butt.

Bolan groaned again. He coughed, almost choking. "Hey, Kleist. You've got to help me. I have to go to the john."

"The john?" Kleist sounded dubious.

"Hell, the washroom, the lavatory, the WC. I have to—"

"This is a loft in the stables. There's no such place up here."

"Well, you better find me someplace," Bolan groaned. "I'm going to throw up any minute."

Kleist got up hastily. "Here. Over here," he said after a swift look around. "There's some kind of basin—"

Seizing the Executioner by the shoulders, he levered him off the bed and propelled him toward a pile of junk in the far corner. Bolan, holding the loose wire together over his wrists, stood over a galvanized washtub.

The warrior brought up one knee with stunning force, at the same time freeing his hands, linking them and bringing them down savagely on the back of the German's neck.

Kleist dropped to the dusty floorboards with a thump that shook the building, blood spraying from his broken nose. He was down and out.

Dust raised by the scuffle was already coating the rivulets of blood as Bolan scooped up the Browning. It was one of the 1922 models made by the FN arsenal in Belgium. There were four rounds in the 9-shot magazine. He pulled back the slide, slipped the automatic into his pocket and climbed cautiously down the ladder to the garage below.

The area was a complete contrast to the junk-filled loft. He saw graded ranks of shining tools gleaming in the moonlight above a professionally equipped workbench, a block and tackle attached to one of the overhead beams, neat regiments of gasoline and oil in cans and drums. There were four cars beyond the inspection pit—a Range Rover, a Volvo wagon, a Fleetwood stretch limo and the Rolls that had ferried him from the railroad station.

He checked each in turn, but none had keys in the ignition. Hot-wiring one in the darkness would be too difficult, and in any event, he had to locate the Freeman woman before he did anything else.

The garage was closed by heavy double doors that rolled on rails. As Bolan expected, having seen the state of the workshop inside, the rails were greased and the rollers well oiled. The door that he opened slid soundlessly aside to let him out into the yard.

He stole past an open-fronted section of the stables where most of the guests' cars were housed, crept behind several others parked nearer the yard entrance and sidled beneath the arch onto the main driveway.

Someone was running toward him from the front of the house. He made it fast to the shrubbery and ducked among the bushes.

The driveway was brightly lit by the moon. The runner, he could see clearly, was Vanderlee. The guy was panting, and his crimped hair was awry as if nervous fingers had been run through it.

A dark figure emerged from an unlit side entrance halfway along the shadowed wall of the manor, stepping suddenly into the milky illumination. It was Rick Salter.

"Where the hell are you going?" he whispered angrily. "What's the hurry?"

The Dutchman skidded to a halt in front of him. "Stables," he choked. "We must go back there and revive that bastard at once. He—"

"What the hell for? I thought we agreed. The police—"

"Lies!" Vanderlee gasped. "All lies—everything he told us! He's no bloody newspaperman. We just went through the stuff in his room. There's a carryall with a false bottom. He's got a Beretta automatic in there with a shoulder holster, a knife, a garrote and God knows what else in the way of burglar's tools. This man's some kind of professional. I say he's got to be questioned again. And then eliminated when we've squeezed him dry."

Bolan cursed under his breath. He'd hoped to be able to recover his gear before he left. Feet crunched on the gravel driveway as the two men hurried away. "We should have thought of this before," Salter was saying. "Searching his room, I mean. We'll help Kleist get him out of that loft and back to mother so he can be roused. One does so hope..."

The PR man's voice faded as they rounded the corner and walked under the arch. Bolan was already on his feet, poised to go. But where to start? Which direction would the illusionist have taken when she left the summerhouse? If she had left it.

He didn't have to decide. A whisper floated his way, scarcely louder than the night breeze sighing through the treetops. He cocked his head, straining to hear, to separate the sound from the innumerable tiny noises that made up the silence of the night.

Yeah, there it was—a soft voice breathing his adopted name.

He could see her now that he knew which way to look, her face a pale blur against the somber mass of the woods in back of the stables, the body lost in shadow. Crouching low to keep out of sight himself, he ran through the bushes to join her.

"Thank God you're free," Freeman murmured. "Are you all right? What did they—"

"Right enough to run," he cut in tersely. "We've got to get out of here before they call up the army."

"The army?"

"Mercs down in the valley. Professionals. At any minute they'll find out that I've escaped."

He listened again and heard a shout from the far side of the stables. "What I thought," he rasped. "We have to move before they get it together." Mind racing, he charted the options.

Main gates?

No way. They'd be closed. Salter would phone down; they might have armed men there at night.

An estate this size would have rear entrances, service tracks, gates for tractors and agricultural stuff to pass through, but he didn't know in which direction they were.

They needed transport.

"So which way do we move?" Freeman asked.

"We hole up long enough to get motorized," Bolan replied. "But not so long that their hired guns have time to spread out."

"Okay. Where's the hole?"

"Where's the best place to hide?" he countered. "The place they're least likely to look? For my money, the place you just escaped from."

"So we go back to the stables?"

He nodded. "Once those two guys have split to call up the mercs on their walkie-talkies. But we have to let them get clear first. The Dutchman carries a gun, I know. And I only have four rounds in this baby." He showed her the Browning.

"You aim to take one of the cars parked there?"

"Right. But not one of the guests'. The yard—even the open part of the stables—is too exposed. We'll use one of Joliffe's. I doubt the old guy drives himself. Where would a chauffeur regularly stash the keys?"

"In his pocket when he was on call. Someplace in his quarters, I guess, when he wasn't," she said doubtfully. "There'd be spare sets, of course."

"Right. Where?"

She blew out her breath, shrugging. "You tell me. In the boss's room? The chauffeur's? Hanging on a hook behind the kitchen door? Even in the garage, maybe, if the doors lock securely."

"The doors are fine. I'd go along with that, if I knew where to look. Could be a hook, a locked drawer, a cupboard. Could be the wall where the tools are racked. But we can't turn on the lights, and it could take a half hour to locate them in the dark. If they're there. Same thing if I tried hot-wiring."

"There's a small flashlight with my gear," the woman offered.

"Okay. Where's the stuff?"

"Behind the trash cans in the yard."

"That's my girl!" Bolan enthused. "We'll go get it once those clowns have taken off."

They tiptoed to the arch and peered into the yard. Vanderlee and Salter were running for the house, the Dutchman carrying the inert figure of Kleist over his shoulder.

"Come on," Bolan whispered. "If we're lucky, the garage doors are still open."

They were lucky. He passed behind the cars parked in the yard and eased himself into the garage while Freeman hurried across to recover her equipment.

The thin beam from the flashlight played around the garage walls. There were keys hanging from a hook at one side of a board used for pinning up sheets detailing mileage, gas consumption and checkup dates for each of the cars. But they were heavy iron mortice keys—for the door to a spare parts storeroom, a drawer below the workbench, a padlocked chest containing car documents dating back several years. Working quickly and silently, Bolan used them all, rummaged through the chest, emptied the drawer, glanced inside the store.

No spare car keys.

He cursed. From somewhere outside, excited voices called. Guiding the woman's flashlight beam, he searched the workbench, found pincers, wire, a roll of adhesive and a small pair of scissors. "We'll take the Range Rover," he decided. "It's the nearest thing to a genuine off-roader. It's big and it's fast."

"It's also nearest to the doors," Freeman observed.

Bolan grinned. He opened the car door, leaned in beneath the wheel, rested the flashlight on the transmission tunnel and began to work. "Shove the right-hand garage door back," he called quietly. "Slow and easy. It's well oiled."

She leaned her shoulder against the iron grip and pushed. The door rolled noiselessly away from her. This, she knew, was the moment of maximum danger. In the moonlight anyone watching from the house could clearly see that the garage was open.

The Range Rover's starter motor whirred, and the engine rumbled to life.

Bolan stretched across to open the passenger door as he flipped the gearshift into first. Freeman tossed the case containing her equipment onto the rear seat and clambered up beside him. The Range Rover jerked forward and shot through the open doorway into the yard.

The luxury off-roader laid down rubber as Bolan spun the wheel and raced for the arch. Once on the driveway beyond, the Executioner took in the scene with a lightning glance.

The doorway on the shadowed side of the huge house was open again, but this time there was light streaming out to lay a wide bar of brilliance across the moonlit pavement. Five men stood on the steps leading down from the door, and there was a Jeep with the soft top raised parked on one side of the drive.

Bolan knew four of the group—Salter, Vanderlee, Ley Phuong and the Nevada rifleman's double. The fifth man was a beefy, hard-eyed gorilla, clearly some kind of heavy employed by the conspirators.

Salter was speaking into a transceiver with the aerial pulled out. Vanderlee held a pistol loosely at arm's length, a Combat Master or a Desert Eagle by the look of it. The ringer was armed, too, a silenced automatic in his left hand. Once again Bolan sensed the familiar tingle at his nape. The rifleman had been left-handed; his weapon had been modified so that the bolt was operated from that side.

Alerted by the sound of the Range Rover's engine, the five were already registering astonishment, anger, determination, as Bolan careered through the arch and headed their way.

Vanderlee's mouth opened in a shout, and the ringer raised his pistol. But Bolan had wrenched at the wheel as soon as he was wise to the situation, sending the tall off-roader plowing through a herbaceous border and across a lawn at one side of the rose walk. Wood splintered and spun away as the Rover smashed through a rustic pergola and bucketed among the bushes of the shrubbery.

Bolan downed the electric window and reached forward to drag away leaves, stalks, blooms and the tendrils of some exotic creeper that were trailing across the windshield. Only two shots had been fired at them as far as he could tell, both from the ringer's silenced weapon. He reckoned Vanderlee and the others were scared that the sound of gunfire would not only awaken the guests who weren't in on the racket, but clue them in also to the fact that Sir Simon Joliffe's spiritist congress wasn't what it seemed on the surface. One of the ringer's rounds had shattered the rear window; the other shot had smashed the outside mirror on the driver's side.

"Two or three of them have piled into that Jeep," Freeman reported. She'd twisted in her seat and was staring out past the jagged shards of glass still held in place by the rear window frame. "They just crossed the lawn. The driver has switched on the headlights."

"They'll be radioing the mercs to get in their armored truck and cut us off. Me, I'll stay with the moonlight. Makes us tougher to locate." He'd already noted the Jeep's lights in the rearview mirror.

"Tougher to locate on the way *where?*" the woman asked.

"I wish I knew. Out, anyway. Although I'd feel better if I had a map of the property."

Behind them the twin shafts of the Jeep's headlights bounced over the rough ground, lanced skyward and swept over a stand of young birches.

Zigzagging between bushes and clumps of furze, Bolan hurtled the Range Rover along the lip of the valley. There were already lights moving among the trees in the woods below where he had encountered O'Hara. The Jeep was two hundred yards behind. "If we're going to make it," the Executioner said tightly, "we have to make it on the far side of the lake."

"But isn't that...? I can see water shining between the trees on the far side of that field."

"We have to cross the meadow to make the lake, yeah."

"And this stone wall?"

"There's a gate," Bolan explained, "in a couple of hundred yards. Hold tight. We're going through without opening it."

The Range Rover slewed almost to a halt, throwing up clods of earth as he braked fiercely and engaged the four-wheel drive. He jerked the lever and fed the full horsepower from the V8 engine to the drive shafts.

Heavy ribbed tires scrabbled for a second on the moist surface, then the vehicle leaped forward, leaving deep furrows in the turf. The stone wall shot past. Bolan swung the wheel, careening the car through ninety degrees, and charged the gate that had saved his life the previous night.

The iron grille protecting the radiator and lamps struck the gate's diagonal crossbar in the center at almost forty miles per hour. The bar snapped, carrying with it the rail at the top of the gate, and the wreckage of the remainder exploded away like splintered matchwood.

A spar from the gatepost, still attached to an iron hinge, rapped the windshield and starred the safety glass on the passenger side, but otherwise, barring dents and scratches, they appeared to have suffered no damage.

They rounded the end of the lake, bounced across the track that led to the bridge and the island and continued through a belt of trees. Beyond the lake the land shelved steeply downward, and they saw that the valley curled around the lakehead. They'd have to descend, after all, unless Bolan was prepared to chance a dense pinewood on their left.

He wasn't. The Range Rover broadsided down between thicker clumps of furze and outcrops of bare rock as the slope steepened more still. "My God, what kind of country *is* this?" Freeman gasped as she bounced up and down like a pea on a drum. "I thought lakes were supposed to be in valleys, not on a plateau above!"

"When you have as much money as Joliffe," Bolan said grimly, wrestling with the wheel, "you can have lakes wherever you want."

He swore as the off-roader tipped almost onto its side, steering straight into a bramble patch to slow their headlong plunge. The Rover bucked, left the ground, then slammed down on three wheels, sending flakes of weathered rock skating into a cut. Freeman cried out as her head hit the roof.

They'd lost sight of the mercenaries when they turned into the meadow, but now, slipping and sliding down the bank with the engine roaring, they could once again see the lights of the armored truck weaving through the trees below, racing to cut them off while the lightweight Jeep bumped in pursuit down the slope above.

"How far up the other side of the valley do we have to go?" Freeman queried, staring anxiously through the starred screen at the moving gleam, now bright, now half-obscured, threading the shadows beneath them.

"I wish I knew," Bolan replied. "From what O'Hara told me, I'd say not too far. It seems there's a high wall. Hell, the property has to end somewhere."

"Will they be shooting again?"

"Sure they will. We know too much. Or at least they think we know too much. They can't afford to have us escape."

"Will the mercenaries have machine guns?"

"SMGs. Submachine guns. But I don't expect them to use them."

"Why not? Aren't they more, well, effective?"

"Certainly. But this is rural England on a summer night. The sounds of automatic fire would have the whole country asking questions," Bolan explained. "They can't afford that, either. Single shots on the other hand..." He paused, correcting a slide that was dislodging an avalanche of earth and stones from the hillside, then continued. "The hunting season's not open yet, but I guess there's nothing to stop a guy shooting game on his own land. Especially someone as rich and eccentric as Joliffe. That's what folks will think, anyway."

"The man who shot at us up by the house, the tall one who was left-handed, he had a silenced handgun. Aren't there silenced submachine guns, as well?"

"Yeah. But that's pretty sophisticated stuff. I can't see the boys on the payroll here being that far ahead of the game."

They had reached the bottom of the slope. Behind them the Jeep had caught up to within a 150 yards. The lights of the armored truck, half-masked by the trunks of trees growing beside a dried-up riverbed that snaked along the valley floor, were still some distance away.

Bolan drove straight over a four-foot bank that threatened to shatter the Range Rover's suspension, scrambled the car through the pale stones marking the old watercourse and shifted down into first to attack the slope on the far side.

The hillside was wooded, and there were stacks of lumber waiting to be carted away in most of the clearings. Two hundred yards beyond the riverbed the land dipped again into a small depression. Trees grew more thickly here, but among them, bone-white in the moonlight and perhaps a quarter of a mile away, the high demesne wall could be seen beneath the massed branches. Bolan sighed with relief. "You still have your throat mike and the other transistor speaker?" he asked.

"Yes, here in the case with the other stuff. Why?"

"Take them out and get them ready."

"I'm sorry. I don't understand. What can they—"

"Just do it."

He maneuvered the Rover as fast as he could up the grade between the scattered trees, rocketing over the rough ground as the pursuers converged behind them. There was no chance of concealment now, no way of disguising his intentions. He switched on the headlights.

In the sudden, blinding illumination of the main beams, the wall—pale, ancient bricks and twelve feet high, as O'Hara had said—seemed frighteningly close. The Rover shuddered to a stop. "Jump out and wait for me," Bolan ordered.

This time Freeman obeyed without question. The door was still swinging open when he powered the V8 and shot away. She dropped behind a screen of bushes. The Jeep was skidding through the riverbed; the armored truck was perhaps three hundred yards away and climbing. The lights hurled black shadows ahead of the trees.

Bolan rammed the Rover against the wall with the lever in second and the pedal flat against the floor.

The sound of the crash was deafening. The wall bellied outward; a semicircular crack looped down from the top and several layers of bricks crumbled away and fell; a little to one side a fissure streaked from top to bottom of the stonework. But there was no breach wide or deep enough to drive through. Bolan backed off and tried again.

The fenders had been pushed back and crumpled almost onto the front wheels, the hood had buckled and spun away, and the remains of the windshield had vanished. But the wreck could still stagger and growl up to twenty miles per hour, deformed panels screeching as the tires thumped over the rough ground.

He aimed the Rover a couple of yards to one side of the first hit, hoping to strike the fissure smack in the middle and tip the whole wall into the country lane beyond.

What he failed to see, lying diagonally across his path, was a trench several feet deep and partly concealed by dead brushwood. The offside front wheel dropped into the cut and the car lurched sickeningly. Then the offside rear followed, and the Rover, powered still by the laboring engine at maximum speed, toppled over onto its side with a shattering of glass. The big engine screamed, stalled and died. Bolan flipped the driver's door up and open. He clambered out, leaped to the ground and raced back to the bushes where Freeman was hidden. The Browning was in one hand; the other was clamped around the speaker and mike she'd produced.

The pursuers were dangerously near. The truck's headlights picked up the stranded Range Rover and the driver braked to a halt between two trees. The Jeep stopped lower down the hill, and Bolan could hear an exchange on the walkie-talkies.

"It will waste one round out of the four," he whispered to Freeman as he dropped beside her, "but I've got to show them we're armed. Otherwise they'll just walk in on every side and take us."

"All right, Mettner, or whatever you're called," Vanderlee's voice bellowed through a bullhorn. "You're surrounded. We have the drop on you and you can't get away. Give yourself up and we'll let the woman go."

The voice came from beside the Jeep. Bolan leveled the Browning, aimed carefully and shot out the headlight nearest to it. At once three single shots ripped out from the armored truck. Slugs spit through the leaves above Bolan's head; somebody cursed.

The moon slid out of sight behind a cloud, and suddenly everything outside the swathes of illumination cast by the three remaining headlights vanished.

Bolan pressed Freeman's arm. "There's a giant oak beside the wreck," he whispered. "Creep up there and climb into the lower branches. I'm going to put my money on the dark. I can't shoot all of them with three rounds, anyway."

She nodded and crawled silently away across a carpet of last year's pine needles. Bolan shot out the Jeep's second headlight.

He lay flat and slithered ten yards downhill. With the two shots left in the magazine, he shattered the wire-fronted lights on the armored truck.

Flame stabbed the dark now from inside the Jeep and on both sides of the truck. Bolan lobbed the empty Browning another ten yards downhill. He pried two stones from the earth and threw them into the undergrowth after it, drawing more fire in that direction. Then, having established a pattern of movement away from the wall, he drew back his arm and sent the miniature speaker spinning even farther. He heard it crash into the leaves somewhere below.

Two guns belched flame from under the soft top of the Jeep. Bolan whispered into the throat mike, "Try to make the streambed. I'll draw them off this way."

And from thirty or forty yards away, his voice uttered in a louder, hoarser undertone, "Streambed, I'll draw them off. . ." The rest of the sentence was lost in a volley of small-arms fire.

Bolan used the mike one more time to project a realistic cry of pain from the bushes below. Then, as the thin shafts of flashlights probed the dark, and men began creeping toward the noise, he was on his feet and stealing noiselessly toward the wall.

He climbed up into the oak tree. He could make out the shape of Freeman, a faint blur lying along a branch that overhung the wall and stretched across the sunken lane beneath.

Downhill, angry voices called questions and answers among the leaves. A penetrating odor of gasoline rose into the tree from the smashed Range Rover. Straining his ears, the Executioner could hear a faint gurgle of liquid. The fuel tank must have ruptured under the final impact.

"That's a fifteen-foot drop into the lane," he whispered. "Can you make it without twisting an ankle?"

"Of course I can," Freeman replied.

"Okay. Away you go. I'm going to make sure they can't use the same route to follow us."

The thump and clatter as she landed on the ground seemed very loud. One of the mercs below heard it. There was a shout, and the flashlights, advancing through the undergrowth, vectored on the wreck.

Bolan held a box of matches in his left hand. Leaning out over his branch, he struck one, held it until the flame grew, then dropped it into the fumes rising toward him. The flame flickered, fanned out, then died before the matchstick hit the ground.

He tried again, throwing the match farther away. Still alight, it hit one of the Range Rover's buckled body panels, slid groundward, then stopped. The flame guttered, dwindled, died.

Bolan swore beneath his breath. He held four matches, struck them together and threw. Same result.

The pursuers had registered the tiny shafts of flame, and shots whistled Bolan's way. He pushed open the box of matches, struck one and held it so that the flame played on the heads of those still in the box. The box spit fire, flaring suddenly in his hand as the inflammable heads ignited.

Bolan tossed the miniature fireball as far out from the tree as he could, and it fell straight into the volatile vapor rising from the vehicle's ruptured tank. The soft explosion split open the sky. A tower of flame whirled upward, roaring among the branches, setting leaves alight. In less than two seconds the wreck and the area around it were transformed into a crackling inferno.

The pursuers halted, barred by the scorching wall of fire.

Bolan was already in the lane. Seizing Freeman by the hand, he began running toward the village.

CHAPTER FOURTEEN

From a private hotel in Bayswater on the seamier side of London's Hyde Park, Mack Bolan called Hal Brognola in Washington, D.C.

"Hal, this is an open line. You have any Intel on the four people our newspaper friend asked you to trace?"

"Why an open line?"

"I'm on the run and can't make it to the embassy. The British police 'wish to interview a man they think may be able to help them in their inquiries.' The inquiries concern the murder of a medium. And they want me."

"Oh, shit."

"The guys who called in the cops thought I was Mettner. Mettner was staying in a nearby hotel. He was able to clear himself, so now the dragnet's out for Belasko, M., special correspondent."

"Striker, you sure have a talent for—"

"Trouble is my business, like the man said. You have the Intel?"

"Some, but not much."

"Pour it on."

"The Dutchman's executive head of an Austro-Netherlands consortium producing aerospace components. The German, he's a macromolecule research chemist specializing in styrene polymers with an abnormally high resistance to heat.''

"Like in jet engines and rocketry?"

"You got it. He's a board member of Kemtex-Elektron GmbH."

"They're UPI's business rivals?"

"Rivals, associates, you tell me. They're both clean as far as Interpol's concerned. Stony Man, too."

"Not in my book they're not. What about Salter?"

"Like you said, he has a reputation for being too damn smart for his own good. He's had his wrist slapped several times for misrepresentation, and he was almost inside on some gambling charge before casinos were legal in Britain. But so far as the law is concerned it's still 'nothing known.' "

"Okay. And the lady?"

"She was once suspected of running a cathouse in Acapulco. End of story."

Bolan laughed. "That figures. Anything on the occult side?"

"Only some kind of license to run a charity group in Rio."

"Confirmatory, all of it, but it doesn't get us far. And you?"

"One thing only. The Bureau identified the rifleman. He's a pro hit man by the name of Frank Scarff. It seems there's a twin brother Lem. Both left-handed. They used to work as a team. Useful for alibis."

"That's the obvious answer."

"Come again?"

"The brother's here, employed as an odd-job man at the hall. Makes the link complete, right?"

"It certainly suggests UPI was in some way connected with the attempt on our lives, yeah. Keep digging, Striker. And keep in touch."

"You bet."

FELICITY FREEMAN CALLED Colonel Williams from the Red Lion in Peverill-St. Mary.

"I can see where it might be useful, having the house wired for sound," she said when she made her report. "But I have to admit, I find myself foxed by the movie cutting room. Can't see where that fits in at all, even if the whole thing is somehow bogus."

"It's the most interesting part of the scenario. And I'm beginning to think it *is* a scenario in some way. I was afraid at first you might be wasting my time. Now I'm glad you called."

"I should add there was no sign that Joliffe was a home-movie buff. The stuff was far too professional for that—even for a man with his money."

"Understood. What did you do after Belasko fired the getaway car?"

"Shoved him under a blanket in the trunk of my own car and drove like hell for London. He thought by then he'd be a murder suspect, so the city'd be the safest place."

"Good thinking. Any roadblocks?"

"One, as we came off the Western Avenue expressway at Chiswick. I must have made it just before they set up the local ones."

"And that one?"

"No problem. You know the constabulary mind. They'd been told to watch out for a couple. Once they saw I was alone they waved me through."

"And, of course, a pretty girl couldn't be part of a murder mystery. Where's Mr. Belasko now?"

"In an old ladies' hotel in Bayswater. Can you pull strings and at least have the police hunt called off?"

"Not really. It would involve a lot of interdepartmental fuss. My people prefer not to disclose their existence if possible."

"Yes, that's all very well, but—"

"You're right, of course. There's clearly something very odd indeed going on down there. Not least the murder of the real Hanslip Cahill. Apart from the coincidence that your friend used it to trick his way into Joliffe's party, it hasn't been followed up in any way. I mean, the killer hasn't made a single move since."

"Unless it was this Duhamel woman. Would she have let Mike get away with the impersonation just because she wanted to get him into the sack?"

"My dear girl, you know more about feminine wiles than I do. What I find most baffling of all is the extraordinary ferocity with which these folks reacted when Belasko was unmasked. It can't just have been because they were mad at being fooled. The normal thing to do with a gate-crasher would be to throw him out, maybe teach him a bit of a lesson first, okay. But, I mean, this drug and torture routine… People who go that far must have something big to hide. They must be *very* determined not to have it found out."

"And the next move—for us, I mean?"

"I'm going to check out this spiritist thing. I'll call you."

"Very well, Colonel. But may I come back to Mike Belasko? Surely it's not fair that he should be left fearing he might be arrested at any minute for a murder he didn't commit? Couldn't you—"

"I already gave you my decision on that, Miss Freeman. Belasko himself is one of the unsolved puzzles in this affair. It will suit us quite well to keep him on ice while certain inquiries are made," Williams said crisply, then hung up the phone.

THE INTELLIGENCE AGENT identified by the code AX-12 called Colonel Williams from a pay phone in the lobby of a movie theater in Exeter.

"It wasn't possible to do anything to help this man Belasko, sir. Any overt action would have compromised my cover. I might have been blown altogether."

"Quite right. The important thing is to stay close to Joliffe. Did you have any joy with Belasko himself?"

"Negative, sir. I accepted him as the South American until he fucked up, uh, that is to say until his act went sour on him, sir. I didn't have much chance to get near him before that. He was having it off with the Dumahel lady most of the previous night."

"Was he, indeed? Did that strike you as a good thing?"

"Well, depends on what you fancy, sir, doesn't it?"

"I mean, how did you read it? Was he with her because it was purely a sex thing, or do you think he was using her, trying to find out something, the way you are, by getting next to someone in the inner circle?''

"Really, I couldn't say."

"The thing is, you see, well, Mr. Belasko is said to be a journalist. But like Mynheer Vanderlee and Herr Kleist, we're interested in knowing what *kind* of journalist. Because since he came into the country he hasn't, in fact, filed a single line, sent a single service message to his editor or made one genuine inquiry. We find that odd, and should he appear again, we want you to report on the smallest move he makes. Do I make myself clear?"

"As a bell, sir. You can rely on me."

MACK BOLAN CALLED Jason Mettner from a booth in back of a bar at Paddington railroad station, not far from his hotel. "There's a story here, a big one, I promise. But I have to ask you to stay with me a while longer while I check things out."

"So ask."

"That's what I'm doing. Meantime, my apologies for giving your name when they wanted one. I needed the time while they checked, and there *was* a Mettner around, so I reckoned that would stall them until I was ready."

"No sweat," Mettner said. "I'm already halfway through my first piece, 'The Day They Took Me for a Murderer. Grilled by Country Cops in Britain's Cider Belt,' by Our Special Correspondent. Just keep feeding me this material, and I'm your man."

CHAPTER FIFTEEN

Colonel Gregory Williams looked like an assistant bank manager—the kind who'd never make manager or even be transferred to a more interesting branch. He was a spare man, below medium height, with a toothbrush mustache and thin gray hair surrounding a bald pate. Customarily he wore circular gold-rimmed spectacles.

He was a nonentity, the kind of man you could never remember meeting before, or if you did remember, you'd forgotten where. But this anonymity had been his greatest asset when, as an SAS major, he'd led a penetration team with spectacular success in the Middle East, and later as a counterintelligence operative in Europe.

Colonel Williams was, in fact, a top-level spook. He was wasted, some said, now that he was no longer active in the field; irreplaceable, enthused the security chiefs whose undercover work depended so much on Intel funneled through from the AX organization he headed.

On the Thursday after Sir Simon Joliffe's weekend house party, Williams drove to Peverill-St. Mary after dark with the intention of making an illegal entry to the old manor house and checking out for himself some of the conflicting data supplied by Felicity Freeman and, through her, Michael Belasko. The woman accompanied him. "It'll be good for you," the colonel said, "to experience a spot of live tradecraft."

She resisted the urge to mention that she'd received a reasonably impressive initiation into the more active side of the business seventy-two hours earlier. Instead she asked to be filled in on the department's interest in Joliffe's plastics empire.

"It's because of the sensitive stuff they make," he told her. "Among all that other stuff, I mean. The government is a minority shareholder in UPI, but it's a big minority. And Whitehall does like to feel that the rest of the stock—or at least a majority of it—is held by people who are, well, all right."

"How is the stock distributed, as far as you know now?"

"Joliffe's family has a controlling interest when their shares are added to those held by the government. The remainder is distributed right and left, all over the market. But there's been movement recently, and we're having that checked."

"Are you talking about a takeover?" Freeman asked.

"No," the colonel replied, "not really. Not in the normal sense. But we have to watch extremely carefully any movement that could affect that vital fifty-plus stake held jointly by Joliffe and the government."

"Do we know how this occult routine started?"

"Oh, yes. We checked, naturally. It's all in the Central Register. The old man's interest is genuine enough, and it goes back years, long before he met any of these gentry."

"Odd for a ruthless and hardheaded businessman."

"Joliffe is old," the colonel said. "Like a lot of people with power, he's looking, as the end of his life approaches, for some assurance that it won't all stop like a light switched off. Along with Arthur Conan Doyle and a stack of other important people, he finds solace in any cult that promises an afterlife."

For a while the woman was silent. Williams's Jaguar sedan purred down the tunnel of light hollowed from the night by its powerful headlights. The moon wasn't up yet, and the rolling countryside lay silent beneath the stars.

"So we're faced with two alternatives," Freeman said at last. "Either Vanderlee and the others really do share the old man's belief that some kind of crossreferencing is possible between the different mediums and their guides—"

"In which case," Williams said mildly, "they were overreacting to the curiosity of outsiders."

"Or, for some reason they're deliberately cashing in on Sir Simon's fads and fancies."

"That's the way it looks," the colonel agreed. "Perhaps we'll find out which once we get inside the manor."

It was three o'clock in the morning when they finally stole toward the vast facade of the remodeled mansion. Williams's agent, to maintain his cover, had been obliged to leave with most of the house party and go to Exeter for the occult congress. But Vanderlee, Kleist and Salter were still there with Joliffe, he'd reported, preparing for additional séances the following weekend. The mercenaries, at least temporarily, had been withdrawn.

The sensors and infrared video cameras around the perimeter of the estate could nevertheless, he'd warned, still be operative.

Williams took the country lanes and drove around the property once before deciding to make it the simple way. He parked the Jaguar out of sight in a disused quarry a quarter of a mile from the main entrance and approached on foot. The huge wrought-iron gates were closed and locked, but there was a pass door in the high wall on one side, and the gatekeeper's lodge beyond was in darkness.

The door was locked, too. It took the colonel less than a minute to open it with the aid of an instrument he took from a flat leather case stowed in his hip pocket. They walked the rest of the way on the fringe of the woods sheltering one side of the driveway.

They saw nobody and heard nothing but the expected country sounds. The only thing that was unexpected was a Harley-Davidson motorcycle.

It was lying on its side behind a clump of bushes, the chromed mufflers gleaming faintly in the starlight. Freeman almost tripped over the polished handlebars as she skirted the bushes. "Why would anyone leave a machine like this out here half a mile from the house? It looks brand-new, too. Poachers, do you think?"

"Unlikely," Williams murmured. "You can't carry much game on a bike, and there are no panniers, anyway. Poachers are going to leave their transport outside an estate, not inside with the gates locked. My guess would be a boyfriend, shacking up secretly with one of the girls in the servants' wing."

"Whoever it is," Freeman said, "they were late arriving—the mufflers are still warm."

"Let the housekeeper worry about that," Williams replied, moving away from the hidden motorcycle. "We have more important work to do."

Twenty minutes later he was tapping a slender steel spike into the mellowed brickwork of Joliffe Hall with a padded hammer. Working on the side of the house away from the stable entrance, he ran an insulated lead to the spike from a fuse box above one of the window embrasures, then paid out more wire to a second spike inserted on the far side of the window. Finally he patched this into a small plastic box that he attached with a special nylon claw to the burglar alarm circuit farther along the wall.

"It's called a shunt," he grunted in reply to Freeman's whispered question. "Bypasses the window without cutting the circuit or putting the alarm out of action. There isn't enough current left in the window wires to operate the siren. When we leave, we simply dismantle the gear and the alarm's all-systems-go again. Nobody knows we've been in."

Williams had unzipped the leather case. He was flexing his wrist outside the window lock, trying one slender instrument from the case after another. Finally there was a barely audible click and the casement swung open. He swung his leg over the sill and went inside. The woman stepped up silently onto the woodwork and lowered herself to the floor beside him.

The colonel shone the beam of a penlight right and left. They were in an anteroom at one side of the entrance hall. "Good God," he muttered, "your friend was right. It does look like the transit lounge at Kennedy. Which way is this blasted tape room?"

"Down a flight of stairs someplace behind that stainless-steel spiral, according to the rough plan Mike gave me. There are two passages, one leading to the kitchen wing. The stairs are behind a door halfway along the other."

They found the door easily enough. But in the corridor below there was no sign of a door on the right-hand side, where Bolan had said the tape room was located. "You're sure it was this side?" the intelligence chief inquired. "There are several doors on the left."

"Those lead into the ballroom and the lecture theater."

"Maybe it was a staircase off the other passageway."

"Uh-uh. Mike was definite. He was looking for the kitchen wing corridor, so he could get out into the stable yard. The right staircase was the one off the gunroom corridor."

"Then we'd best look more carefully." The colonel returned to the foot of the stairs and began examining the paneled wall inch by inch.

Upstairs a darker blur momentarily obscured the stars showing in the dark rectangle of the open window. There was a small slithering sound as a leather-clad thigh slid across the windowsill, a minute jar as two running shoes hit the floor. Then a shadowy figure dodged the plinths islanding the huge hallway and vanished into the blackness of the library.

Williams was almost at the end of the passage. "How did your friend find this room, anyway?" he asked.

"He was just passing. The door was partly open, and he looked inside."

"Did he say what kind of door it was?"

"An ordinary, flush-fitting modern door, I guess. He said—" Felicity broke off in midsentence. Williams had uttered a faint exclamation of satisfaction.

"Flush-fitting is the clue," he murmured. "Lucky he took the wrong turning and passed when he did."

"What do you mean?"

"I mean, he'd never have known the room was there otherwise. Look at this!" He was playing the flashlight beam over the paneled wall. A hairline crack marked a rectangle against the woodwork. "The room isn't meant to be seen at all. This door's not just flush. It's concealed. Beautiful job, too. See how they made use of the grain here... and again here... to disguise the fact that there *was* a crack?"

"Yes, but there's no handle."

"There seldom is on secret panels," Williams grunted. "Trouble is to find the knob that operates it.

Piece of the molding moves in all the horror stories, except there *is* no bloody molding on these panels."

"Mike said there was kind of a control cabin," Freeman offered, "at one side of the platform where they held the séance. Do you think there might be?"

"An idea," Williams agreed. "Where is this place?"

"At the foot of the stairs, leading down from the entrance hall."

"We'll give it a whirl. Stay here and see if anything happens."

He disappeared into the dark. Felicity watched the slender ray of light dwindle and vanish. For a moment she could see reflections lightening the ceiling, then they, too, dimmed and she was totally alone.

The house was utterly silent. She was uncomfortably aware of those different levels of steel, plaster and wood above her, each carrying their sleepers, each capable of spelling disaster, possibly even discovery and death if some false move or untoward noise should awake the conspirators.

The woman shivered, then started as there was a loud buzzing noise on her left and the secret door swung open and hit her elbow.

Seconds later Williams was at her side. "Good thinking," he muttered, giving her arm a squeeze. "Same principle as the entrance to an apartment building, only here there's no intercom. We'll take a look in there before we go any farther."

They crept through the tape room and stole down the iron spiral to the movie setup below. The place was no more than twelve feet square. Shelving that covered one wall was stacked with two 35 mm film cameras, several optical instruments in leather cases, cartridges of stock for loading the cameras and several dozen reels of film in cans. The moviola editing machine stood on a steel table flanked by filing cabinets and a sink loaded with photographic equipment. The plastic garbage can beneath the moviola was empty, but the flashlight beam picked up three short strips of discarded celluloid beneath the sink. He held them up and shone the light through them.

"Interesting?" Freeman whispered.

"Depends on how serious you are about spiritualism," the colonel replied. "We'll do a random check."

Easing out three of the cans, he saw that each was identified by coded letters and numerals printed on an adhesive strip with a felt-tip marker. He noted their respective positions, then pried off the lids. Two contained full reels, the third only a few dozen feet of film.

The colonel began threading the strips between his fingers while his companion held the flashlight. Neither of the full reels interested him much, but he spent some time squinting through one of the short samples. Finally he fed it into the moviola and pressed a switch. Light flooded out through the side panels of the editing machine as he pulled the strip through manually and bent down to peer through the eyepiece.

Freeman used the additional illumination to check out the rest of the room. The colonel was rolling one of the full reels back into its can when she saw the crumpled ball of paper underneath the developing sink.

"What about this?" she asked, smoothing a creased sheet of typescript on top of a filing cabinet.

He slid the cans back into their correct positions on the shelves. "What have you found?"

"Background notes, just a few lines, but significant in view of what Mike Belasko heard at the dinner party."

Williams took the paper and held it so that light from the moviola fell on the lines of smudged typing.

XANGÔ—Head of the Fifth Line of Umbanda: the Orixá ruling thunder and lightning, earthquakes, rain and rocks. Equivalent to Thor in European theogony...equated with St. James in Brazilian. Derived from West African Yoruba god Shango, said to be son of Yemanja, the Earth Mother. Many myths concern him, most including resurrection. All myths include transubstantiation of...

The notes ended in midsentence. He turned the paper over, but there was nothing on the other side.

"Significant is right," he said slowly. "Especially when the images on some of those film strips are taken into account. Wasn't Xangô the spirit whose mouthpiece Joliffe is supposed to be when he's in a trance?"

"That's what Cleo Duhamel told Mike."

"What we have to discover now is whether this secret film and tape complex has been installed with Joliffe's knowledge, or whether it's been equipped by enemies to work in some way against him. If he knows about it, the facts we have can be interpreted in a totally different way."

"And if he doesn't," Freeman added, "we still have to isolate the real villains of the piece, and their motives."

Upstairs in the tape room Williams played the flashlight beam over the console. "This has been built by an expert," he said admiringly. "If all those input channels led from microphones in the same room, they could record a symphony orchestra."

"But they don't, do they? Come from the same room, I mean."

"It would have to be the size of a tennis court if they did. No, I imagine they're distributed around the house, one at a time. Someone, either Joliffe or those working against him, likes to know what everybody is saying about everybody else." The colonel moved the flashlight. "Like the cans downstairs, the channels are identified only by numbers and letters. But there must be a key to the codes somewhere, so they can check who's talking and what they're going to record. And it can't be far away."

They found it in a locked drawer at one side of the console frame. Williams had it open in thirty seconds. The list was interesting. Of the twelve microphones, one was in the entrance hall, two in the library, one near the huge open fireplace in the drawing room, and two in the kitchen quarters. But none of the guest rooms was bugged. The remaining half dozen were all in Sir Simon Joliffe's private suite on the top floor.

"Concealed no doubt in the phone, in vases, pictures, table lamps, beadings, whatever," Williams said. "Happily we don't have to check. It's enough to know that all this expertise must be directed *against* the old man in some way.... Hello? What have you got there?"

At the back of the drawer she'd found a flat leather case, not unlike the one holding the colonel's housebreaking tools. She snapped it open. Bedded in satin within were two gleaming hypodermic syringes.

Williams snorted. "The pieces of the puzzle are almost ready to assemble," he said. "But it's time we got out of here. Put them back where you found them and I'll relock the drawer."

"I wish I could see through all this as clearly as you seem to."

"All in good time, my dear. But this isn't the place to hold a seminar. Besides, we have to check out those Brazilian nymphs in the huts behind the stables."

In the corridor upstairs the door swung shut with a faint click. Freeman started, stifling an exclamation.

"What is it? That was just the latch—"

"No, no," she whispered. "It was in the reflection, up there near the entrance hall, where the other passageway branches off toward the kitchens. Shine the flashlight that way. I think I saw something move."

Holding the light well away from himself, Williams complied. The corridor was deserted; there was no sign of movement at the corner. "The inside of the house is too new to have rats," he said. "Probably that means no cats, either. Your nerves are playing tricks on you."

"Perhaps."

To reach the stable yard they headed toward the kitchens. They were almost there when she snatched the flashlight from Williams and swung the beam swiftly in the direction of the hall.

Again the hallway was empty. At the far end a curtain stirred slightly in front of a window. She ran up and twitched it aside. The window was closed and locked. Through the glass she looked out across a stretch of lawn. In the distance the surface of the lake was silvered with the reflection of the moon as it rose above the trees. But nothing moved and nobody was to be seen. "Perhaps I *am* getting jumpy," she said, "but I could have sworn . . ."

No lights showed from the windows of the young priestesses' living quarters. The colonel ran across a strip of moonlit grass and dropped down among the bushes surrounding the nearest cabin. A few minutes later she heard him call softly, "It's all right. These aren't wired at all. You can come over."

She hurried across to join him. Behind her the giant flower heads on a rhododendron shrub, livid in the wan light, nodded heavily as the leaves were parted and a pair of eyes stared at the intruders.

Williams was standing by the window frame, selecting instruments from his kit. Soon they were standing together in the piny closeness of the hut. The atmosphere was stifling. There was no sound of sleepers— no snoring, no labored breaths, no creaks or rustles from the covers.

Warily they moved from room to room. In a hanging closet they found rows of gaudy dresses, saw beads, shells and bright trinkets mixed up with lengths of colored ribbon on a night table. In another room a shelf was loaded with pots and paint, and a cardboard box crammed with eyeliners, mascara and lipsticks.

But of the occupants there was no sign. The place was deserted. The bunks had been stripped of sheets and blankets; all the drawers were empty. And each of the other huts was similarly bare.

"Which proves more than anything else," Williams said ten minutes later, "that the entire occult side of this rigmarole is phony."

"Why do you say that?" Felicity asked.

He turned toward her and murmured, "Because I went to the library and got some information on various occult sects before we came down here. And I can tell you that if the initiation ceremony he saw had been genuine, those novices would have been bound under the very strictest penalties to stay fasting in those quarters for another seventeen days."

CHAPTER SIXTEEN

Mack Bolan realized he was under surveillance the day after his phone call to Mettner. His hotel had been fashioned from three consecutive town houses in a dingy gray Victorian street; his third-floor front room, high-ceilinged with plaster moldings at each corner, had one advantage—a bow window that allowed him to see left and right down the length of the street.

And to see the pale gray Ford sedan parked all day in the line of cars to the left of the hotel, with a different man behind the wheel, apparently reading a newspaper, every couple of hours.

There was a similar car, this one black, also with a watcher behind the wheel, eighty yards to the right.

Once Bolan was sure he wasn't mistaken, he went to a washroom at the rear of the hotel and pushed up the frosted glass window. A long narrow yard with a row of trash cans, a German shepherd sleeping in front of a doghouse and two drooping lilac bushes ended in a wall blocking off a service lane.

A door in the wall led to the lane. Between two delivery trucks a man in a pinstripe suit leaned against a lamppost reading a newspaper.

The Executioner whistled softly to himself. Back in his room he glanced again at a copy of the previous

day's *Independent*. The story had been downgraded to
the bottom of an inside page now, but there was still a
short follow-up piece paneled in boldface type.

Scotland Yard detectives searching for Michael
Belasko, the missing American journalist, were
today concentrating their inquiries on hotels in
West London. Belasko was last seen at Joliffe
Hall, near Peverill-St. Mary (Devon), the country
home of multimillionaire plastics tycoon Sir Simon Joliffe, four days ago.

Superintendent Charles Heath, who with De-
tective-Inspector Fogarty of the Devonshire
County Police heads the "Murdered Medium"
investigation, told our reporter: "We are anxious
to interview this man as we have reason to believe
he may be able to assist us with our inquiries."
Information has been received, the superintendent added, that Belasko had been seen at a Mayfair nightclub and near the U.S. embassy in
Grosvenor Square.

Bolan smiled wryly. There were always people who
had seen the wanted man somewhere. But the shadows outside the hotel were something else. He didn't
believe Vanderlee and his confederates would be capable of mounting a team whose members were regularly spelled. But if it was a police operation and he was
a murder suspect, why didn't they move in and make
an arrest? Surely there couldn't be another guest in this
seedy hotel on the wanted list?

He reckoned not. So for some reason they were keeping him on ice.

Why?

Was it just on account of the Cahill killing, or did the British have some other reason for watching him? Were they expecting him to lead them somewhere? Did they know who he really was? Was the surveillance team, so obvious to the expert eye, *meant* to be recognized—as a ruse perhaps to stop him going anywhere?

Too many questions and not enough answers.

He was sure of one thing, though—they weren't going to stop him from going anywhere, and he was going to make it without a tail.

There was a lot to do before he picked up the UPI trail once more. He had money. The conspirators hadn't taken that from him. He had clothes, bought the morning of his arrival in London. But he needed to replace the Beretta and his other weapons of war. He needed papers and a base from which he could continue his mission in secret.

First priority was a phone. By now the hotel lines would be tapped for sure. The police had to have gotten onto the hotel in the first place, either through his call to Brognola or the one to Jason Mettner—which meant the Red Lion at Peverill-St. Mary was also bugged.

Felicity Freeman would be back home in Exeter, and in any case he couldn't impose on her anymore; she'd done enough already.

It had to be the lone wolf routine then, not a role that bothered the Executioner. He'd been waging his personal battle against animal man single-handed for more years than he cared to remember.

And this time, as it had been so many other times, the solo spot meant a night spot.

Bolan spent the rest of the day checking out the exact timetable used by the watchers. The guy behind the wheel of the car on the left of his window was spelled after a shift that lasted two hours and fifty-seven minutes; the team working the black Ford on the right changed places after three hours and nine minutes. He guessed the odd times were supposed to make it look less like a military operation. There were four men in each team.

Working alternately, the cars took a turn around the block every half hour, at which time a fifth man, obviously called in by radio, would appear, wearing a telephone linesman's uniform, and open a manhole in the street to keep the parking space for the car when it returned.

Four men, sometimes working in pairs, sometimes singly, handled the lookout spot in back of the hotel— the pinstripe gentleman, a blue-overalled man from the utility company, an unshaven kid in jeans and a leather jacket, and a white-coated delivery boy.

With fourteen cops on the detail, Bolan had to be smart if he wanted to make a clean getaway. He decided to make it across the roofs, before the moon rose and lightened the tiles, in the twelve-minute gap between the car changeovers. During that period, he reasoned, the new man in the gray sedan would still be settling in and the guy in the black car, looking forward to his relief, might relax his concentration.

The hotel wasn't full. The few guests there—mostly retired people with modest incomes—seemed to spend their time in the television lounge.

None of the rooms on the floor above his own were occupied. He'd explored that story between spells of keeping watch during the afternoon. At one side of the creaking counterbalanced elevator cage an unnumbered door led into a housekeeper's room, with shelves that were used for storing linens. And in the center of the room's high ceiling, a rectangular trapdoor was outlined.

Giving access to an attic floor, to storage rooms or straight to the roof? He guessed the roof. Attics in these old houses were usually reached via a narrow wooden staircase.

In a closet full of brooms, pails and an ancient vacuum cleaner, he found a six-foot whitewood stepladder. Standing on top when the ladder was opened, he could reach up and touch the trapdoor.

It took a lot of heaving at the full stretch of his arms before the heavy wooden trap would budge; clearly it hadn't been opened for years. But finally he made it, and the flap crashed open.

The hotel remained silent. Nobody seemed to have noticed. Bolan returned to his room and continued his vigil.

Projecting the watchers' timetable ahead, he worked out that he had a choice of two twelve-minute periods to choose from if he wished to make his bid after dark

but before the moon rose—one around nine o'clock,
the other soon after midnight. He'd have to take a
chance on the quartet in the lane. Their movements
were too complex for any pattern to have emerged. If
he kept to the street side of the roof slope, and was one
hundred percent successful, avoiding any kind of sil-
houette above the ridgepole, they wouldn't spot him.
But success would depend on how the chimneys were
placed and on which side of the roof the skylights were.

There were no skylights.

Not in the normal sense, anyway. Bolan played the
beam of his flashlight around once he'd dragged himself up through the open trap and saw that there were
indeed no attics, no storage areas up there. He was in
an echoing cavern of joists, plasterwork and spider-
webbed beams, a triangular tunnel blocked here and
there by huge water tanks and the brick shafts of
chimneys.

He shone the light as far down as he could. No
lighter patch relieved the darkness of the twin roof
slants. The loft seemed much wider than the three old
houses that formed the hotel. It was clear that it ran the
entire length of the block.

Stepping warily from joist to joist, Bolan advanced.
He knew that if he placed his weight on the lath-and-
plaster spaces between, he'd probably burst through
and drop into a room below. Every few feet he stopped
and listened. He heard the gurgle of water, a ticking of
hot pipes, a scurry of rats or mice in the distance.

For what seemed an eternity the Executioner crept
forward. Above some buildings the owners had insu-

lated the roof and the spaces between each set of joists with a slab of fiberglass. In other cases the undersides of slate roofing tiles were visible where they hung from the rafters.

In no case was a skylight, a trapdoor or any means of access to the roof to be seen.

The twelve minutes were long gone. There had to be some way out onto the roof!

There was a way, over the very last house—a dormer projecting from the rear slope, flanking a chimney breast wide enough for a dozen flues. It was closed off with vertical wooden double doors fastened by rusting bolts. Bolan laid the flashlight on the cover of a cistern, stepped over a network of pipes and examined the bolts. They were rusted almost solid. He had no tools, and it took him ten minutes, scraping the rust away with his nails, before the first bolt moved. He slammed the heel of his hand against it.

The bolt shot back with a screech of metal, showering him with dust. He stifled a cough and began to work on the remaining bolts.

When he coaxed them back, he shoved gently at one of the doors. It creaked loudly, dried-out wood scraping a stone sill, and opened a couple of inches.

At once the space beneath the roof was suffused with blinding light. Bolan started back, blinking his eyes against the dazzle. Even through that narrow crack the illumination was bright enough to make the dusty, cobwebbed space look like a studio set for a Gothic horror movie.

Squinting against the brilliance, the Executioner leaned forward and peered between the doors. The police were going all out. The street in front was brightly lit. The roofs or the dark lane in back of the hotel were the obvious routes a guy wishing to make a discreet exit would take. So they'd covered that, too, in an ingenious way.

At the end of the lane there was a concrete pillar above an electricity transformer. Leaning back against a sling, apparently working on a fuse box between the green glass insulators, the man in blue overalls was perched on top of the pillar.

The portable floodlight, angled up from the rear of a flatbed truck below to illuminate the wiring, just happened to bathe the roofline of the entire block in its cold glare.

Bolan drew back and eased the door shut. They really had the place sewn up tight. So which of the well-covered exits would give him the best chance of making it and getting away without a tail?

Somewhere on the street side for starters.

Bolan turned and looked back along the raftered tunnel to the place, maybe twelve houses away, where the shaft of light from the open trapdoor was still faintly visible. It would be at that point in the street that the watchers' attention would be concentrated. And where he was was as far away as he could get. So instead of going up onto the roof he'd have to go down somehow through the house below.

There was only one way to do it, and it meant taking a deliberate risk that he'd carefully been avoiding ever since he'd climbed through the trap. There was no tar paper, no fiberglass insulation, no planks covering the joists in this final loft—lightweight laths supporting a plaster ceiling in the room below filled each space between the beams.

The Executioner took a deep breath and stepped off the joist he was standing on, resting his whole weight on the thin wooden crisscross below. There came a rending, tearing, splintering crash, a cloud of plaster dust and a dazzle of light. Glass smashed; a woman screamed.

Bolan shot through a gaping hole in the ceiling and landed on an overstuffed couch covered in green velvet amid the ruins of a small crystal chandelier. The screaming woman was sitting up in a high old-fashioned bed on the far side of the room with her hands pressed to her mouth. She was middle-aged, wearing a white calico nightgown, with her gray hair in curlers and a pair of spectacles pushed up on her forehead. An open book lay on the floor below a bed lamp on the night table.

Bolan picked himself up, slapping white dust from his clothes. Without a word he ran to the door, jerked it open and stepped into the hallway outside. He saw white-painted doors, a wall-to-wall carpet, an elevator shaft with the car empty behind a grille.

Someone was shouting downstairs; the screams in the room he'd just left had subsided into hysterical sobbing. He snatched open the gate and pressed the button for the basement. The elevator whined downward. The warrior reckoned the basement a better bet than street level.

With luck he'd be able to creep unseen to the street and take cover behind one of the parked cars. From there he could make a dash across the street to the far sidewalk. With better luck he might even be around the corner at the end of the block before the watchers caught on. At street level, on the other hand, he'd be visible on the steps beneath the huge square portico before he made the sidewalk at all.

The elevator was fairly modern. The descent was swift and smooth. Bolan was out and across the tiled floor of a large kitchen. The outside door had a simple mortise lock, and the key was in place. He twisted it, turned the handle, opened the door and made it up the iron stairway to the sidewalk.

Seconds later he was flat on his face beneath a fat-tired Chevrolet Blazer. The hubbub inside the house was just audible. Somebody was yelling into a phone, probably calling the police.

The Blazer was built high off the ground. He was able to crouch on hands and knees and check the street both ways. No sign from the nearer car. Not yet.

His first thought had been to wait until one of the cars made its half-hourly prowl around the block, then sprint across behind it. But his timing was shot to hell now, and he couldn't risk running into the local cops when they answered the call. Maybe the noise from the house would distract the attention of the watchers from the road.

Yeah, the driver's door on the gray Ford had opened, and the man had taken a few steps down the sidewalk his way.

Bolan pushed himself upright on the far side of the Chevy and made it over the fifteen feet of pavement. He plunged between the fenders of two parked sedans.

No sweat. No shout from the man on the sidewalk; no reaction from the black car beyond the hotel.

A youth on a moped zoomed down the street. A taxicab with its For Hire flag illuminated cruised past in the other direction. Bolan got to his feet, bent low and raced for the corner.

Rounding it, he heard the warble of police sirens and saw the pulses of blue light reflected from the stucco facades of the block he'd left. What he didn't see was the Audi Quattro sedan that pulled silently out of the line of parked automobiles and tailed him down the adjoining street. It was driven by a tall, muscular man with craggy features and white hair, who carried a silenced automatic in his left hand.

CHAPTER SEVENTEEN

Paddington railroad station would be too obvious, Bolan judged. Not only had the call he made there previously helped tip off the police that he was in this part of London, it was also one of the busiest places in the city and therefore the most likely for a wanted man to try to get lost in. He decided to make his calls in full view of passersby, a bold move most likely unexpected by the police.

He walked to the ritzy Gresham Continental Hotel at the corner of Oxford Street and Park Lane. Inside the opulent lobby he tipped the maître d', drank a beer in the American Bar and was then shown to a table. When the waiter delivered the outsize embossed menu, Bolan asked for a phone to be brought to the table.

The man driving the Audi Quattro tipped the top-hatted doorman and asked for the car to be kept ready just outside the entrance canopy. He took a seat in the American Bar from which he could keep the exit from the dining room under observation. He ordered a Scotch on the rocks. His gun, the silencer unscrewed now, was in one of the deep patch pockets of his brown leather jacket.

Bolan called Hal Brognola in Washington. Using a thinly disguised speech code, he filled in the big Fed on the current situation and requested replacements for the ID and weaponry he'd lost down in Devon. Brognola told him where to collect it at noon, British time, the following day.

Bolan called Jason Mettner in Peverill-St. Mary.

"I have spies at the embassy," the newspaperman said guardedly, "with Company connections. According to the head of station's assistant, certain Brit sources not unconnected with spookery have been asking discreet questions about, well, a colleague of mine with initials M.B."

"Interesting."

"That's what I thought. It seems they're aware of his activities in the southwest, and it's been noticed that he never shows at press conferences, never interviews anyone or asks for press facilities and has never filed a single line."

"More interesting. Who handled the queries?"

"At the embassy? The press attaché passed them straight to the top."

"The ambassador's the last guy to know anything about your colleague."

"Yeah," Mettner said, "fortunately."

"You know which branch of the spooks' club was asking?"

"Defined by two letters, one at the beginning of the alphabet, the other almost at the end."

Bolan's eyes narrowed. Department AX. "That's most interesting of all," he said. "Because it seems those were the guys there before us. At UPI, I mean. I found...let's say there's written testimony proving they have some kind of undercover agent in there. And the guys running the party know about it, but they haven't figured the mole yet.''

''Hell!'' Mettner exploded. ''I'm the guy giving out the information here, and I don't know from nothing. I don't know why you're here, I have no goddamn idea why a Ministry of Defense department should infiltrate a plastics factory, I'm lost in all this occult crap—''

''Welcome to the club.''

''Okay, okay, so you're in the dark, too. But you're on the inside, kind of, and like I say, I don't know squat. I mean, I can tell this could build up into one hell of a story, but, jeez, I don't even know what *kind* of story.''

''Try military,'' Bolan advised.

''Military?'' There was silence on the line. Then Mettner said, ''You're not putting me on? Well, uh, you're not coming down this way by any chance? I mean, so maybe we could meet?''

''Don't call me. You know the rest of the line.'' He hung up the phone, paid for a meal he hadn't eaten and left.

The driver of the Audi hurried through the lobby, fired up the big sedan's engine and cruised slowly down the street behind the Executioner. He turned into Culross Street, a wide alley that led to Grosvenor Square and the U.S. embassy, now less than one hundred yards behind Bolan.

The small two-story buildings, originally designed as coach houses, had mostly been transformed into elegant Mayfair residences, with yellow front doors, bay trees in tubs and expensive security systems. Some of them still maintained two-car garages at street level. But the Rolls-Royces and Aston Martins were all locked away now. The street was deserted.

It was as good a place as any, the Audi driver thought. If his mark was heading for the embassy, he could lose him for good. He coaxed the Quattro into low and leaned on the gas pedal.

Bolan's fighter's instinct saved him. Since leaving the high-density traffic area, he'd been aware of the Audi's low growl some distance behind. He flashed a glance over his shoulder as the engine's whine suddenly rose in pitch. The big car was fifty feet away and closing fast, the four-wheel drive biting on the shiny cobbled surface of the roadway.

The warrior took a couple of fast steps and hurled himself into a recessed doorway as the Audi lurched toward him. The heavy bumper struck sparks from the brickwork, missing him by tenths of an inch, knocked over a green-painted wheelbarrow decorated with pots of geraniums and skidded to a halt in the center of the alley.

Bolan ran. He was unarmed, and there was nothing he could do against more than a ton of car driven by a man wielding a silenced automatic—a man he recognized as the Audi swept past on its first run. He knew there would be others.

The car backed up with a screech of rubber, turned and headed for another pass. Bolan was level with two sets of double garage doors when the sedan caught up

with him. It would be child's play for the driver to
smash him through the wooden doors. This time there
was no recessed entrance within reach. A simple twist
of the wheel and a swerve could mow him down if he
raced into the middle of the street. The only way he
could go was up.

A carriage lamp on a wrought-iron fixture jutted
from the wall above one set of doors. He leaped desperately and grabbed the fixture, drawing up his knees
as the Audi's radiator grille and hood streaked past
beneath. Before the car was clear of the doors he
dropped with a heavy thump onto the roof.

Tires squealed as the Audi rocked to a halt. The two
suppressed shots were just audible, a pair of heavy-
caliber slugs drilling through the roof panel. One
whistled within a hairbreadth of the warrior's chin.

The driver's door jerked open, and the tall man with
the white hair erupted onto the cobbles, gun in hand.
Bolan slid off the roof fast on the other side of the car.
A narrow passageway separated two of the houses on
that side. Weaving from left to right, he sprinted for it,
hearing the tinkling of toughened glass as the gunner
fired at him through the sedan.

By the time Bolan reached the passage the man had
him in his sights. He fired twice more, chipping brick
dust from the alley walls. "Come out and die like a
man," the white-haired killer called.

Bolan was halfway along the four-foot passageway,
crouched behind a trash can filled with stinking ref-
use. "Come and get me," he growled. "Lem Scarff,
isn't it? Brother of a hired gun who couldn't make it?"

Scarff yelled with rage, "Shut up, you bastard! The mission only got fucked up because he was murdered by you and your fat friend."

"We were targets. Frank might have been able to make it, but he sure couldn't take it. He bit on a cyanide pill because he was a coward."

"Goddamn you to hell!" Scarff raged. "You think I buy that crap? Frank was a brave man, and he's going to be avenged, I'm telling you. Just you wait until—"

"Sure," Bolan needled, "brave like you, chasing an unarmed man with a specialized piece. Very courageous."

"I don't need no piece to tear out your guts." The hit man was beside himself with fury. "I'm going on in there with my bare hands," he seethed.

"Try me," the Executioner said, and stood up.

Scarff raised the silenced automatic, then suddenly lowered it. At the far end of the alley the street lighting was momentarily blocked out as two men turned in and strode toward the trash can.

Scarff swore, then turned back to the car. "You won't be so lucky next time," he spit over his shoulder. "And I'll be waiting. So you're in deep shit as long as I'm around."

A door slammed, and the Audi's engine was gunned. Bolan heard the crunch of tires over broken glass as it roared away.

The two men drew level—a tall, thin man in a light jacket and a stocky, bearded guy. "Mr. Belasko, I believe?" the shorter one said.

Bolan remained silent.

"Thought we'd lost you for a moment there when you disappeared from the hotel so suddenly," the tall man said. "And all that dinner wasted! Scotland Yard, sir. Criminal Investigation Department."

Bolan sighed. As he had suspected, the three-box surveillance operation in Bayswater must have been no more than a blind, staked out deliberately for him to discover... while the real watchers formed a separate unit, ready to move when he did. "I'm not armed. Not even a blowpipe."

"Never mind. If you'd like to come along with us, there's someone who wants to see you. The car's just around the corner."

Bolan shrugged. "Where are you taking me?"

"Paddington station, sir."

CHAPTER EIGHTEEN

"The name," said the short, spare man with the gold-rimmed spectacles, "is Williams. I don't think you need to know any more, except perhaps that I speak only in a semiofficial capacity." The voice, as clipped as the man's mustache, was like that of an officer in a stiff-upper-lip British war movie.

Bolan said nothing. He was sitting outside Paddington station on a hard, uncomfortable chair in a wooden shack that seemed to be some kind of yardmaster's office. Williams was perched on a swivel chair behind a scarred desk strewn with worksheets and timetables. The plainclothes CID men had gone home.

"Inquiries in certain quarters," the colonel continued, "have shown that it might not be inapposite for us to have an exchange of views. I'm referring, of course, to events of the past few days in Devonshire. Information from your own country, furthermore, leads us to believe that you are... How shall I say?" He hesitated.

"Say it any way you want," Bolan cut in. "But get to the point."

The colonel permitted himself a wintry smile. "We've been told off the record that you're reliable."

"That makes my day."

"No government department ever admits anything to any other. But apart from that character testimony, it seems you may—I only say may—be over here as a result of certain reservations concerning the plastics business passed on from a department here to another one stateside."

"No comment."

"It should be fruitful, therefore—especially as you've been, quite literally, on the inside—if we traded information. Do you agree?"

"Maybe," Bolan said cautiously. "So if I'm clean, what's with all this..." He gestured at the office decor. Outside the shuttered window, bumpers clattered as a locomotive pushed a line of freight cars into a siding. "Why the secrecy? Why the stakeout at my hotel?"

"A surveillance team I must compliment you on evading so professionally. Ah, that is to say... What I mean..."

Bolan grinned. "You loused up that sentence, didn't you? Come on, Williams, give! Drop the gobbledygook and start talking."

The Briton tilted back in his chair and brushed the two sides of his mustache outward with a forefinger. "These people are important," he said. "They have clout. If they knew we were too interested, they'd be capable of pulling strings at the highest level and having the dogs called off."

"They do know," Bolan said.

"What!" The chair banged forward. "Are you telling me—"

"I found a paper in Vanderlee's room," Bolan went on. "It was an official memo about experiments on the TASM missile guidance system at UPI. The paper was a photocopy, and there was a message scrawled on it—probably by this man Salter—warning Vanderlee that there was some kind of mole in there."

"And the memo? What was it about?"

"It told the recipient to watch out for leaks at UPI."

"Who was the recipient?"

"You should know."

"What do you mean?" the colonel demanded angrily.

"If you want cooperation, don't fool around," Bolan snapped. "The mole was referred to by the code AX-12. I got tipped off tonight that the spooks checking me out at the embassy and elsewhere were from a certain Department AX. Since you yourself tell me I've been given a five-star rating, it doesn't take an Einstein to work out that you—" He broke off as someone rapped on the door.

"Come!" Williams called sharply, his voice still angry.

"We located Miss Freeman, sir. She's here now."

"Have her come in."

"Don't tell me I've been working with one of your agents all the time!"

"Miss Freeman helps out the department from time to time," Williams explained stiffly. "She has specialized knowledge."

"I'll bet!"

She sat on a chair beneath a notice board pinned with block-section diagrams of the railroad's western region.

"I was telling our transatlantic friend," Williams said, "that because of the drag our targets have, we can't be *seen* to interest ourselves in this investigation. I was about to explain that this is why we meet—" he waved around the office "—under such theatrical conditions. And why *he* mustn't be seen with *us*. And why, therefore, it's best that he remains officially a wanted man. For the moment, anyway."

"Just how long is that?" the Executioner asked. "When you say officially, do you mean the police are in the know, or will they really be looking for me?"

Williams cleared his throat. "Scotland Yard and the CID will be, as you call it, in the know. As far as all the regular police forces are concerned, it's a genuine murder hunt."

"Perhaps," Freeman said quickly before Bolan could reply, "it might be helpful if we left that for now and summarized what we know between us as far as UPI is concerned?"

"Right you are. From your end?" Williams looked at Bolan.

He shrugged. "The way I see it, one, the old guy is crazy about the occult. Two, he surrounds himself with mediums, with the idea of finding some kind of relationship between their guides, if that's what they're called. Three, he believes he's a medium himself, and a mouthpiece for this god Xangô. Four, the guys selling this Joliffe-is-Xangô line fix an initiation ritual as part of the local color. Five... Well, five, Miss Freeman and I fake a séance and the equipment goes crazy!''

''And they beat the hell out of you for your pains,'' Williams said with uncharacteristic force.

''Do you have anything to add?'' Bolan asked.

''In one way, yes. It's like the other side of the coin. Against the points you note—what we might call the innocent view of what's going on—consider the following. A hidden two-room suite professionally equipped to make movies and record videotapes, with a dozen different mikes to bug the house, though Joliffe's apartments are the only private rooms wired for sound. A sheet of paper in one of the secret rooms filled with notes on this Xangô character. A case with a couple of new hypodermics and the discovery that your initiation ceremony is the biggest phony of all.''

Bolan was surprised. ''I figured at least that was real.''

''We've been doing a little research,'' Freeman told him. ''Billed as a Candomblé session, wasn't it? Well, part of the ritual was Quimbanda—the black magic side of Umbanda—and even that was wildly inaccurate. The whole thing was a mess, bogus from beginning to end. If it was genuine, the so-called priestesses would still be down there fasting. In fact, they're all back here in London, looking for work at the theatrical agency that booked them.''

''The real tip-off,'' Williams added, ''was the second movie room.''

"A second room? With the same kind of equipment?"

"Part of Joliffe's suite. AX-12—that is, our contact there—reported on it. It's not concealed, and the gear's all fairly normal home cine material. Expensive but not up to professional standards."

"Tell him about the cans," Freeman suggested.

"In the secret movie room," the colonel explained, "I pulled out three at random. Reels in two of them seemed to record normal séances in that basement theater place. The third was different because the medium was Joliffe. And this was the one someone had edited. We found a couple of cuts on the floor." He drew the celluloid strips from his pocket and handed them over.

Bolan held them up to the light one after the other, peering at the different frames.

He saw a man sitting at a table—it could be Joliffe—with two men and a woman grouped around him, either manipulating or rearranging objects too small to identify on the 35 mm negative. The woman was clearly Cleo Duhamel.

Another sequence showed the man standing with hands outstretched. Supporting him from behind, identifiable by the lock of hair over one eye, was Rick Salter.

Bolan handed the strips back. "So?"

"The point," Williams said, "is that the same scenes were on the finished reel in the can, only in each case Joliffe was alone. What do you make of that?"

Bolan whistled. "The way I read it, the old man's séances are as phony as the rest of the setup, but he doesn't know it."

"Hole in one. It's clear now that the whole damn scene is directed against Joliffe. He knows nothing about the tape room, the mikes, the initiation fakery. He thinks the entire thing is for real."

"Yeah, that figures. The syringes are the key. They drug the old man, probably with some South American hallucinogen, and when he's out of it, they manipulate him, move props around, record 'spirit' voices and film the whole thing. Then they edit themselves out, splice what's left together and tell Joliffe it's a record of what he did when he was in a trance."

"Joliffe's no medium," Williams said. "He's been made to think he is. Vanderlee and his associates are trading on his craze for spiritualism, duping him into believing this rubbish about being the mouthpiece of Xangô."

"But the people who come to these parties," Freeman objected, "surely they can't *all* be in on the deception. A lot of them are perfectly respectable—"

"No, no," Williams interrupted. "Most of the guests on these occasions are, well, at least perfectly sincere. They are there to set the scene, to create a genuine atmosphere. I imagine there are occasional fake séances seeded in among them, with special dialogue designed to refer to Joliffe's so-called powers. Did you ever wonder, Belasko, just why your own fake séance failed, why that high-tech speaker let you down?"

"Sure," Bolan said, "negative feedback. You used to get that kind of squealing when tuning primitive radios. You still get it when someone else uses electronic gear too close to you."

"In other words there were other mikes and other speakers nearby."

"Right."

"You mean the other séances were faked, too?" Freeman queried.

"One at least must have been," Bolan said. "Probably Cleo Duhamel. Her material was so close to ours!"

"AX-12 thought perhaps the reason she was so 'friendly' to you was to stop you finding out that the initiation was a fake, too," Williams suggested.

Bolan shifted in his chair. He cleared his throat. "A little extreme, don't you think?"

"It worked, didn't it?" Freeman said sweetly.

"One thing has me puzzled," Bolan said, "and that's the second movie rig. If it was in the old man's suite, he must have known about it."

"My guess," Williams said, "would be that they pretended that the edited footage so carefully prepared in secret was, in fact, *unedited* film shot with Joliffe's own limited equipment."

"It seems strange that all this could go on in a guy's home without his knowing anything about it."

"Folks as rich as Joliffe never know half of what goes on in their own homes," Freeman said, unconsciously quoting Bolan's comments on the lake. "This all goes on, don't forget, either in the basement or the servants' quarters—literally below stairs. The servants could be on the conspirators' payroll. In any case, they could keep tabs on them, and on the other guests, through the bugs.''

"And remember Salter is a high-powered PR specialist," Williams added. "A pro with a reputation for stage-managing stunts."

"Yeah, but..." Bolan was dubious. "Okay, this squares with the facts as we know them. But why? What are they getting out of it? This isn't the kind of deal you dream up over a beer. A lot of time, money and thought have been spent here."

"Exactly." Colonel Williams was genial. "We all want to know why. And this is precisely why you're here tonight, Mr. Belasko. Do you have anything special in mind for tomorrow?"

"I have to be in Exeter at noon."

"Perfect. Miss Freeman will drive you to Devonshire tonight."

"Why?"

"At this stage of the game," Williams told him, "there's little or nothing *we* can do. So far these people have broken no laws, committed no crime. Dabbling in the occult isn't illegal. All we can do officially is monitor things from the outside. And unofficially..." He blew out his breath and shook his head. "The slightest hint of any cloak-and-dagger activity, the tiniest false move, and heads would roll. These people, I tell you, have power and influence. Do you read me, sir?"

"Yeah."

"Very well. Unlike us, you aren't hamstrung by protocol and procedure. As far as your real self is concerned, you're not even in the country. That mythical wanted man, Mike Belasko, can be discarded at any moment. He doesn't exist. You're in a unique position, therefore, to help us, and help your principals at home."

"Which, being interpreted, means?"

"Before we can make any move," Williams said, "we have to know what's going on, and we have to know that it's wrong. That foul play is involved, we're certain, but we don't know how foul, or what play. Put it this way—before we can act, we need action."

"And you want me to...?"

"We want you, Mr. Belasko, to go down to Peverill-St. Mary and—how shall I put it?—stir things up a little!"

CHAPTER NINETEEN

There were fifteen cars parked in the stable yard of Joliffe Hall. Another weekend of spiritist experiments, AX-12 had told Williams, was to culminate in a very special séance at which revelations of mind-blowing significance were promised.

It was Bolan himself who discovered that the mercenaries were back. He was driving around the area in an inconspicuous Renault, checking out country lanes that surrounded Joliffe's property, when he saw movement in the branches of a tree above the high wall eighty yards ahead.

Bolan resisted the desire to lift his foot or raise his head. He coasted beneath the overhanging branches, squinting up to see a man in camou fatigues paying out a wire among the leaves.

Three-quarters of a mile farther on, where a dying elm drooped branches over the wall much lower down, he saw men with a chain saw, lopping off any dead wood that might offer a way onto the property.

The Executioner returned after dark for a detailed recon. This time he came prepared. He wore a snug-fitting nightsuit, a military harness attached to a quick-draw shoulder rig for his Beretta 93-R and a hip holster carrying a Desert Eagle automatic. A plastic stun grenade, a small canister of CS gas and a waterproof neoprene pouch were clipped to the harness waist belt. Inside the pouch were wire cutters, lockpicks, a looped garrote, a spool of adhesive tape, a suction cup and the Beretta's silencer.

He'd been asked to stir things up, to provoke the conspirators to action. Preferably illegal action, which might give Williams the excuse to move in. But it must be clear at the same time that the nuisance was in no way connected with the police or the British intelligence services. Vanderlee and his confederates had to know that the troublemaker was the same American newsman who'd infiltrated their party and tried for reasons unknown to fake a séance.

Bolan, in fact, had to make sure he was spotted and recognized. And make sure he got away when it was all over.

"Plus anything that you find out, anything you see or hear that might throw light on the reasons behind this chicanery," Williams had said, "will naturally be more than welcome."

The warrior repressed a smile. Government departments were the same the world over.

He reckoned the part of the perimeter least likely to be watched closely would be a sector the mercs had worked on that very day. He'd make it over the wall via the dying elm they'd been trimming as he'd passed.

Bolan took the longest way around to approach that part of the wall, because from this direction there was a long, shallow grade leading down the lane. He cut the Renault's engine at the top of the grade, pushed the gearshift into neutral, released the brakes and allowed the little sedan to coast down under its own weight. At the foot of the slope he used the last vestige of momentum to run the car in behind a stand of young willows on the far side of the lane.

He was checking the hardness of the ground when a dull gleam of metal in among the slender trunks caught his eye. He crept closer. The long grass had been flattened at one side of the stand and a passage forced through the undergrowth beyond. He switched on a penlight, shielding the beam with one hand. At the end of this short trail was a motorcycle leaning against a tree.

He risked a flash of the full beam. The machine was a Harley-Davidson, quite new, judging by the state of the chromework on the mufflers and high-set handlebars. He put out a hand to touch one of the finned cylinder jackets, which was cold.

Bolan's face was thoughtful as he crossed the lane. Did his discovery imply a second intruder in the Joliffe estate that night, or was the rider engaged in some activity, clandestine or otherwise, in the sleeping fields beyond?

One thing was certain—nobody was going to abandon an expensive motorcycle like this one. The owner was around somewhere, and he'd be back. Sometime.

Bolan filed the information away for later evaluation. He unwound a coil of lightweight nylon cord from around his waist and stared up into the dark, leafless bulk of the elm. The mercs had carried out their task well. The nearest projecting branch that remained was a good thirty feet above the wall surmounting the bank.

Bolan shrugged. Sometimes you had to try harder.

A three-prong grappling hook had been spliced to one end of the cord. He paid out a couple yards and swung the weighted end experimentally around his head. When he had the feel of rope and hook, he shifted his grip, altered the plane in which the loop was spinning and whirled it faster, faster, finally letting go so that the weight shot up into the dark.

There was a rattle of loose wood, and a few twigs dropped onto Bolan's face. The grappling hook fell on the far side of the wall. He hauled it back, hand over hand, and tried again. On the third attempt the prongs caught on something and held. Bolan pulled, testing it with his full weight. If the tree was dying from Dutch elm disease, there was a risk that branches under strain could crack and break away. The cord remained as steady as a rock.

He grasped it with both hands and walked himself up the wall, hoisting himself onto the branch after he reached the top. The branch creaked alarmingly as he sat astride it, but no wood splintered away. He disentangled the hook, pulled up the cord and rewound it around his waist.

A plane tree grew close to the old elm, its leafy branches within easy reach. As far as the Executioner could see, it should be an equally easy ten-foot drop to the ground from its lowest limbs. But first he was going to watch and wait.

He waited a full hour, every sense alert to the sights and sounds of the night. Still creaking, the tree swayed slightly in a breeze carrying the odors of farm and field. Leaves rustled. In the distance a truck engine started and a dog barked. Voices spoke quietly in the woods maybe two hundred yards to his left, and from time to time he heard footsteps swish through the undergrowth. Clearly there were patrols.

Soon Bolan was able to identify the nearest. One guy, passing every fifteen minutes on a sinuous route that took him within forty feet of the elm, continued through the woods, and must have returned to base along the bed of the dried-up stream because the man always passed in the same direction. The mercenaries' base, he assumed, was where the voices had come from.

He paid a lot of attention to the exact route—not because he intended to avoid it, but because he wanted to follow it, as far as he could check it out from the top of a tree in the dark.

The point being that the path taken by the sentry would be free, for sure, of trip wires and sensors. And they'd hardly waste IR cameras or night vision video equipment recording the passage of their own men.

When he had it fixed as accurately as he could, Bolan transferred himself from the elm to the plane tree and began working his way down among its thick branches. It was slow work, brushing aside the big leaves, feeling his way past shoots and twigs that could snap off and alert the guards, testing each branch before he trusted his weight to it. But eventually he was lying along a limb that projected horizontally, roughly a dozen feet from the ground.

He waited for the patrol to pass for the fourth time, allowed the guy to make another seventy or eighty yards, then hung at the full stretch of his arms and dropped.

It was more like twenty feet than ten. He hit the ground with a thump that jarred his spine, went limp, rolled and came up in a combat crouch with the Beretta in a two-handed grip.

The voices two hundred yards away hadn't altered their pitch. No challenge was issued. Bolan's landing, which had seemed very loud to him, had passed unnoticed.

Stepping cautiously, he arrived at the path taken by the sentry. The man was a long way ahead now. Bolan could only just hear the scraping of branch and bush as he passed through the undergrowth, the faintest jingle of equipment. Silently he flitted after him.

From the treetop it had only been possible to chart the route a certain distance. After that the Executioner would have to shadow the guard by ear or risk losing his way and straying into one of the zones monitored by cameras or crisscrossed by wire.

Assuming it was the same guy passing every quarter hour—and assuming his circuit started and ended at the base—then Bolan's tree had to be about halfway along the outward leg. Which, at seven and one half minutes per leg, meant the sentry would be turning back anytime. Bolan accelerated his pace.

He was drawing near when the merc turned sharply to the left, then almost at once left again, so that he was at the inner edge of the woods, facing back the way he'd come.

The swishing sounds ceased, to be replaced by the crunch of boots on gravel. A second man was approaching the first, walking along the dry riverbed. Bolan crouched behind bushes, peering toward the paler gloom beyond the trees.

He saw two dark blurs, heading dead on. When they merged, a murmur of voices carried to him. A match flared, and two points of crimson glowed against the darkness. Seconds later the two men parted, one continuing toward the base, the other returning to Bolan's right.

In the brief glimpse of features revealed by the light of the match, he was fairly sure that neither man was Reagan O'Hara or Lem Scarff. He nodded grimly to himself in the dark. There would be an account to settle with Mr. Scarff some other time.

It was just as well that he was close to the first guard when he turned, otherwise he could have blundered straight ahead until he tripped a wire or activated a camera shutter. It was useful, too, to know that the patrols RDV'd at the limit of each sector and then turned back.

Would they be linked that way around the entire perimeter of Joliffe's huge property?

He reckoned not. There would have to be dozens of mercs. But there would certainly be outposts in radio

contact and men stationed among the farm buildings
on the far side of the estate.

Bolan stole out from beneath the trees and approached the streambed. He didn't need to shadow the
patrol now; he knew where he was—farther along the
slope he'd skidded down with the Range Rover, below
the lakehead. And the wires, cameras and other security equipment would surely be confined to the belt of
trees just inside the wall.

Error.

The big guy had crossed the valley, stepping carefully on smooth, flat stones among the gravel, and
scrambled halfway up the slope when something
caught his leg and he pitched headlong. At the same
time he was blinded by the blue lightning dazzle of a
flashbulb.

Bolan cursed, rolling ten feet downhill in a shower of
earth and stones. Someone shouted in the woods below.

On his feet again the Executioner hurled himself at
the hillside, fists grabbing for outcrops and tufts of
heather, feet scrabbling in the soft soil as he willed
himself to the top of the slope before the mercs below
got their act together.

Fortunately it was a single-shot still camera, not
movie or video equipment whose flash he'd tripped. So
they'd know soon enough who the intruder was.

What the hell—he'd been asked to stir things up and
to make sure they knew who was responsible for the
stirring.

They'd know who he was, yeah, but not where, not if he made the lip in time. The camera couldn't track him, and he had the additional advantage that he'd been there before; he knew the lay of the land.

Down below O'Hara was shouting orders; Bolan recognized the voice. A searchlight beam lanced out from beneath the trees. He redoubled his efforts to make the top. The beam was swinging. They might not know where he was, but they'd know where the camera that flashed was.

The spot climbed the hillside, questing left and right, limning each bush and rock in brilliance, throwing black shadows. It homed on the place where Bolan had fallen, snaking past a camera on a post.

The beam overtook him as he was hoisting himself over a crumbling outcrop on the lip. It swept ahead, spearing the night sky, dropped back, then steadied, pinning Bolan to the hillside as vulnerable as a moth on a display board.

A single shot rang out.

Flakes of weathered shale erupted from the outcrop two feet to Bolan's left. A second shot plowed into the soft rock beside his head.

He was almost over. They were too far away to use handguns, and for the same reasons as before, O'Hara would confine himself to single-shot small arms in the hope that, outside the property, they'd be taken for hunters' weapons. At close quarters, though, Bolan would have to contend with silenced automatics.

Two rounds—from assault rifles, he guessed— sounded almost as one. A slug nicked his sleeve and gouged a strip of leather from the harness belt. Another ricocheted off a core of harder rock with a shrill scream. Splinters of shale stung his ear. Then he was over, out of the glaring light, and running.

He vaulted the stone wall and sprinted across the meadow toward the mansion. A splitting roar erupted behind him. Thin beams of light waved crazily over the lip of the valley. They were chasing him on dirt bikes by the sound of it, howling up the slope. He wasn't going to make the rose walk before they were on him.

Running, Bolan glanced swiftly right and left. The lake and the trees surrounding it were too far away. On the other side the land rose to a plantation of young firs, but that was even farther. The meadow stretched ahead beneath the stars, dotted here and there with darker patches where clumps of furze grew. In the distance a yellow glow was visible above the ornamental shrubs sheltering the house. Joliffe and his party must be having a late night.

The bikes were over the lip and roaring his way, the long fingers of their headlights reaching out for him, probing the meadow grasses.

It would have to be a furze clump—and the nearest one at that—if he wasn't to be shot down like a hunted stag. He turned toward the spiny bushes.

Twenty yards. Fifteen. Ten. And suddenly Bolan's shadow was dancing ahead of him. The nearest biker had him pinned in a shaft of light.

Bolan dived beneath the lowest branches and dragged himself farther inside the clump as a hail of bullets thwacked through the spines above his head.

Sir Simon Joliffe was throwing a party. Light streamed from the mullioned windows of the mansion, the driveway was jammed with cars and a tent had been set up on one of the lawns.

To the spiritist enthusiasts who were houseguests, the party was to celebrate an important event; to fifty outsiders who'd been invited—after careful vetting by Rick Salter—from the surrounding countryside, it was just one more social event in a crowded summer calendar. Although, true enough, it was a rare event when old man Joliffe threw his expensive premises open. When he did, however, there was nothing to criticize about the quality of the hospitality offered.

A whole, huge Scottish salmon lay on the white-clothed buffet table in the tent. It was surrounded by dressed lobster, crab, crawfish and prime cuts of lamb, beef and different varieties of game. There was even wild boar and venison specially flown in from France. Smaller tables groaned with selections of salads, cheese, pies and French pastries.

The night was warm; many guests stood around on the floodlit lawns, drinking champagne cocktails served by white-jacketed waiters moving unobtrusively among them. The basement ballroom was closed, but for those who wanted to dance a jazz quartet played in the vast entrance hall.

For the spiritists, who kept the news very much to themselves, the celebration was in honor of the fact that Vanderlee, Salter and Kleist had formally registered their cult as a British Umbanda Association, officially accepted as a "charity," which meant firstly that there were advantages taxwise, and more importantly that, as in the case of a club, the authorities were blocked from too close an inspection of its activities.

Joliffe, surrounded by the usual coterie, was sitting at a special table beneath a jacaranda tree when the snarl of motorbike engines was first audible over the strains of music and the guests' chatter.

Kleist lifted his head. "What's that?" he queried. "It sounds like—"

"Motorbikes," Vanderlee cut in. "More than one. Surely there couldn't be latecomers at this hour?"

"All the guests on the list have arrived," Salter said.

Cleo Duhamel looked apprehensive. "There wouldn't be gate-crashers, would there? You know, local gangs who heard there was a party and thought they'd crash it?"

Salter shook his head. "The gates were closed when the last guest arrived. And there are private security men along the driveway."

"In any case," Ley Phuong said, "the noise is coming from the other side of the house. Over there." He nodded toward the stables and the rose walk.

"I know." The PR man drew Vanderlee aside and murmured, "I told O'Hara to keep his men away from the gardens and the driveway, but they do have a couple of dirt bikes down in the valley where they park the command car. I hope this doesn't mean..." He left the sentence unfinished.

The Dutchman bit his lip. It had been tough enough explaining the burned-out Range Rover to the old man without revealing the presence of armed strangers in the valley. Both that and Kleist's marked-up face had been explained by burglars, surprised before they got into the house. "Cahill's" disastrous séance had been more difficult still; they'd gotten away with that by citing the gutter press. But if there was more trouble brewing, on this night of all nights...

"Laugh it off," Vanderlee said brusquely. "I'm going to go into the house and call up O'Hara to check."

Five minutes later Vanderlee was back beneath the jacaranda tree, scowling. Salter raised an inquiring eyebrow. "All hell's breaking loose down there," the Dutchman growled before he was near enough for Joliffe to hear. "Some bastard managed to get over the wall without tripping any of the alarm circuits, but they caught him with a flash camera this side of the valley."

"Who was it?"

"Well, of course they don't know yet. But O'Hara's sent a man to collect the neg and they'll rush it through. Maybe a half hour. Meanwhile the fellow's apparently heading this way. O'Hara was obliged to send the bikes to cut him off. He was too far ahead for anyone on foot to catch up with him."

"The bikers had better succeed," Salter seethed. "One will have a few things to say to Mr. O'Hara! I understood the man was a goddamn professional."

"Rick, my boy!" Joliffe was calling from his chair. "What's all this I hear about motorcycles? Don't tell me you've laid on some kind of circus act, as well! You *are* an enterprising young fellow!"

"It's not exactly that, sir," Salter called, hurrying across. "The fact is, well, some sheep escaped from their pen at the farm, and it wasn't noticed at first. But now the animals are coming toward the house and the farmer thought he'd better send some chaps on bikes to head them off in case they spoiled the party. One does so apologize."

"Quite right, my boy. Quite right. Sheep, indeed." The old man chuckled. "What a performance!"

"Oh, Sir Simon, is it true?" A pretty girl in a red silk cocktail dress called out as she passed the table. "Are you really planning to give us a circus act? After all this?" She swept a plump arm around to encompass the tent, the well-dressed couples ornamenting the lawn, the expensive machinery glistening in the driveway, the music drifting from the floodlit manor. "You *are* a sweetie." She sauntered away with her blond head on her escort's shoulder.

Joliffe was saved the embarrassment of a negative reply. But Kleist, moving across the lawn with Salter, muttered venomously, "There'll be a bloody circus here all right if O'Hara doesn't fix this fuckup and earn his goddamn pay!"

The rasp of the dirt bikes' exhausts had settled into a regular singsong rhythm, rising and falling.

DUST, SPINY TWIGS and chips of bark showered over Bolan as he lay beneath the furze clump with a stream of .45-caliber death pumping into the branches all around him.

The bikers, three of them, circled at a distance of thirty yards, the shafts of their headlights bobbing up and down, swinging left and right as the dirt bikes lurched over the rough ground.

They were firing silenced MAC-10 submachine guns, steering with one hand, the fingers of the other wrapped around the gun's pistol grip while the muffler was supported by the handlebars. This was the close-quarters situation Bolan had wished to avoid, especially now that the mercs had silent firepower, but luckily for him any kind of accuracy in such conditions was a matter of pure chance. As long as the bikes were moving, they were unlikely to score.

Bolan's task was to keep them mobile. If they dismounted and advanced on foot from three sides, he'd be finished.

For the moment, he figured, they aimed to do it the easy way—saturate his cover in the hope of blowing him away without any risk to themselves. And they kept on the move because they didn't know if he was armed.

Not yet.

They'd know as soon as their 30-round magazines were exhausted. And with the concentrated bursts they were firing, at a cyclic rate of 114.5 rounds per minute, that wouldn't be long.

Bolan held his own fire and waited. Once they'd established a regular course around the furze and checked out where the bumps and hollows were, the bikers killed their headlights.

They continued to ride in the dark. Bolan could see them as moving blurs, now lost against a wooded background, now dimly silhouetted against the stars. Muzzle-flashes escaping from the silencers were points of fire twinkling only when the guns were aimed directly his way.

One of the riders peeled off and rode fifty yards away, pausing to reload where he'd be a tougher target to hit. Over the growl of the idling engine, Bolan heard a metallic snick as a fresh magazine was rammed home.

He crawled to one side, where the furze was thickest, and let loose a single shot from his Desert Eagle at the nearest bike as the man who had reloaded joined his comrades. The huge muzzle-flash and thunderous report of the heavy Magnum made too tempting a target for the killers to ignore. Each aimed a burst into the clump where the big gun had flamed.

But the Executioner wasn't there anymore; he was flat on his face in the least expected place, where the furze was thinnest, now fisting the silenced Beretta. The bikers, he reckoned, would be alert for a repeat performance from the Desert Eagle. Meanwhile, silent death would stalk them from behind the 93-R's flash-suppressor.

Bolan flipped the semiauto on to 3-shot mode and shifted his position so that he could get a shot off at the next man around. As the bike's engine grumbled and snarled, Bolan held his breath and squeezed the trigger. The gun bucked in his hand. He heard the metallic thuds as the silenced rounds impacted against the chromework. The bike's engine screamed, then stalled.

He had a momentary vision of the machine rearing up and throwing the rider, then the heavy clatter as it fell onto the man's body.

One of the other riders shouted. The bikes accelerated, speeding around the clump now with only occasional bursts flaming from their weapons. They would be holding their fire, waiting for another muzzle-flash, wondering why they hadn't registered the shot that had wasted their buddy.

Bolan believed that the element of surprise was invaluable. Case in point here. The bikers knew there couldn't be two men concealed in the furze clump. It would soon occur to them that one man could have two different guns.

The Executioner had to make his move before that realization. The unexpected worked more often than not. So why not use it now?

He was on his feet, merged into the dark mass of the furze clump, when the first bike passed, spraying a short burst. Bolan started running the instant the second man fired. He hurled himself across the meadow, feet pounding the rough ground, and dropped into the long grass. He'd timed the circuits, and he hadn't been wrong—the Yamaha was fifty feet away when he was ready to fire.

Bolan watched it approach, his trigger finger poised. It was a piece of cake. The rider was turned away, watching the furze. The range was no more than ten yards, with the target between the warrior and the clump. The biker was pressing the trigger of his SMG when the Beretta delivered his death warrant.

Two 9 mm hornets smashed through the top of the man's spine, spilling him lifeless to the ground. The third, elevated by the climb of the Beretta's muzzle, furrowed the top of his head as he fell. But by that time the guy was feeling no pain.

Bolan raced forward, seizing the bike's handlebars almost before they touched the ground. He swung his leg over the saddle, wrenching the twist-grip so that the engine roared and the bike took off, popping a wheelie.

He accelerated fiercely around to the far side of the bush, hoping to catch up with the remaining gunman before he was wise to the fact that he'd lost another buddy. But something must already have alerted his quarry. The last biker had swung wide and steered away from the furze. When Bolan rounded the corner, the guy was already seventy yards away.

Skidding his machine in a half circle, the biker switched on his headlight and raced back toward the Executioner. Momentarily blinded by the shaft of light, Bolan was slow to react. Then he switched on his own light, wrenched the bike around and careered toward his adversary.

The two powerful lightweight machines hurtled toward each other, lights blazing, like latter-day equivalents of knights at a medieval joust. And, as in olden times, the result of the contest would be a matter of nerve. Each man would be gambling on the hope that the other would cry chicken and be the first to turn aside.

Neither of the riders was shooting. In this test of nerve at speed it was a must to have both hands free to steer. The guns, like the medieval knights' lances, would be reserved for the contact, the moment of truth.

Exhausts bellowing, the two machines drew nearer. It was only Bolan's icy determination that allowed him to make it. The bikes were only feet apart when the merc finally realized that his adversary wouldn't veer off. At the last moment, the final second, he leaned away and tried desperately to haul his Yamaha out of the Executioner's path.

Bolan's front wheel rammed the rear of the other bike with a shattering impact. It could have been a deadly maneuver on a roadway, but the rough ground and the long grass slowed the machines to an extent that there was a good chance a head-on collision would prove less than lethal. Bolan had bet his life on it.

As the warrior expected, the bike's momentum catapulted him from the saddle on impact. He shot over the tangle of twisted machinery, hit the ground fifteen yards beyond, shoulder-rolled and arrowed up in a combat crouch with the Beretta in a two-handed grip.

The gunman, too, had been thrown clear, but he'd landed on his back with the wind knocked out of him. Astonishment had retarded his reflexes with deadly effect. He staggered to his feet, groping for the SMG in the grass. Bolan raised the Beretta and took him out.

The warrior releathered the autoloader and turned aside. Should he pick up the remaining Yamaha and ride to the house? Maybe not. He could hear faint strains of music now, and a distant babble of voices. It would be better to make a silent approach. Treading carefully over the rough ground, the Executioner strode across the meadow toward Joliffe Hall.

VANDERLEE, KLEIST and Cleo Duhamel stood in a corner of the library. Outside the windows Bentleys, Jaguars and Mercedeses burbled discreetly to life. Some of the older guests were leaving, although there were still couples dancing and the tent buffet was by no means deserted. Salter and Ley Phuong had escorted Joliffe to his private suite.

"I don't like this," the Dutchman said. "O'Hara's men haven't returned, and I can no longer hear the motorcycles. O'Hara thinks he heard shots from a heavy-caliber revolver a few minutes ago."

"Maybe we should organize a search party," Kleist suggested.

"I find it extraordinary," Duhamel said. "We spent a fortune hiring this man O'Hara and his cutthroat gang. Why? To make sure our plan can progress without interruption. And what happens? We spend more money, installing sophisticated detection equipment at his suggestion . . . and at once an impostor and his accomplice succeed in infiltrating the house. The first series of séances is wrecked and we risk losing our credibility. Kleist is attacked, the wall is partially breached and an expensive vehicle is destroyed by fire."

"You have to remember, Cleo—" Kleist began.

"And now, tonight," the voluptuous woman went on, ignoring the interruption, "yet another intruder is allowed to slip through the net. There's shooting. Our soirée could be compromised. And still the person is at large. What kind of organization are we running, for God's sake?''

''It's probable that we're dealing with the same man,'' Vanderlee said. ''And if we are, he's some kind of professional.''

''The same man? You mean the impostor? But why would he wish to return? What kind of a man is he?''

''You tell me, Cleo,'' the Dutchman said dryly. ''You know more about him than we do.''

She flushed. ''He'd taken Cahill's place. I thought he might be schooled in spiritism. It was important to prevent him paying too much attention to our little pleasantry on the island.''

''As long as it was enjoyable,'' Kleist said.

''What's this professional line you're handing me?'' Duhamel demanded, clearly anxious to change the subject.

''Scarff says the man who tried to fake the séance here is one of two men we paid his twin to take out in Nevada,'' Kleist replied. ''He wasn't certain at first, but it seems he saw the fellow again in London, and now he's sure. He blames him, he blames both of them, for his brother's death.''

''We could use that,'' Vanderlee said grimly. ''Keep Scarff on call.''

''I never understood,'' the woman complained, ''quite why you found it necessary to dream up that Nevada fiasco.''

"Oh, come on, Cleo!" Vanderlee expostulated. "You know very well why. We discovered the memo, tipping us off that the British were interesting themselves in UPI, that they knew there was some kind of leak. Then a couple of so-called experts were called in for the guidance trials. Hell, it was the obvious thing to eliminate them before they spoiled everything."

"For my money," Cleo said, "it would have been smarter to shadow them, see where they went, find out who briefed them and why, then take it from there."

"Yes, darling, but it wasn't your money, was it?" Vanderlee said acidly. "It's so easy to be wise after the event, isn't it?"

"All right, all right. So what makes you think to-night's break-in is by the same guy?"

"I should have thought that was obvious, too," Kleist replied. "The man probably killed Cahill, knowing nobody here had met him, as a means of getting an in here first time around."

"With a blowpipe? Your all-American boy?" The woman was scornful.

"Whatever. After he's roughed up a bit, he escapes through the woods, besting O'Hara's men and the security stuff. Tonight's intruder knew how to avoid the security devices in the woods. Most of them, anyway, and he chooses, out of the whole damn estate, to penetrate at almost exactly the same spot. Surely the conclusion's obvious enough?"

"Perhaps. But supposing it is the same man, what does he want? Why should he keep trying to get in here?"

"Oh, Cleo! He's some kind of agent. He's on a fact-finding mission, either for the Brits or the Yanks. He's looking for clues, a follow-up to that damn memo."

Lem Scarff walked into the library, holding a sheet of photographic paper that was still damp. "Colonel O'Hara asked me to give you this," he said to Vanderlee. "It's just developed. From the camera on the hillside."

The Dutchman took the paper and held it so that the light fell on the shiny surface. The picture showed a man in the act of falling forward on a steep slope, his arms outflung, a tall, muscular man wearing a close-fitting dark suit and a harness bristling with weaponry. The harsh flashlight left very little modeling on the face, but the likeness was unmistakable.

"That settles it," Vanderlee said. "It's the same son of a bitch. The guy who said his name was Mettner, only it wasn't. And he's armed to the bloody teeth!"

"Two can play that game," Kleist rasped. "Four or five even better. Get Salter and Phuong. There are guns in the movie room. Between the house and O'Hara's men we'll flush him out, and this time we'll find out who he really is. Scarff, you can come along for the ride."

"Bastard already dusted three of my buddies," Lem Scarff growled. "Just let me get my hands on the bastard and you'll have the info you want."

CHAPTER TWENTY

Bolan wouldn't have made it if there hadn't been a party. AX-12 had concentrated his report on the sé-ance planned for the following day and its "mind-blowing" revelations, saying only that there would be outside guests on the night before. But as soon as the Executioner saw the tent and the couples still moving between the brightly lit house and the lawns, he knew there could be no serious search for him until every-one had gone home. Everyone but the cultist house-guests, that is. And he was sure they'd be dragooned indoors and up to their beds once the last car had passed the main gates.

Meanwhile, as long as he kept to cover, he had a free hand—the conspirators could never cover the whole area around the manor on their own, and they wouldn't call up the mercs until the genuine spiritists were tucked safely into their beds.

His primary aim was to make a second visit to the secret rooms to see if he could uncover evidence that Williams had missed. He figured also on stealing some of the film cans the colonel had mentioned. Then he'd check out the living rooms and pocket any written ev-idence he could locate. With luck.

For the moment, anyway, he was going to lie low and let the conspirators sweat. He'd hit upon the ideal place—one of the cabins where the phony priestesses had been staying.

Once he'd reached the hut, getting inside posed no problem. He used the window as Williams had, the lockpicks from the pouch at his waist doing the job in seconds. Then he settled down to wait.

IT WAS THREE O'CLOCK when the last guests drove away. As Bolan had expected, Salter shooed the spiritists indoors at once. "My dears, for tomorrow night one feels one will need all the sleep one can get!"

Ten minutes later five armed men strode down the driveway to meet Reagan O'Hara. The hunt was on.

Vanderlee, Salter, Kleist, Phuong and Scarff were all openly carrying handguns; the mercenary leader cradled a MAC-10.

Bolan wondered how they were going to handle it. The estate was vast, much of it wooded. Certainly he'd been heading in the direction of the mansion when the mercs last saw him—but that was back in the meadow, some distance away. There were plenty of other places he could have gone, especially as the party was still in full swing when the bikers were sent after him. The lake island, the fir plantation, another belt of trees near the main gates, a row of outbuildings on the far side of the stables—all were possibilities. So were the priestesses' cabins.

O'Hara was pointing directly at Bolan's hideout. The general plan became clear a moment later. Although he couldn't hear any voices, the pantomime the Executioner could see through the window told him all he wanted to know.

The mercenary leader was now gesturing toward the lake with a wide sweep of his free arm. He pointed at the men surrounding him, at the house, down the driveway. Vanderlee said something, and O'Hara jerked his head toward the front of the mansion. A Jeep with a powerful spotlight fixed to the windshield rolled around the corner, driven by the beefy hardguy Bolan had seen before. At the same time several headlight beams sliced through the dark beyond the rose walk. O'Hara was calling his soldiers up from the valley.

Three more dirt bikes approached the house, as well as a squarish four-wheel-drive vehicle. O'Hara was briefing his team.

Bolan read the battle order. The bikes, maneuverable and swift, would quarter the more distant parts of the property, probing with their headlights; the 4X4, which looked like a Toyota and had a searchlight on its roof, was to concentrate on cover from which it would be harder to flush a fugitive; the Jeep had been assigned the area between the house and the main gates; and Vanderlee's confederates, with their superior knowledge of the terrain, would cover the mansion itself and its immediate surroundings. Including the priestesses' cabins.

Scarff and Salter were making for Bolan's retreat right now. The driver of the Toyota, a thuggish goon in combat fatigues, was handing out radio transceivers to the rest of the party. The Jeep swung around and headed for the gates; the bikers roared off; the four-wheel drive lumbered toward the lake.

The two armed conspirators were eighty, maybe ninety yards away. Bolan hurried to the rear of the cabin. He had to get out before they arrived, and he had to make sure they weren't looking his way when he scaled the wall surrounding the stable area.

He'd closed the window he'd climbed through, and with luck they wouldn't realize it was unlocked. What he had to do was open the rear door and relock it before they were inside the hut.

The door was at the end of a short hallway, and fortunately it was secured with a simple dead bolt that one of his instruments mastered in less than a minute. He heard a key grate in the lock at the entrance as he swung the door open.

From the far side of the pass door separating the passageway from the front room, he heard Lem Scarff's hoarse voice.

"One up the spout, nice and ready. And believe me, my trigger finger's itching. Shooting that bastard would be a real pleasure, believe it."

"Oh, but you can't do that, dear boy!" Salter protested. "One has to take the man alive. There are so many questions to ask."

"You can ask," Scarff growled. "I don't aim to kill, just to hurt bad."

Bolan heard the banging of closet doors, the shifting of chairs and a table as he slipped past the open door, pulled it shut and locked it. He ducked below window height and dodged around to the one place they'd be unlikely to look for him—outside the door they'd just entered. Seconds later the rear door opened again and Salter's voice said, ''Completely empty in there. One thought it a nonstarter, but one has, I suppose, to check all the others.''

Peering around the corner of the small building, Bolan saw the two men going into the second hut, immediately behind the one he'd just left.

Still keeping low, he catfooted to the rear wall of the stables. Partly sheltered from view by a poplar that grew against the wall, he unwound the nylon cord from around his waist and launched a powerful cast upward.

This time it caught on the first try. The warrior tested the cord for secureness, then climbed up to the roof of the stables. He drew up the nylon, rewound it, then lay flat on the tiles at one side of the clock tower. Crawling up to the ridgepole, he could look down into the stable yard. Kleist and Vanderlee emerged from Joliffe's private garage, casting a flashlight beam behind the parked cars, then into the open part of the stables. There was a second flashlight in the vegetable garden on the far side of the wall. Over the gabled roofs of the mansion Bolan saw the Jeep's headlights reflected from the belt of trees near the gates. Nearer, perhaps a hundred yards away, a voice rasped unintelligibly from the speaker of a walkie-talkie.

Conditions seemed right for an attack on the main building. Bolan began edging along the steep slant of tiles. Behind him lights came on and then went off in the cabins. He was vulnerable, moving along this side of the roof, if Salter and Scarff finished their search and happened to flash a light upward as they returned.

He moved cautiously, concerned that the Desert Eagle's holster and the plastic grenades clipped to his belt would scrape the tiles and alert the men in the yard below. But he made it to the gable end without incident.

He hoisted himself over the ridgepole, lay on his back and let himself slowly down the far slope. When his feet touched the eaves trough, he raised himself on one elbow and looked below. The top of the wall was twelve feet beneath him.

Bolan looked beyond. The flashlight was now bobbing among the bushes at the far end of the garden. Judging from the direction of the beam, he guessed the man holding it had his back to the wall.

The Executioner unwound a dozen feet of the nylon rope, affixed the hook to the eaves trough and lowered himself to the wall. It took several hard throw-and-jerk casts to free the hook, and there were telltale metallic sounds each time. But the man in the bushes didn't turn around; Vanderlee and Kleist were walking out of the yard beneath the arch. Bolan's luck was holding.

So far.

He crept to the inner end of the wall. Then the pendulum swung the other way.

It was an easy step up from the brickwork to the curved roof of the breezeway that joined the stables to the house. What Bolan hadn't realized was that the

roof was glass, each panel covered with dark mat paint
to minimize the heat of the summer sun immediately
outside the kitchen quarters.

He cursed silently. From the junction of the breezeway and the house wall it was an easy twenty-foot
throw to lodge the grappling hook behind a sandstone
coping from which he could climb to a third-floor balcony. And beside the balcony there was a fat pipe rising to a slope of roof between two dormer windows.
But first he had to make the far end of the breezeway.

The glass panes were located between curved iron
spars fishboned out on either side of a central spine
supported on slender wrought-iron pillars. The pillars
were cemented to the tiled pavement linking the kitchen
quarters and the stables.

Since they were beneath the center of the canopy,
there was no way he could climb the last one and reach
the top of the breezeway if he was to drop down and
make the distance across the yard on foot.

And the canopy was too wide for him to make a
throw that would lodge the hook safely behind the
coping. The hook would fall and smash the glass.

There was no alternative—he'd have to walk the
slender spine between the two curves of glass if he
wanted to make the house wall in the right place at the
right height. Stepping gingerly, with arms spread on
either side to maintain his balance, he started out.

Bolan was well aware of the danger. The iron spars
of the canopy framework were rigid but very thin. The
spine was a little thicker. If, halfway between two of the
supporting pillars, his weight deformed the spine even

by one-tenth of an inch, the spars on either side could buckle and the glass would break.

Advancing one foot with extreme care, he drew the other up behind it, held his breath, then pushed the first one forward again. Raised voices floated up to him from the far side of the arch. The Toyota was grinding along in first, somewhere between the shrubbery and the fir plantation.

The Executioner kept going. At one point the glass on his left creaked alarmingly, and he froze for a full minute, agonizingly conscious of the perfect target he'd make if anyone flashed a light his way. Fifteen feet farther on one of the curved glass panels cracked with a noise like a pistol shot. He stopped dead, senses alert for discovery, but the damaged pane stayed in place.

He was at the wall. The canopy spine was cemented into the brickwork here, and the concrete had weathered and gone soft. As soon as the Executioner's weight was applied to the iron framework, the spine shifted, grinding into the concrete, which flaked and fell away. The glass on either side split, erupted and dropped onto the tiles with a clatter.

At once there were shouts from beyond the arch. Flattened against the wall behind the buttress, Bolan heard footsteps race across the cobbled yard. O'Hara's voice, alternating with garbled speech from a transceiver, yelled on the far side of the house. The stutter of a dirt bike, faint at first but increasingly loud, advanced from the direction of the lake. He could see the headlight beam brushing the pale canvas of the empty tent.

Kleist and the Dutchman were almost level with the breezeway. Once their flashlight revealed the shattered glass on the tiles, they'd look up and see him through the jagged hole in the canopy. He eased the Beretta from its quick-draw rig and pulled back the slide.

"Over here, quick! He jumped down from the wall!" a man's voice called from the far end of the vegetable garden. "He ran behind the outbuildings, heading for the woods! This way. You can cut him off!"

Confusion reigned. Incoherent phrases from Kleist and Vanderlee were echoed by the two men searching the huts. The pair in the yard changed direction; the door in the wall crashed open and they ran through. The bike accelerated around the front of the house.

Bolan breathed a sigh of relief. He had no idea who or what the guy in the bushes had seen, but the interruption was appreciated. He levered himself away from the wall, uncoiled the nylon cord and threw. Once again the hook lodged on his first cast.

He raised himself to the coping, coiled up the cord for the last time and began working his way along the narrow ledge to the balcony. It was fifteen or twenty feet, no difficult task.

Facing the wall with his arms outstretched and his cheek pressed against the rough stonework, Bolan was looking straight ahead to his goal and the dark landscape beyond and below it. Light flickered here and there in the distance, among trees, up into the sky, across smooth swells of ground. But there was no way of telling which sections of the search party produced it, or whether, in fact, some of it might have been coming from vehicles outside the estate. Nearer at hand Bolan could see flashlights moving across a stretch of wasteland between the vegetable garden and the woods, and hear the negative responses of the hunters as they called to one another. He clambered over the balustrade and crept to the far side of the balcony.

The pipe was wide enough to be gripped between the knees and the soles of the feet. Bolan reached his two hands around the pipe and hauled himself up.

The slope of roof between the two dormers was too steep to climb. He had to make it to one or the other of the two windows, balance on the sill and break in. The only way to get there was hand over hand, along the eaves trough.

He was halfway there when one of the brackets supporting the trough pulled out of the stonework. Bolan's weight dragged the shallow metal conduit downward, and at one place where it was particularly corroded, the trough snapped.

Luckily the break was just behind the Executioner. The section he was grasping swung crazily down at a forty-five-degree angle, over the courtyard cobbles sixty feet below.

For a timeless instant he almost lost his grip. His right hand slipped from the curved metal and flew into space. His feet thumped against the wall. Only the fighter's lightning reflex, clamping steel fingers, contracting the left biceps and screaming shoulder muscles, saved him from dropping to his death. Then, laboriously, the sweat running into his eyes, he brought back the right hand, gripped the eaves trough and held on.

He hung there, panting, allowing the adrenaline to race back through his veins, until his breathing returned to normal. Then, feeling more vulnerable than at any time since he arrived in Britain, he started the agonizing task of hoisting himself once more upward at the full stretch of his arms, desperate to reach the next bracket and the rigid, secure portion of eaves trough that would stretch beyond it.

He moved the last couple of feet, reached up and wrapped aching fingers around the projecting iron spike. Tentatively, ready to switch at any moment, he transferred his weight to that hand.

The bracket held.

Like a drowning man surfacing at last, Bolan shifted his grip to the far side of the bracket. Seconds later he was beneath the dormer.

One of the two white-painted window frames was open to the balmy summer night. From inside floated the sounds of heavy, rhythmic breathing. Bolan pulled himself up onto the windowsill. He eased his lean, muscular body across the ledge and dropped silently to the carpeted floor beyond.

CHAPTER TWENTY-ONE

Even with the window open the room was close. It smelled of a light floral perfume, with something more aromatic—incense, perhaps—in the background. The bed was a pale blur in the darkness.

Outside the open casement the stars shone less brightly. Trees bordering the eastern boundary of the estate were now silhouetted against the milky radiance where the late-rising quarter moon was about to appear. The warrior trod softly forward. He had to be out of there before moonlight disturbed the sleeper and revealed his presence.

He could make out the door, six feet away from the bed with a night table in between. Gliding toward it, he reached for the handle, wrapped wary fingers around a porcelain knob and twisted.

There was an audible click.

Bedsprings creaked. Bolan heard a rustle of covers, the slither of silk. He opened the door, then heard a sharp intake of breath.

Outside, an unlit hallway led to a stairwell illuminated from somewhere below. In the faint light penetrating the gloom he saw a figure sitting bolt upright in the bed—a wispy-haired woman with wide-open eyes and a sheet drawn up to her chin. It was Mrs. Haytor, the Scottish clairvoyant who'd been his dinner companion the night of his arrival at Joliffe Hall.

Bolan's mind raced. He was faced with a credulous woman, in the confused state that resulted from an unexpected awakening. Could he pull off a crazy trick? It was worth a try.

Whipping up both arms, he crossed them in front of his face, effectively hiding his features. "I come," he announced in a deep, sepulchral voice, "with tidings for the one who is to be the chosen of Xangô!"

Fading into the corridor, he pulled the door shut on a gasp of surprise from the bed, then ran for the staircase. Halfway down the first flight, he heard a door jerked open, a patter of bare feet, a soft, insistent knocking on another door, then Mrs. Haytor's loud, excited whisper. "Mary! Wake up! Come quickly, dear. I just saw a spirit in my room, a full manifestation! A man with a message for Sir Simon..."

Bolan sped to the lower landing and on down to the floor below. It wouldn't be long before common sense persuaded Mrs. Haytor that it was no ghost she'd seen.

Bolan finally arrived at the stainless-steel spiral that led to the entrance hall. Soon, the early-morning staff would be in to clear up after the party, but right now the place was a mess. Champagne bottles stacked in a wicker crate stood beside a table that was covered by a white cloth spotted with food stains. Dozens of wineglasses waited on a cart by the hallway that led to the kitchens. Empty cigarette packs littered the floor around the overflowing pedestal ashtrays.

Bolan looked down through the haze of stale smoke at the tall picture windows in back of the hall. Light pouring through the glass striped a curve of lawn and one corner of the buffet tent. To anyone out there beyond the illumination, a man creeping down the staircase would be as obvious as an image on a movie screen.

The Executioner half closed his eyes, straining to see farther into the garden. If there was moonlight now, it was negated by the glare from the house. He could see nothing. Nothing moved.

It was a chance he'd have to take. He couldn't stay there all night. Hoping that O'Hara had shifted his base location nearer the false alarm beyond the vegetable garden, Bolan catfooted around the spiral, took the corridor past the library and went down into the basement.

Zero reaction.

He knew from Colonel Williams that the secret door to the movie-tape complex could be opened from the electrical control booth at one side of the rostrum in the room used for séances.

The room was adjacent to Joliffe's miniature ballroom. Bolan hurried to the door and found it locked. That was no problem to the sophisticated implements he carried in the pouch clipped to his waist belt. Nor was the wider, heavier door with medieval iron hinges beyond. It took him four minutes and eleven seconds to make the control booth.

The switchboard was equipped with tumblers, buttons and levers. The latter, it was clear, could have nothing to do with opening doors. Selecting one in the beam of his penlight, Bolan tried a tumbler switch.

He started. With a subdued whine of machinery, an antiglare gauze slid down behind the desk on the dais in a sickly green twilight that seemed to emanate from the paneling at each side of the stage. At the same time thin spirals of violet smoke wreathed up in front of the desk.

The setup was evidently designed to blur the outlines of anyone seated at the desk and hide anyone close behind who was in on the act. He cut the switch and thumbed a button. A brilliant white spot shafted a dazzling beam at the desk.

Bolan cursed. He switched off the spot and pressed another button. A green pilot light glowed. In the darkened room nothing moved, no light appeared. Maybe this was it.

In the corridor the thin beam showed him the displaced panel, the door sprung open six inches. He walked inside and pulled it shut after him.

He wasn't sure what he was looking for, but he knew that the longer he stayed, the more difficult it would be to make a getaway; it was essential that he was out of the house and under cover somewhere in the estate before daylight. Any kind of search he made would therefore have to be selective.

What was expected of him?

He'd already filled the first two items of Williams's shopping list—he'd stirred things up, and the conspirators knew who was responsible for the stirring. The third demand? Find some kind of evidence that threw light on the activities of Vanderlee and company. And find proof that the activity was wrong.

Planning a selective search, he started on the assumption that anything that was locked would be worth investigating and might reveal sensitive material. Even in a secret room, putting such stuff under lock and key was just human nature. Bolan unzipped the pouch and bared his specialist tools for the third time.

Basically what he had to deal with were steel drawers in the desk and filing cabinets, and wooden cupboards set into the walls. He'd have a stab at the film cans below, but he reckoned it wasn't worth wasting time on the audio reels—the bad guys weren't going to bug their own conversations.

The drawers were no problem; the cupboards, with heavy locks, were more difficult. But in minutes he had them all open. It was in the less secure drawers that he hit pay dirt.

A small notebook listed the addresses of a dozen companies in Austria and Eastern Europe, most of them manufacturing aerospatial hardware and sophisticated armament with their guidance systems. Some of the companies were annotated with the names of individual managers and their departments. Each entry was followed by a coded series of numbers and letters.

Fax sheets in another drawer related to transactions between these companies and government departments in Poland, Egypt, Iraq, Pakistan and Syria. A third was stuffed with memos detailing different financial operations of Universal Plastics' research department. Bolan crammed them all into his neoprene pouch.

He ignored a drawerful of UPI promotional material headed with Rick Salter's office number, and a wad of typescript backgrounding the different spiritist organizations in South America. Given the circumstances, that was predictable and proved nothing.

Bolan hesitated over another notebook filled with the names and addresses of private individuals in different countries. They were entered in what looked like various categories, but the heading over each section was again in code. Finally he shoved that book in with the rest.

He could find no correspondence files, and most of the folders in the steel cabinets contained manufacturers' instructions—some for the complex electronic products marketed by UPI, some for the high-tech recording and movie equipment installed in these two rooms. There was no sign of any written material concerning the séances and nothing to do with Sir Simon Joliffe's supposed mediumistic gifts.

There were four cupboards, two in each room. Each was lined with thin sheet metal that Bolan guessed might be some kind of antiradiation protection, but there was no indication whether this was designed to shield ultrasensitive material within the cupboards or to protect the occupants of the room from such material. Only one cupboard had anything in it.

He removed, one after the other, more than a dozen small pieces of electronic equipment whose use baffled him. Each of the items was fashioned around a different pattern of rigid plastic chassis. Bolan stared at diodes, transistors, complicated circuit boards and a series of purpose-built holes and projections clearly designed to accept accessories or allow the component to be fitted into some larger piece of equipment. The electronics bore no relation to the promotional material or any of the diagrams he'd seen, but each item was embossed beneath the plastic chassis with UPI's logo, a Made in Britain slug and a part number in letters and figures.

Bolan saw no point in taking any of the items. In themselves they proved nothing and clarified nothing. But he took a ballpoint from the recording control desk, tore a leaf from a memo pad and carefully copied the reference number of each part.

He folded the paper, stowed it among the notebooks and went downstairs for the last time to collect a couple of the film cans at random from the selection racked on the shelves. Then he killed the lights, allowed the secret door to close behind him and headed up the stairway toward the kitchens.

As he came out from the hallway, he saw that he'd miscalculated and dawn had already broken. Rosy light flooded through the picture windows of the entrance hall.

Bolan's pouch was zipped and clipped back onto his belt. He hefted the wide, circular movie cans into the crook of his left arm and unleathered the Beretta with his right. Then, stealing down the second corridor, he turned a corner and walked into the first of the kitchens.

The hardguy who'd been driving the Jeep stood at the far end of the long stainless-steel sink. As the Executioner appeared, he raised a heavy-caliber revolver and fired.

CHAPTER TWENTY-TWO

The shot, echoing back from tiled walls, was as loud as a thunderclap. Bolan's cat-quick reflexes had him on the floor behind an old-fashioned, heavy kitchen table while chips from a smashed tile were still falling onto his shoulder. The slug had passed so close to his head that hairs just above his ear had stirred.

From where he was he could no longer see the gunman, but there was a slatted rack carrying nests of aluminum cooking pans hung from the wall just behind and above the guy. The rack was suspended by chains from two hooks screwed into the wall.

Bolan sighted the Beretta very carefully. It was a difficult shot but not impossible.

The hardguy must have seen the tip of the Beretta's silencer, for he let loose another thunderous round. A long splinter of white wood was gouged from the tabletop above the Executioner.

Bolan squeezed the trigger. His 9 mm slug hit the right-hand hook smack on the nose, snapping the curved part off the shank set into the wall. The supporting chain fell away, and the rack tipped down from the horizontal to the near vertical, spilling the entire collection of pans over the gunner. The noise was deafening.

While the hardguy, cursing, was fighting off the metal shower, Bolan sprang to his feet, took a running dive at the table and slid facedown across the scrubbed top to hit the flags, shoulder-rolled and came up between a freezer and a restaurant-size dishwasher with his autoloader spitting fire.

He'd already snicked the gun into 3-shot mode. One round was deflected by a pan as the gunner fisted it away; another narrowly missed his head and shattered a second tile; the third nicked the top of his right shoulder, plowing a red-hot furrow through flesh and muscle.

The guy yelled with pain and fury, clapping his left hand over the wound. The revolver in his right roared once more, but shock slowed his reactions and the bullet flew wide, breaking a windowpane and spinning into the yard. With blood spurting between the clenched fingers of his left hand, the hardguy dropped to one knee and backed off through the open door of a laundry room.

Bolan knew he had to get out of there and into the open. Already he could hear shouts from somewhere beyond the stables, and feet were pounding on the floor above. "What the hell is going on?" a querulous male voice called from upstairs. "I thought I heard a shot!"

"Damn right, buddy," Bolan muttered. "Here's another." He blazed a 9 mm trio at the framework of the laundry room door to help the gunner keep his head down while the warrior got to his feet.

After the clatter of aluminum, the gunner's cries of rage and the earsplitting detonation of his revolver, the thuds from the subsonic rounds were almost unnoticeable, especially when the big gun blared yet again as the guy fired blind around the edge of the doorframe.

Bolan didn't know where that one went. He'd vaulted onto the top of the dishwasher, which was backed by a tall Tudor window with small leaded panes.

Tensing his muscles, he crossed his arms over his face and hurled himself backward at the window. The soft lead bulged outward, split and propelled glass rectangles into the yard. Bolan burst through in a cloud of sharp, glittering fragments and landed on his back on the cobbles.

Wounded though he was, the hardguy had guts. He was out of the laundry room and racing across the kitchen floor while Bolan was doing his backward leap. As the Executioner hit the ground, he appeared in the ruined window with a murderous glare in his eyes. He raised his revolver, then homed in on the warrior.

Still lying on his back, Bolan fired two-handed before the hardguy could press the trigger, the three shots smashing into the gunner's chest. He reared up under the impact, then flopped forward to slump through the breached window. The gun dropped to the flagstones among shards of broken glass already tinted rose by the rising sun, and now darkened by splashing blood.

Bolan was on his feet and sprinting along the side of the house, away from the stable yard. The nearest hunters were approaching the arch behind him.

A bullet chipped against the wall ahead of him, another ricocheting off stonework facing a window and whining away. Lungs pumping, he zigzagged as he ran, willing every muscle to increase his pace.

The hardguy he'd just taken out of play had been driving a Jeep, and he'd been alone. So where was the vehicle now? In front of the mansion near the entrance porch? It was worth a look.

He was approaching steps leading up to a side door when a lightning glance over his shoulder revealed Vanderlee, Kleist, Phuong and Salter outside the arch. Mercs on foot were running down the rose walk.

Bullets hummed around him as he threw himself at the door, grabbing the handle. He pushed, and the door burst inward, tumbling him into a hallway on his hands and knees. He whirled, snatching the Desert Eagle from its holster. Still kneeling, he let loose three rounds from the heavy automatic. The range was too great, but he wanted them to know that he had firepower.

The warrior sprinted down a short corridor, through a TV room and into a small room off the main hallway that seemed to be used as a study. Beyond a rolltop desk and leather armchairs he could see the stainless-steel spiral.

Two cleaners were in the outer hall, and they stared, openmouthed, as he raced for the double doors at the entrance and the porch beyond. Neither made any attempt to stop him.

Bolan pulled open the glass-paned outer doors, and, yeah, the Jeep was there, standing at one side of the broad, shallow steps. The Stony Man warrior cleared the steps and launched himself into the driver's seat.

Expertly he hot-wired the vehicle and slammed the gearshift into first. The engine bellowed, and the Jeep skated away, showering gravel from its rear wheels.

Bolan glimpsed pursuers grouped outside the glass doors, saw in the rearview mirror that they were firing. All of the bullets missed their mark. Then he was around the corner of the house, speeding toward the arch—and O'Hara.

The man stood yelling into his radio, three mercs with assault rifles standing behind him. Bolan wrenched the Jeep's wheel and smashed through a flower bed onto the lawn where the buffet tent was erected.

He was vulnerable, perched behind the wheel in the open-sided vehicle, but he was a hell of a lot better off mobile than he would be on foot. Just the same, those assault rifles were too close for comfort. Metal screeched and thumped as quick-fire rounds smashed into the bodywork.

Bolan spun the wheel again, churning up Sir Simon's lawn, turning his back on O'Hara and his men. He aimed the Jeep straight at the unflapped entrance to the tent, shoving the gearshift into second and tramping the gas pedal flat.

The vehicle leaped forward, sped through the tented interior, knocked over a stack of garden chairs and rammed the long table on the far side of the tent. Trestles disintegrated and planks cartwheeled aside as the Jeep hurtled through. It plowed into the canvas rear wall, pulling all the guy ropes free of the earth on the far side, and burst out into the open air again as the canvas split from top to bottom.

The heavy bumper bar protecting the fenders and radiator grille had saved the Jeep from serious damage, but the windshield had cracked, there were fragments of tortured wood bouncing on the roof and hood, and a section of ripped canvas had wound itself around an outside mirror and was now plastered to the windshield. Bolan snaked the vehicle over the rough ground before the meadow to dislodge the wood, and reached around the windshield to pull away the canvas.

As his view cleared, he saw the Toyota rocketing toward him from the direction of the lake. The off-roader was crammed with mercenaries toting silenced MAC-10s. He slewed the Jeep to the left and saw three Yamaha trials bikes, ridden by men in combat fatigues, speeding toward him from the fir plantation.

There was nowhere Bolan could go: he was trapped in a pincer movement. His only chance was to try to shake them on foot in the encumbered area containing the stables, the yard, the parked cars and the cabins. But to get there he had to outdistance the mounted pursuit and at the same time keep far enough away to be out of range of O'Hara's men.

In third now, he twirled the wheel and braked, spinning the Jeep in a U-turn, and raced in a wide arc for the priestesses' huts. Ahead of him O'Hara's riflemen were running; behind, he could see in the mirror that the bikes and the 4X4 had closed ranks to give chase.

If the gunners kept running, he reckoned, he could make it; because the motorized stuff was over a hundred yards behind and not closing the distance. But if they were smart enough to stop, take up a position and aim properly, it would be close.

They were smart enough. Or O'Hara, the veteran, was smart enough to give the right orders.

The three men dropped to one knee and raised their rifles. As Bolan drew level two hundred yards away, heading off now at an angle to make a tougher target, they opened fire. There was automatic fire from the Toyota, too. The soft top of the Jeep was in rags. Then a tire burst, crippling the Jeep as Bolan headed in among the trees behind the huts.

The Jeep ground to a halt with the tire off the rim and the damaged wheel furrowing the soft ground. Bolan got out and raced past the first row of huts, then past the second. There was no point making a stand where he could be enfiladed and fired on from behind; Vanderlee and the other principals, directed by O'Hara, had to be pretty close by now.

Beyond the back wall of the stables a stretch of rough ground waist-high in weeds separated the enclosed vegetable garden from a long, low row of sixteenth-century outbuildings. From what he'd seen before, Bolan reckoned their lower floors were unused, although there might be servants' rooms above.

He approached the area facedown in the grass, worming his way toward a Dutch door whose top half was open. Behind him the hunt fanned out among the cabins. The Toyota and the dirt bikes had cut their engines, and now there were at least a dozen armed men with itchy trigger fingers, eager to flush him out as they patrolled the edge of the woods on foot.

"He's got to be within a couple of hundred yards," O'Hara's voice rasped. "It's only been a couple of minutes since he left the Jeep."

"If we see the son of a bitch, do we shoot to kill?" one of the mercenaries asked.

"If you see him, shoot," O'Hara replied. "We'd rather he was alive because there are questions to ask. But if not, what the hell? The important thing is to bring him down."

Bolan had reached the Dutch door, and he wriggled inside. He was in a dusty storeroom stacked with rusting garden tools, the blade of a harrow, a pile of flowerpots, most of them broken.

The sun, hovering above the horizon now, beamed a shaft of brilliant light through a cobwebbed window and threw across the beaten earthen floor the elongated shadow of a very tall man.

Bolan saw the feet first. From his prone position he twisted his neck and looked up. It was Ley Phuong, the huge, hairless man who seemed to belong to Joliffe's inner circle. He held an automatic loosely in his right hand.

There was no chance for Bolan this time. Phuong was less than ten feet away, and his weapons were snug in the shoulder rig and hip holster. He'd be drilled three times before he could reach either of his grenades, let alone draw a pin.

"Into the next room, quick," Phuong whispered. "There's a trapdoor and an underground passage, a brick tunnel that leads to ruins behind the huts. None of them know about it. Move!"

Bolan stared at him. "I don't get it."

"Get going! They'll be here any minute." The tall man gestured toward an open door, a dark space beyond.

The coin dropped. "You're the inside man, the one they call AX-12."

Phuong hesitated. "What if I am? I know you have to be on the same side, but I don't know exactly who or what you are."

"Ask Colonel Williams."

"I see." The big Oriental paused again. "We don't have time to talk here. Come on. We'll make it to the tunnel."

Bolan scrambled to his feet and followed the man into a utility room containing chopped wood stacked along two of its walls. A huge wheel leaned against a third wall, and a halter and several dusty lengths of harness hung from pegs. The trapdoor was beneath a window whose small panes were grimy with dust. It was set in a brick floor and half-covered with empty sacks.

"My private escape channel," Phuong said, pulling at the iron ring set in the trap, "in case I have to make a fast getaway. The sacks are glued in place so that they fall back over the cracks when the flap is lowered." He shoved the gun into his belt and produced a powerful flashlight. The trap creaked open.

Bolan saw iron spikes hammered into a brick shaft that was about twelve feet deep. At the bottom an arched opening led to the tunnel. "Go on down," Phuong advised.

The Executioner lowered himself through the open flap, feeling with one foot for the first spike. He looked up.

"I'll come with you as far as the ruins."

Bolan climbed carefully to the floor of the shaft. Phuong followed, letting the trap down after him and cutting off the sound of the pursuers' voices, which had been getting too close for comfort.

The underground passageway was four feet high, the ancient vaulted brickwork still dry and in good condition. A current of fresh air fanned their faces as they bent double and forged ahead.

"Nothing personal," Phuong said, "but I don't understand why you were sent when I'm already here in deep cover as a department head in the UPI research section."

"I know Williams," Bolan replied, "but let's say we work for different bosses."

"You mean you're from the American end? Even so—"

"Look," the warrior said, "you work at UPI, you're close to Joliffe, you're in with Vanderlee and the others, okay. But do you have the entry to the movie and recording rooms on your own? Can you fool around in there without exciting suspicion?"

"Negative. Officially I don't even know about the room. I'm only close to them in my capacity as UPI section chief. I'm not in their confidence when Joliffe isn't there.''

''But you keep close by faking an interest in spiritism?''

''That's right.''

''Which is why you can row yourself in with the hunters anytime there's a risk of someone rocking the occult boat?''

''Right again.''

''Okay. So you have an ear to the ground. You inform Williams of anything that comes your way, but you can't dig any deeper because it could blow your cover.''

''That's affirmative.''

''Well, I can. Williams wants to stampede them, but he wants them to see that it isn't a spy on Her Gracious Majesty's payroll that's blowing the whistle. You read me?''

''Loud and clear.''

Bolan stared ahead. Some distance in front of them the tunnel curved. In the glare of light stroking the brick walls he saw a flash of movement as some underground creature startled by their presence scampered into the dark. ''You know why I'm here,'' the warrior said. ''Now fill me in on two things, okay?''

''Try me.''

''One. Apart from the occult link with its boss, what exactly do Kleist, Duhamel and Vanderlee have to do with UPI?''

''They hold stock,'' Phuong explained. ''Just as Joliffe does in their companies. You know these multinationals. And they have subcontractors in common, manufacturers of nonclassified components, that kind of thing. And that's it. End of story.''

"Number two,'' Bolan said, "and talking of components. Do you know they have a copy of a memo sent to you warning of leaks concerned with the TASM guidance system?''

"I know the memo was lost. Fortunately not from anyplace connecting it with me.''

"Okay. So tell me what exactly they're worried about. What kind of leaks, what kind of material?''

"Nonspecific,'' Phuong replied. "Not blueprints or specifications or test data. But it seems classified components, ultrasecret and highly sensitive experimental parts relating to the TASM guidance sensors, might have turned up in the hands of certain Central European arms dealers. It may be a coincidence. None of our people have seen them, and it could be that Warsaw Pact technicians are working along the same lines. It happens. But naturally we have to check.''

"You're talking about actual, physical components, three-dimensional stuff, genuine working parts?'' Bolan asked, thinking of the items he'd found in the secret room cupboard.

"That's correct.''

"And you're checking whether any are missing from the UPI stores, is that it?''

"As far as possible, yes. But these are experimental bits and pieces. The high-tech freaks might fashion half a dozen different examples of any model, differing only in the smallest detail, and the less successful ones don't necessarily get logged.''

"Are you saying that your people are afraid that the missing parts, if any *are* missing, might be touted around Europe as samples?''

"Something like that,'' Phuong said, suddenly evasive.

The tunnel turned again, and suddenly the flashlight was no longer necessary. Ahead of them daylight filtered down dimly from the top of another shaft.

"The iron steps have been pulled out of this one,'' Phuong told him. "There's a wooden ladder I use and pull down after me anytime I come this way.'' He walked ahead, lifted the ladder from the side of the tunnel, fed it into the shaft and leaned it against the curved wall. "On your way... partner.'' He smiled.

Bolan shook his hand and climbed the ladder.

After Phuong withdrew and his footsteps died away, Bolan took stock of the situation. He was beneath a dense tangle of briers that choked the space between three walls of what had once been a summerhouse. A lot of the crumbling stonework had fallen away, but it was clear that the original design had included niches for statues and a pyramid roof. Rotting rafters still projected from the top of the least-weathered wall. From the open front of the structure, cracked steps led down through a chaos of underbrush toward the woods. The Toyota 4X4 was parked under the first row of trees.

This could be the chance he'd been waiting for. He moved spiny brambles aside to look closer. The five-man crew of the Toyota was standing nearby. One held up a transceiver, and Bolan could make out the voice of O'Hara issuing some kind of operational orders.

He edged toward the front of the ruins, checking out the options. One hundred fifty yards of waist-high scrub separated him from the mercs, three of whom still carried their silenced MAC-10s. The driver and the guy with the radio wore hip holsters.

Any frontal assault was impossible. They'd mow him down before he emerged from the briers far enough to get off a single shot. Forcing his way through beneath the brushwood, even if he could make it unobserved, would take him all of ten to fifteen minutes—and it was possible that the men would pile back into the vehicle and take off at any minute.

The only answer was an overt action, and the resulting noise that would bring O'Hara and the others running. But by then he should have the Toyota.

Bolan unclipped a plastic stun grenade from his harness, then drew the Beretta from its shoulder rig and eased back the slide, holding the autoloader in his left hand. With his teeth he drew the grenade pin, wrapping the fingers of his right hand tightly around the plastic egg to secure the spoon. Then he thrust aside the briers and stood.

One of the mercs spotted him at once and yelled a warning. Another spun around and choked out a silenced blast from his MAC-10. As the slugs zipped through the foliage around him, Bolan drew back his arm and hurled the grenade.

The flash of the explosion was lost in the early-morning sunlight. Less effective in the open air than it would have been in a confined space, the concussion was nevertheless enough to lay out all five of the mercenaries.

Bolan was down the steps and running, forcing his way past bushes and clinging brambles, while the flat crack of the detonation was still ringing in his ears. Four of the men were out cold. The fifth merc had dragged himself onto hands and knees and was groping for his MAC-10. A single shot from Bolan's Beretta blew him away as his fingers closed on the butt.

The Executioner leaped into the Toyota's driver's seat and keyed the engine to life. He spun the vehicle around in a tight circle, zigzagging away through the trees as Vanderlee, Kleist and O'Hara ran into sight on the far sight of the summerhouse. Kleist and the Dutchman opened up, but if any slugs made the distance, they were absorbed by the tree trunks surrounding the careering Toyota.

Bolan had made the meadow and was tearing toward the lake when his mirror showed him the first of the bikers. The guy was two hundred yards away, coming from the front of the house and going like the hammers of hell. The warrior twisted in his seat and saw a second bike speeding from the fir plantation. But that one was too far away to worry about. At least for the moment.

Bolan was aiming for the valley. The shortest way down was on the far side of the stone wall, the slope where he'd been caught by the camera. But it was too steep for the Toyota. If he wanted to make it with the vehicle remaining on its own four wheels, he'd have to follow in the Range Rover's tire tracks and drive around the lake before he headed downhill.

But before he set the Toyota at the slope, Bolan had to deal with the first biker. The guy was closing fast and would clearly be able to draw level before the warrior started his vehicle over the edge. As usual, he decided to meet trouble head-on.

When the dirt bike was thirty yards away, he stood on the brakes as he hit a patch of bare, sandy soil, at the same time wrenching the wheel. The Toyota skidded around with the engine screaming until it faced the astonished rider.

Now Bolan stamped on the gas pedal, and the Toyota shot forward. Braked to a halt, with both feet on the ground, the biker hefted his subgun by the pistol grip, then aimed with both hands. Bolan ducked as the windshield exploded, showering him with glass.

He held the wheel steady and the Toyota kept going. It slammed into the bike at forty miles per hour, shearing the front wheel and fork off the frame, mangling the engine and catapulting the rider into the air. The gas tank ruptured, spilling fuel over the overheated engine, and the bike erupted into a fireball.

Bolan swerved the Toyota around the miniholocaust and looked for the rider. But the mercenary had had enough. He turned his back and ran, limping, for the safety of a belt of trees. Bolan let him go.

He was broadsiding the Toyota down the slope between outcrops and clumps of heather when he saw the second biker. The guy was manhandling his machine with ferocious skill, showing all the expertise of a professional as he covered the hillside at near-top speed.

The warrior squealed the Toyota to a dead stop, opened the driver's door and raised the Desert Eagle. The big gun's backblast drowned out the yowl of the attacker's bike—and the Yamaha was sliding riderless down the hillside in a cloud of dust.

Bolan backed up and drove down as fast as the terrain would allow. He could see movement among the trees away to his right. Metal gleamed somewhere in the woods below as the armored command car was called to intercept him. But this time, he reckoned, he could make the wall with time to spare. It was only as the 4X4 bumped over the streambed that he realized he wasn't the only game the hunters had in their sights.

In the distance he saw a running figure streaking for the wall. On either side mercs moved in to intercept. But the fugitive, a slight guy in a black leather biker's suit, was too quick and too smart for them. Bolan thought the pursuers were firing—their guns were raised—but he couldn't hear over the grinding of gears and the growl of the Toyota's laboring engine. The leather-clad figure had jumped onto the blackened frame of the burned-out Range Rover, made it to the wall and dropped from sight before they closed in.

Bolan had crammed on a fair speed by the time he reached the trees on the far side of the streambed. He roared up toward the wall, ignoring the few mercs one hundred yards away on either side—last-ditch troops, he guessed, left to hold the fort. And unless they had mortars, the command car was too far away to count.

They didn't have mortars.

The Executioner was aiming for the damaged section of wall between the carcass of the Range Rover and the tree he'd climbed with Freeman. As bullets thudded into the rear of the Toyota, he let go of the wheel and hunched close to the door to keep clear of the steering column when the crunch came.

The Toyota ran full tilt into the wall. This time the wall, weakened by the shock of being previously rammed by the Range Rover, fell, crashing down the bank into the lane with a thunderous billowing of yellow smoke that blanketed the area with a choking fog.

Bolan extricated himself from the wreck of the 4X4 and jumped into the lane. Coughing out the dust in his lungs, he heard the bellow of a powerful motorcycle engine. When he crossed the lane to retrieve his rental behind the stand of willows, he saw that the Harley-Davidson was gone.

The drive back to Exeter generated many thoughts. And few answers.

CHAPTER TWENTY-THREE

The voice in the telephone receiver was sharp and incisive. Jason Mettner's ballpoint covered sheet after sheet of the memo pad with figures, percentage breakdowns and shorthand notes punctuated by names spelled out in caps. He was installed in Felicity Freeman's Exeter apartment, three rooms on the top floor of an old town house in a quiet street not far from the cathedral.

The woman herself was away, doing a one-night stand in a Southampton club. Bolan was asleep in a guest room cluttered with stage props, vanishing-lady chests and glove puppets. Mettner had been summoned from Hull, where he'd been investigating a North Sea oil rig scandal.

When the voice stopped talking at last, he put down the ballpoint and lit a cigarette. "Thanks, Roger," he said, blowing out smoke. "You're a pal. Don't know what we'd have done without you."

He paused, listened again, then added, "Can't tell you right now. Honest. I know it's a lot to ask, picking your brains for all this inside stuff and not letting on what the story is. But I have sources to protect. As soon as they're clean, the moment the story stands up, if it does stand up, I'll cut you in. Word of honor."

The voice quacked a short question. "Only one thing, buddy," Mettner replied. "The scoop on the share transactions *since* Easter. What? You can't? Oh, shit! Who? Stanley Karsh on the *Herald?* Yeah, I met him once on some city freebie. He's their stock-market wizard, right? Okay, I'll pump him. And thanks again." He hung up and reached for his portable typewriter.

Mettner was on his fifth cigarette, tapping out his notes, when Freeman's key scraped in the lock. "My God!" she exclaimed, coming in from the short hallway. "This place stinks. I thought we were in a smokeless zone!" She threw up a window, fanning away smoke with a newspaper. "I see Mike Belasko was spotted in Cardiff today," she said, tossing the paper onto an occasional table. "Getting warmer, aren't they!"

"That one of the late editions? What page?" Mettner asked absently, the cigarette still in his mouth as he scrawled a footnote on one of his pages.

She picked up the paper and opened it out. "Page seventeen, column seven."

"Must have been a last-minute report." The newspaperman underlined a row of typed figures and dropped the ballpoint beside his machine. "There, honey. One more page of deathless prose and your spycatcher friend is satisfied."

"You got it all? Everything the colonel wanted?"

"All except the very latest figures on the share transactions. I have to make one more call for those later."

"That's terrific, Jay! Aren't you clever!"

"I won't lie to you, my beauty. It's no more than knowing the right guy to call. The Intel comes from the finance editor of the *Courier*. Real mine of information... And what he couldn't produce from his own lode he dug up for me elsewhere. Phoned every newspaper morgue in town, had half the clerks in the City scouring the files all afternoon."

"Without saying what it was for, I hope?"

"He doesn't *know* what it's for. Mrs. Mettner's boy isn't that stupid, sugar! Anyway, Roger Cameron's on that kind of kick every day of the week. They'll have assumed it was for him."

"Well," the woman said, "I think you deserve a drink."

"Me, too," Mettner agreed. "Our adventurous confederate was sniffing around for breakfast when he hit town this morning. I had to go down to the corner store to buy a bag of oranges! My God, what I do for my friends!"

SHOWERED, SHAVED and refreshed, Mack Bolan was going over his probe of the estate with Mettner and Freeman when Colonel Williams dropped by early that evening. Mettner had already typed out a summary of the material Bolan had taken from the secret rooms at Joliffe Hall.

Williams read the summary three times, then began sifting through the originals the Executioner had brought. "Very, *very* interesting," he said at last.

"Maybe you'd like to share the secret," Bolan suggested.

"It's all here in these documents. Half of them relating to the how, the other half to the why."

"It's the why that's been bothering me," Bolan commented.

"The ultimate aim, of course, is money," Williams said. "When isn't it? But it happens that the way of getting it—through control of Universal Plastics—affects the security of my country and yours, indeed of NATO as a whole."

He poked a finger at the first notebook Bolan had discovered. "What do we have here? A list of companies manufacturing modern armament and space hardware. Along with the names of friendly contacts and a series of reference numbers. The companies are subcontractors supplying government departments in Eastern Europe and the Middle East. Here again we have documentary details of complex two-way traffic between UPI's finance department and these other elements."

He picked up the memo paper on which Bolan had copied the part numbers of the components in the shielded cupboard. "You were probably too pushed to notice, but these numbers are the same as the references after the company names in the first notebook."

"You're telling us...?" Mettner began.

"The way I see it," Williams went on, "is this. A consortium of businessmen, tycoons in and out of the electronics world, reckon they could make a killing if they could offer for sale the ultrasecret hardware being manufactured by UPI for NATO."

"For sale to the Soviets?" Mettner asked.

"Not necessarily. Warsaw Pact, Middle East, Far East, Israel. Anyone would be prepared to bid—and bid high—for such material. This no espionage story, no theft and sale of the designs. With UPI in their hands they can offer the actual merchandise, the finished product."

"And meanwhile?"

"Meanwhile, as AX-12 and Mr. Belasko have discovered, they offer sample components stolen from the UPI research labs as a foretaste of what they can produce once they control the company."

"What I don't understand," Bolan said, "is what this has to do with the occult?"

"And how could they control the company, anyway?" Freeman asked.

"Basically you're both asking the same question."

They stared at each other, then at Williams.

"Surely you can see? Look at the figures!" For once the colonel sounded irritable. "UPI's a public company, right? The government is a minority shareholder, but it's a big minority. With the stock held by the Joliffe family, the joint holding makes fifty-eight percent—now a controlling majority. But since the government doesn't play the markets, it really is the family who has a controlling interest. Are you with me?"

They nodded.

"You'll understand," Williams continued, "that with the Stealth, HOTOL and TASM systems at stake here, we aren't unnaturally concerned with the present goings-on. Which was why, originally—" he looked at Bolan "—we breathed in the ear of your Mr. Brognola."

Bolan remained silent.

"It's all here, you see. Kleist, the rocketry genius with power to act for Kemtex-Elektron of Karlsrühe. Vanderlee, the executive boss of an Austro-Dutch consortium that's been buying in to plastics for more than a year. Together with the Duhamel woman they've been secretly buying up UPI shares for months, mainly through nominee companies—because under British law you have to declare publicly a holding in any company that's more than five percent."

"And the nominees?" Mettner said.

"Thanks to you and your financial friends, we can now trace all of them back to these three, and most importantly to the Umbanda Association they registered as a charity. The details from Stanley Karsh on the most recent transactions gave us that one."

"Well, fine," Felicity said. "So they're investing in a—"

"They've swept the marketplace," Williams cut in. "They've got virtually all the UPI shares there are to get now, except the government holding and that of Joliffe's family. If for any reason the Joliffe stake in UPI was to be added to what they have already, they'd be majority shareholders and the government would be powerless."

"And then?" Mettner asked softly.

"Write your own scenario. Once they're in control they can do what they damn well like. Close down the British factory, transfer the research department to Austria or wherever, concentrate on aerospatial material and manufacture in quantity. Name it. And always, of course, they'd be selling to the highest bidder, with bids skyrocketing all the time. Think of all those oil sheikhs who want to be world powers—and all their money."

"But there must be some clause in the UPI-NATO contracts designed to prevent just such a sellout?" Mettner said.

"Of course there is. The contracts would be withdrawn, void. But they'd have the know-how, wouldn't they? All they'd need would be a couple of back-room boys who'd worked on the projects from day one, a couple of good-timers who could be suborned to go where the money was, and they'd be in business, starting production from scratch."

"You think they'd find people like that?" Freeman asked.

"Of course. There are always people like that. Probably on the payroll already. There has to be someone getting those samples out."

"This is some story!" Mettner said. "Provided I ever get clearance from you guys to use it. But the fact is, right now they *don't* have the Joliffe family's shares, do they?"

"Not yet," Williams said soberly. "But this is where the two halves of the puzzle come together."

"Explain," the Executioner demanded.

"They've duped Joliffe into thinking he's a medium, right? He believes he's the mouthpiece of the god Xangô. The fun and games we've been seeing have had only one purpose—to convince the gullible Sir Simon that he's the chosen medium and ultimate high priest of the association they just registered."

Freeman frowned. "Could he be that gullible?"

"Old men, even intelligent old men, are very vain. They want to leave a mark. They also want what the shrinks call psychic security." Williams shook his head. "That's where the bastards have been so bloody smart. What better way to snare such a man than to convince him that, yes, there really is an afterlife... and then persuade him, so to speak, that he's already a big shot in it?"

Mettner chuckled. "I see what you mean. But I still don't see, in terms of share transactions, what help it would be."

"I think I do," Freeman said slowly. "You're saying... ?"

"I'm saying I just got back from Honiton, a small market town not far from here. Joliffe has a first cousin living there, an old woman on her own who's still mourning her husband after twenty years. Like lots of lonely old women, she's interested in spiritualism. She says it keeps her in touch with 'dear Harold.' Unlike lots of lonely old women, she owned a pile of UPI shares."

Mettner sat up in his chair, an unlit cigarette in his mouth. "You said 'owned'?"

"She sold them last week. Dear Harold had said it would be best. She received a message from him at a séance given by such a charming lady—a foreign lady named Mrs. Duhamel."

"Good Lord!" Mettner exploded.

"Exactly. These gentlemen are roping in the departed to con the Joliffe family into selling out. Once the old man's installed as high priest or whatever nonsense they dream up, you'll see the nitty-gritty of the spirit messages alter, mark my words."

"I don't believe I'm hearing this," Mettner said. "You mean—"

"I mean the faked film record of what happens while he's supposedly 'in trance' will show his 'guides' harping more and more on the unimportance to the spirit of material things, the transience of earthly pleasures, the true way through abnegation and self-denial. Then, after the soft sell comes the pitch—to find true spiritual perfection, you must rid yourself of all worldly goods."

"Including shares in Universal Plastics International," Mettner said.

"Precisely. They'll get him to part with the lot. And the diabolical cleverness of it," Williams said, thumping the table in unaccustomed anger, "is not only that it's perfectly legal, but that the proceeds, as well as the shares themselves, will all be credited, in the best good works tradition, to a charity." He paused, then said, "The charity involved, of course, is the Umbanda Association just registered, whose only active board members are... guess who!"

"IT'S NOT ENOUGH," the Executioner said to Felicity Freeman. "It would never be enough just to tip Joliffe off. People caught up in a religious fever are unshakable."

"But this isn't exactly a religious—"

"It's the same principle," Bolan cut in. "What they call the club syndrome. I'm in, you're out. I'm saved, you're not."

"But surely... I mean, if you were to present him with all the evidence we just discussed, couldn't you convince him?"

"That the close friends who just gave him a new lease on life are a bunch of cons? Not a chance. Do that and you're attacking the immortality he just won. You're destroying the guy's own image of himself. You need a lot more than circumstantial evidence to get that one across. And don't forget the nitty-gritty, the disposal of his shares, the aim of the whole operation, hasn't happened yet, hasn't even been suggested."

"Yeah," Mettner said, "I see what you mean. Any lawyer, even a smart PR person like Slater, could lay waste to our case pretty fast. There's nothing on record against any of these men. We can't prove they're crooks. Not yet. And don't forget the evidence we do have was obtained illegally. It wouldn't be difficult for someone on the ball to make mincemeat out of our whole theory—especially to a guy who didn't want to believe it, anyway."

"But the mercenaries!" Freeman protested. "A private army with shoot-to-kill orders? In England? Don't tell me that doesn't count for something."

"As far as O'Hara's soldiers are concerned," Bolan said, "I think that's a subject both sides would want to ignore in any kind of confrontation."

"But if Sir Simon knew about them?"

"For people as plausible as Vanderlee and company, they wouldn't be too hard to explain away," Bolan said.

"That's right," Mettner agreed. "They were hired to keep the place free of the bad guys. Folks like us, people who dreamed up a lot of lies to rock the boat and discredit the old man's intimates. They could probably sell him the line that it was crooked business competitors."

Freeman sighed. "So what do you plan to do?"

The three of them were still in her apartment. It had been agreed that it was safer for Bolan to stay there until the heat was off or the next action phase was on the launching pad. Williams had returned to London in the hope of more news from Phuong. The newspaperman was killing time until the night train that would take him back to the east coast and his oil rig story.

"Like I said," the Executioner went on, "it's a waste of time facing Joliffe with the facts, even if they support our theories. Just as pointless wasting time collecting more facts. What we have to do is create a situation where the conspirators give themselves away in front of Joliffe."

"And just how," Mettner inquired, "do we organize that?"

The warrior grinned. "I'm working on it."

CHAPTER TWENTY-FOUR

"This is what you might call an interim operation," Colonel Williams said, "designed apparently to strengthen Joliffe's belief in his so-called psychic powers. Fortunately the conspirators were a little careless for once, and AX-12 was able to overhear the entire plot. He was out of sight behind one of the book stacks in that library, and they thought they were alone."

"Interim?" Bolan queried.

"That's right. The big one, the definitive 'proof' that he's in personal touch with the divinities, is scheduled for the following weekend before an invited audience of occult fans at the UPI headquarters plant."

"Why there?"

"Security. The site's already guarded and wired in because they're working on classified material, and it's a damn sight easier to patrol than a bloody great country estate."

"Got it. So what's with this interim jazz?"

"They feel the old man's faith in all this might have been shaken when your Cahill séance was revealed as a fake. Only shaken, and only slightly, but they feel a boost would do no harm. Just in case."

"Okay, Colonel. What's the MO this time?"

"It's on a different kick. I could give it to you in a few sentences."

"I'm listening."

"It's quite clever and quite simple. They plan to set up a black mass in an abandoned country church, complete with satanist rituals and a mass orgy, then have Joliffe kill the ceremony stone dead with his 'power for good' after the details have been leaked to him by one of his 'guides.'"

"That's the craziest idea I've ever heard!" Mettner exclaimed.

The three of them were sitting in Felicity Freeman's living room. Mettner was back in town because his oil rig story had turned into a union-management dispute with the threat of a strike and was likely to drag on for weeks.

"What are the details?" Bolan asked. "Not from the old man's point of view, from ours."

"They've roped in a crowd of jet-set sniffers from London," Williams said. "You know—black magic and crack, with a sex free-for-all thrown in. Maybe even a couple of preteen virgins to be ritually deflowered. Bit of a giggle, eh!"

The Executioner frowned. "Nice people. And these, I guess, will be the devotees, the congregation?"

"That's right," Williams agreed. "Those and a few local bikers out for kicks. There'll be one of their people acting as high priest, and the old woman they call Mother will be scripting the whole scenario. The way she did for the island initiation."

"It seems that was a load of bull, anyway," Mettner said.

"That's because the lady isn't South American, as she'd have you believe, but a tough cookie from Tiger Bay, the dock area of Cardiff."

"Okay," Bolan said, "you set the scene. What's supposed to happen?"

"After the playacting and the rituals," Williams went on, "and before the sex bit starts, everybody has to partake of a blasphemous Eucharist." He looked up. Freeman had entered the room with a tray of mugs, a sugar bowl and a steaming pot of coffee. "I couldn't begin to tell you what's in the chalice in mixed company. But I can tell you that this time the stuff will be drugged. Like the fruit drink suicides of Jim Jones, they're all going to fall down and die—only this time it'll be without their consent."

"How does this tie in with Joliffe?" Mettner asked. "Will he appear there, like some avenging angel, and pronounce a spell?"

"Nothing so corny. They can't afford to have his name connected with it officially. No, they'll have him doped up on the usual stuff at home. There'll be a video unit at the church to relay the scene. Then, at a given moment—just after that filth has been consumed—his 'guides' will instruct him to act. He'll go into his number, and presto, they all fall down dead and he's stopped the evil from spreading any farther."

"Do we know what his number will be?"

"No, but whatever it is, you can be sure that it'll be filmed, and the film doctored in the usual way to prove that he did it. The watches of all the victims will have been stopped at the same time, and doubtless there'll be a clock in the background when they shoot the film to show that the times coincide."

"Very ingenious," Mettner observed. "What happens afterward?"

"The police will have been tipped off, but not soon enough to stop the show. By the time they arrive, Vanderlee's stage managers will have gone. So will the video crew and their truck. And so will O'Hara's men. The constabulary will stumble upon a church full of stiffs. End of story."

"But not for the late editions of the sensationalist Sunday papers," Mettner concluded. "What a front-page story." He grinned. "I can see the headline—Devonshire Keeps Up with the Joneses!"

"Won't the papers make a meal out of the drug bit?" Freeman demanded. "They're bound to make a comparison with the Jim Jones tragedy, and they can't keep all the news from Joliffe."

"That's been taken care of," Williams replied. "As you say, they can't get around the drugs. They'll simply arrange it so that the old boy believes his powers—or his fellow spirits—poisoned the Eucharist. I gather the Duhamel lady has some Amazonian rain-forest potion that's pretty hard to detect, anyway."

"You did say O'Hara would be there?" Bolan asked.

"Oh, yes. They'll have the whole place sewn up. They can't afford to have interruptions. The timing will be all-important."

"And was Phuong able to identify the church?"

"Yes, it's on the edge of Dartmoor. If you don't mind," Williams said primly, "I think it better to keep code names."

"Does it matter? We all know who he is, Colonel."

"Security," Williams said for the second time. "When an agent is working in deep cover, it's important never to use his real name. One might get used to it and quote it, just once, in the wrong place."

Bolan shrugged.

"I'm not making a thing out of it. It's just the way we work. Now," Williams went on briskly, "off the top of your head, what do we do?"

"Squash the thing before it starts," the Executioner suggested. "Back home during the Chicago gang wars there was a mafioso famous for saying, 'If there ain't no witnesses, there ain't no case.' For my money it's the same thing here. If there's no black mass, nobody can tell Joliffe he blew away the folks celebrating it."

"My feeling exactly," Williams agreed.

"So we have to get past O'Hara's mercs and scare away the weirdos, the winos and the wastrels before the curtain goes up?" Mettner asked.

"That's about the strength of it," Williams said. "Shouldn't be too hard once we're in. I have a few fairly impressive pieces of official paper in my wallet that give me a bit of clout legally."

"Why don't you just inform the local police," Freeman asked, "and let them wind up the whole unclean thing before it starts?"

"Good question. Same objection as before—there might still be something they could make capital out of.

Claim the old man thought-processed the cops, that kind of thing. Mr. Belasko is right. Only if *nothing* happens can nothing be made of it.''

"Social question, Colonel," Mettner said. "You were talking earlier about 'the big one,' a séance of sorts up at the UPI plant that would prove Joliffe was a power in the hereafter, before a specially invited audience. How does that audience relate to the socialite crew being press-ganged into the black-mass sequence?"

"Another good question. The answer is that it doesn't, except in the case of a few characters seeded in among the congregation for color, who won't be swallowing the poison, anyway. No, the church lot are sensation seekers, out for kicks, shallow people. The folks invited to the UPI party are something else."

The colonel produced a small notebook. "Remember this?" he asked Bolan. "It's the last one you found at Joliffe Hall. We didn't discuss it at our council of war the other day because I'd already handed it over to our cryptologists to decipher. It was an easy enough code to crack, it seems."

He opened the book and kept it spread on the table with two fingers of his right hand. "As you see, it's just lists of names and addresses, all of them people interested in, or likely to become interested in, the occult. The coded headings simply categorize them in terms of that interest. Here, for example—" his left forefinger pointed "—we have men and women already into South American spiritism, Umbanda and all that. On the other page are genuine mediums, clairvoyants and so on."

Williams wet his forefinger and turned a page. "These people, most of them elderly, are listed as 'gullible.' They're mad keen to believe and they'll swallow anything. Here, on the other hand, are seekers with an interest as deep but with open minds, those saying in effect, 'Okay, I'm listening. Persuade me.' They're followed by the real psychic investigators, the pros. There are several subdivisions. And then the 'anything for kicks and the hell with the truth' brigade."

He closed the book, picked up his mug of coffee and leaned back in his chair. "You'll guess at once," he said, "that the special invited audience will be drawn from folks in the first, third and final categories, and that anyone from the fourth and fifth will be rigorously excluded."

"It's the uninvited audiences I'm interested in," Bolan told him, "in both cases. How many of us will there be?"

The colonel adjusted the glasses on his nose. "I should think the two of us could handle it. It would be strictly against protocol to involve an American newspaperman. Mr. Mettner and Miss Freeman will have to stay outside the field of, ah, operations and act as liaisons."

CHAPTER TWENTY-FIVE

"The church is twenty-seven miles southwest of Exeter," Williams told Bolan. "Turn right off Route A-38 at Ashburton, then penetrate a maze of country lanes until you make Hexworthy, on the upper reaches of the West Dart River."

Phuong had reported that the ceremony was scheduled for nine o'clock, soon after dark. To avoid drawing attention with a fleet of different cars, the congregation was to be ferried to the village in a single rented bus. O'Hara's mercs and the people organizing the mass would, of course, be in position much earlier. The agent didn't know how or when the law and the newspapers would be alerted.

"One thing's for sure," the colonel said. "We'll have to make a recon well before the balloon goes up. How do you see us making the approach, assuming we do it the day before?"

Bolan looked up from the map. "I'd say from above, approach the place from the moor. Too much cover for lookouts if we make it along those tree-shaded, sunken country lanes."

"Agreed. There's an army battle course near Okehampton on the far side of the moor. Firing range and all that. The folks are used to the sound of tactical support planes. I'll lay on a chopper to dump us half a mile away from the church, pick us up maybe a couple of hours later. Does that suit you?"

"Suits me fine."

THE CHURCH WAS SMALL, more like a chapel, with a steeply pitched gray roof, two Gothic windows on each side, and a squat, square stone tower surmounted by a pyramid of slates. The granite walls were in good shape, though there were tiles missing from the roof.

It was set in a hollow at the edge of the moor. A weed-grown footpath, broken here and there by a stone slab step, led down to a narrow valley brimming with trees through which the bare chimneys of the village thrust like the spars of a sunken ship.

Bolan and Williams approached it facedown in the heather channeled between granite outcrops studding the final slope of moorland. It was late afternoon; the birdsong below had become more sleepy as the shadows lengthened. The colonel raised himself, checked that the sinking sun was behind him and couldn't reflect off the lenses, then scrutinized the area through powerful field glasses. For ten minutes, motionless except for the slight movement of his arms, he swept the area back and forth on either side of the church. At last he lowered the binoculars and shook his head. "It's as clean as a whistle. Same birds hopping among the tombstones when I started looking."

"Okay. Let's go."

"Mind you," Williams said as they climbed a crumbling stone wall and threaded their way to the porch between moss-covered graves, "there may well be scouts posted below in the valley, or among those ruined houses, but they won't see us as long as we keep to this side of the church."

One of the weathered double doors was half-open. Bolan shoved it with his shoulder, easing his Beretta in its rig. The ironbound foot of the door screeched across the flags, shuddering the ancient panels. When the door swung free, the rusted hinges squeaked alarmingly. "So much for discretion," the warrior muttered.

The building was empty. A bare stone altar stood beneath a circular window with many of the glass panes broken; three steps led down to the barren nave; the wooden stalls had all been removed long ago. There were damp patches and bird droppings on the flagstones, but the air was surprisingly dry.

The two men glanced around. "They'll have to bring in the wrecking crew," Bolan said, "then hire a decorator if they intend to get some atmosphere in here and snare those socialites."

"It's all part of the fun for them—the rustic scene," Williams said, gesturing toward the western end of the church, where dust motes danced in a sunbeam that shone through a pane of colored glass onto a chair with one broken leg.

Outside the sun was about to lower itself behind the hills. Deep trenches of purple shadow lay across the bleak undulations of the moor. "If you were O'Hara," the colonel asked, "how would you deploy your men to cover this place and keep out the unwanted?"

"If I was O'Hara," the Executioner replied, "I'd expect two different kinds of intruders—rubberneckers, country folk curious at the signs of activity in a deserted village, and troublemakers, people like you and me who might have heard of the plan and want to kill it. I'd expect the first bunch to wander up the track from the village, and the second to infiltrate from the moor. I'd place my soldiers accordingly—like heavy on the moor side, lighter on the lanes."

Williams nodded approvingly. "And the best places?"

"We'll take a look."

They cased the churchyard and its immediate surroundings. The evening air was now busy with the hum of insects. At the end of the footpath there was a gate, and below that a rutted track still muddy from the previous day's rain. The track wound between six-foot banks down toward the village. Dense patches of cow parsley and willow herb covered the banks, and in places the long arms of briers curved half across the trail. "They don't need a platoon to cover that," Williams commented. "A single section could do it. And anyone trying a shortcut through that lot would make as much noise as a herd of buffalo!"

"They'll need more to cover the moor."

The ground for several hundred yards on either side of the churchyard could have been purpose-built for an infantry unit ordered to stem an advance at all costs. Buttresses, ledges, dikes and sinkholes in the granite provided enough cover for a regiment, while many of the outcrops were pitted and crosshatched with gullies along which a man could cover a field of fire without himself being visible.

Toward the top of the first rise was a perfect outpost, the remains of a Bronze Age "pound," a six-foot-thick rampart that had once enclosed a hamlet of small round stone huts. On the other side of the church were the walls of a "blowing house," used by medieval tinsmiths to smelt the black ore they dug from the ground. Among the surrounding undergrowth they saw a granite millwheel, half a dozen stone ingot molds, a crumpled cigarette pack.

Bolan was taking notes, scribbling details, the relative positions of possible hazards. He estimated distances and marked in trees.

"It's a gamble," Colonel Williams said, "but for my money all we have to do is get through O'Hara's lines. They'll be using silenced guns, so as not to alarm the congregation. The congregation won't know the mercs are even there. They mustn't know they are there. Because once everybody starts asking questions the time schedule is loused up, and timing's all-important if this blasphemous muck's to be served up here at the exact moment Joliffe does his number at the manor."

"You mean," Bolan said, "that if we make the church, O'Hara won't send in his men after us? At least not at first?"

The colonel nodded.

ON THE NIGHT of the promised black mass the vagaries of Britain's summer weather provided the perfect

decor for the scenario dreamed up by the conspirators
at Joliffe Hall.

At midday the tail of a depression swam in from the
Atlantic, towing a chilly breeze in its wake. After the
breeze came clouds, a low-pressure front drawn across
the sky like a dark gray blind. Then the heat rising from
the previous day's sunny landscape with moisture from
the earth met the cold airstream and there was precip-
itation beneath the clouds. At a quarter to four the
wind dropped. By dusk the chilled air had blanketed
the whole of Dartmoor in fog.

Bolan was thankful he'd taken notes and made
rough plans the day before. Relying on eyesight alone
would have made their penetration extremely dangerous.

Anxious not to raise suspicion by establishing a pattern, Williams and Bolan had turned thumbs down on
another helicopter ride. They'd been dropped a mile
away, on the far side of a local tor, by an army half-
track that regularly patrolled the moor. They both wore
combat fatigues that resembled as near as possible that
worn by the mercenaries. Bolan wore the silenced Beretta in a shoulder rig and a pouch containing other
weapons of war at his waist. Williams carried a long-
barreled Walther with a sound suppressor.

It was a long mile. By the time they'd worked their
way around from behind the tor, the valleys were already brimming with mist, and wisps of white curled
around the lower half of the bleak rock pillar above
them.

After that it was a matter of worming their way toward the church through the rolling swells of heather and furze. When they were still several hundred yards away, they heard an occasional murmured order, the clink of metal equipment and, a couple of times, the swish of heavy bodies through undergrowth.

"Where," Williams whispered, "do you figure is the best place for us to hole up until the countdown starts? This is more your scene than mine, so I'm leaving the tactics to you."

They reached the edge of the hollow before Bolan replied. "The ruins," he whispered, "as long as nobody's staked out there already."

Negative.

What remained of the crumbling walls, half-buried in a bramble thicket and choked with creepers, was behind the vestry on the far side of the church from the entrance doors. From the muffled noises filtering through the mist, O'Hara preferred to position his men on the far side of the hollow, where they could monitor the footpath, the lane, the church and the outer rim of the moor at the same time.

By the time Bolan had crawled back from his recon of the ruins, the mist had thickened to a fog that reduced visibility to fifteen yards. Long scarves of it wreathed the headstones and veiled the tops of trees below the hollow. The church was no more than a bulky shadow without shape or substance.

The two men installed themselves in the ruins. They'd wait there until the organizers and the video unit were in place and the debased members of the congregation began to arrive. "We mustn't jump the gun. We must leave it as late as possible, whatever happens," Williams whispered.

"I thought it was vital to stop it before—"

"Before they're transmitting and Joliffe is scheduled to start? So it is. But we dare not act too early in case it gives them time to tip off Vanderlee at the manor, in which case they might simply call the whole bloody thing off and switch it to a place and time we wouldn't know about."

It was impossible to say when darkness fell. The world closed in until there was nothing but the graveyard, the dim bulk of the church and the stealthy movements of the mercs deployed on the far side of the hollow. Occasionally they could hear a muttered word.

The nearest inhabited village was three miles away. Other than the fretful barking of some distant farm dog, they heard no unexpected sounds until the unmistakable whine of a truck laboring up the lane in first gear announced the arrival of the organizers.

It was exactly 8:15.

Now they heard footsteps, voices. There was a brief exchange in which O'Hara's harsh tones predominated. Bolan recognized the old priestess's singsong Welsh accent, Rick Salter's drawl.

Before long there were sounds of activity inside the church: heavy objects dragged across the flagstones, a gurgle of water from the vestry.

An irregular pulsing light now faintly illuminated the windows. Candles, Bolan thought. Then he heard the thumping of a generator somewhere down beyond the lane. Preparing for the transmission, no doubt.

The subjects of the transmission began arriving at a quarter to nine. As far as Bolan could tell, there was a big bus and at least two cars, perhaps three. There was a lot of backing up and jockeying for position, an occasional brake squeal or a slither of spinning tires, as the vehicles maneuvered after discharging their passengers. Evidently, somewhere off the lane, there was a field that they were using as a parking lot. He wondered how Mettner and Freeman were making out, stationed as a backup or a possible getaway unit in her Mercedes behind one of the village's decrepit barns.

Williams had given the signal when they first heard the rumble of automobile exhausts. Now they were back on the edge of the hollow, staring through the fog at the church doors.

The scene was macabre. Behind them the great bare mound of the moor domed skyward through the murk, vibrant with memories of lost travelers, witches' sabbaths and quagmires that never gave up their dead. In front and below, a long line of men and women, flat featureless ghosts in the moving mist, appeared and disappeared on the path that wound from the lane to the church.

And off to one side, invisible but deadly, the men with guns.

A suffused red glow illuminated the door of the church. Here and there in the file of celebrants was a lantern on a pole that lent the procession the appearance of some medieval sorcerer's feast. Despite himself Bolan felt the hairs on his nape prickle.

The last of the new arrivals vanished inside the church. The red glow faded, then died as the doors were closed. For a while there was silence. Even the generator had been switched off. Then, quietly at first but with increasing volume, a confused murmuring sound resolved itself into some kind of statement and response, with the voice of the Welsh priestess rising above it with manic force.

Williams glanced at the luminous dial of his watch. "How many of them are there?" he whispered.

"From what I've seen at the hall, a dozen, tops. A few have already been taken out, and they wouldn't have had time to replace them yet."

"Right you are. On our way then."

"Drop to the far side of the wall," Bolan instructed. "About ten yards inside there's a stone memorial, horizontal, like an outsize coffin. Get behind it and shoot anyone who comes your way. I'll take the perimeter and deal with any outposts, then join you there to see if we can blast our way through the rest of them. Okay?"

"Okay." The colonel rose to his feet, stole away and was at once swallowed up in the fog. Bolan moved in the other direction.

"Who's there?" The low voice was alarmingly close. A mercenary with a MAC-10 materialized from behind a rock and confronted the warrior.

"Army maneuvers," Bolan replied quietly.

"This is a private function. What the hell do you mean, 'maneuvers'?"

"This," the Executioner murmured. A sudden kick with the heel of his left foot sent the subgun clattering to the ground. At the same time the loop of a wire garrote dropped over the guy's head. Bolan flung his arms wide with the wooden toggles at each end of the wire clenched into his hands.

The hardguy uttered a single choked cry, strangled swiftly into silence. He fell facedown, clawing at the red-hot strand knifing into his windpipe. Bolan placed a heavy foot between his shoulder blades and kept up the pressure. When the drumming of feet on the ground ceased and the last gurgle faded away, he loosened the garrote and straightened.

"Gregoire, what's going on?" The heavily accented voice came from thirty feet away, a little to Bolan's right. He remembered from his plan that there was an outcrop on the rim of the hollow. The guard had to be standing on that.

"I can see you," the man called. This was palpably untrue—the fog was thicker than ever up there. "Who are you? Come a step closer and I'll open fire!"

The Executioner wished he would. Muzzle-flashes, however faint, were a better target than a disembodied voice muffled by fog. He continued his stealthy advance until the miniature bluff and the indistinct blur above it began to materialize from the dark.

Feeling his way over the rough ground step by step, inch by inch, he came up against a stunted oak and crouched behind it. He pried a stone from the spongy ground and tossed it a few yards away. The stone rustled through the leaves of a low shrub, and the gunman opened fire.

Tiny pinpoints of flame stabbed through the mist as the subdued *phut-phut* of the silenced MAC-10 reached Bolan's ears. Steadying his right wrist with his left hand, he got off a trio of 9 mm subsonic rounds that scored all along the line.

The blur topping the outcrop folded to half size, then vanished. The warrior heard a scrambling clatter as the body rolled down a steep slope of rock and crashed into a bush. The subgun thumped into the undergrowth.

"What the hell's happening?" O'Hara's voice bellowed. "Damn this fucking fog! Fleming, do you hear me? Gunter, Pigeon, get over to the bluff and see what happened."

Bolan climbed to the edge of the hollow. O'Hara was a professional. The warrior knew he'd have stationed his men around the church in such a way that, if they opened fire, there would be no danger of them wasting one another. He knew where he'd have posted sentries to cover the hollow, and he decided to act on the assumption that the two of them would think alike. Which meant that he'd score more quickly, more easily, if he circled the depression and zeroed in on the mercs from the rear.

Wading through tall grass, he was surprised by a misty figure that appeared to rise from the ground almost at his feet. One of the mercs had been lying in a shallow trench. "Gunter?" the man began, seeing Bolan's combat boots and camou legs. "Were you—"

The sentence was never completed. Bolan was already behind the man. His left arm encircled the merc's head, wrist and forearm wedged up beneath the chin to choke off any cry. His right plunged the razor-sharp blade of a commando knife, plucked from an ankle holster, into his victim's back. The blade grazed bone, punctured muscle, then slid easily home into soft tissue.

He felt the throat convulse against his arm, and hot blood splash over his left hand. The man stiffened, then sighed. Bolan was familiar with the symptoms. He snatched his arm away and let the limp body slide into the trench.

The warrior wiped his hand on the dead man's shirt, picked up his MAC-10 and started to crawl downhill along the trench. He remembered it from his notes, a stone- and pebble-floored hollow that curved around the rim and ended in a granite lip projecting over the lane. The pebbles could be dislodged and roll, a perfect giveaway, but there was no better way to make a tour of the enemy's positions. Carefully, warily, he advanced.

From out of the fog he heard a sudden surge of voices raised in a canonic dirge. Beyond the lane the generator started up again. Behind him the two mercs sent to check were yelling at O'Hara, away on the other side. They must have stumbled on at least one of the bodies.

Bolan profited from the noise, accelerating his pace, displacing an occasional stone while the shouts continued. Somebody was near enough to get off some shots, bullets smashing into a boulder half-buried in the bank of the waterway. He couldn't see anybody and he knew he couldn't be seen. They had to be firing at the noise. He picked up a pebble and threw it farther down the gully. This time it didn't work. There was no response.

Over the dripping of moisture he thought he heard, very faintly from inside the churchyard, a couple of stifled reports from Williams's Walther. Somebody stumbled and fell.

And then a figure materialized from the gloom only a few feet away. Bolan lay still. Evidently the guy hadn't noticed him. He leaped over the trench and moved cautiously forward. The warrior dropped him with a single shot from the Beretta an instant before his shape melted into the fog. He was on his knees when the merc hit the ground.

Force, unexpected and stunning, slammed into his back and knocked him flat again. One of the guards had leaped on him from behind.

He fell facedown with an arm crooked around his neck and one cheek grazing the sharp granite fragments lining the trench. Bony knees ground into his kidneys; fingers groped for a nerve hold on his wrist; the Beretta skittered away.

Bolan heaved, struggling to regain his breath. He broke the neck lock, humped his back and drew up his knees in an attempt to catapult the attacker over his head. But the man was tough and strong. He was dislodged, but he wasn't thrown. The two men rolled in the trench, locked in a life-or-death struggle.

The noise of the struggle, Bolan knew, would draw the rest of O'Hara's unit, but at first they wouldn't know which of the two figures in battle fatigues was their own man. He had to settle the fight before his assailant could achieve a hold that would immobilize him long enough to be recognized and fired on. And before the others waded in to separate them physically.

Bolan knew all the tricks of unarmed fighting, and used them. So did the merc. But the merc didn't know about the nerve pressure point behind the ear and below the mastoid bone. He died very quickly. Then the Executioner was up and sprinting for the churchyard.

The mercs who'd raced to join the fray were indistinct figures, lacking depth and definition. Before they realized that their man had been beaten, Bolan was fading even faster. They opened up then, but it was too late—he was already over the wall and into the yard.

When he was as close to the church as he could get on hands and knees without risking being caught in the faint light escaping through the windows, he rose silently to his feet among the obliterated names and dates on the ancient tombs. He'd recaptured the MAC-10 before he left the trench, and he now switched it to full-auto.

Fog wreathed the gravestones, lending an illusion of movement to the immovable, so that it was impossible to say in that two-dimensional world whether the dim shapes seeming to appear and then vanish were living men, stone angels or granite slabs.

Bolan started with the silenced subgun parallel with the church wall, held fairly high. He spun slowly through 180 degrees, firing nonstop until the barrel was level with the wall again on the other side and the magazine was exhausted.

His gunplay drew no response.

The warrior dropped the empty subgun and turned toward the church. Within a few paces light flickering behind arched windows began to dissolve the mist. In the illumination he saw the figure of a crusader lying on his back on a boxlike tomb.

The crusader was wearing combat fatigues in camouflaged material.

Colonel Williams sat up and swung his feet to the ground. "I got two of them," he said, "maybe three. How did you do?"

"We're not drawing return fire."

Together they walked into the porch and thrust open the doors.

CHAPTER TWENTY-SIX

Williams and the Executioner remained unobserved as they entered the church and stood behind a heavy, semicircular velvet curtain that had been fixed just inside the doors.

The first thing that struck Bolan was the smell. The air was heavy with the odors of candle grease, incense and burning herbs, spiced with some other indeterminate agent that was both sour and unpleasant.

The second thing was the fact that all the members of the "congregation" were stark naked—thirty men and women, sitting on six rows of wicker chairs that hadn't been there when he checked out the church the previous day.

The lanterns carried by the procession were arranged in a half circle in back of the nave. Black candles burned in wall niches and at each end of the altar, which was now covered in purple velvet. Behind it, on the end of a chain suspended from the roof, a life-size cross was hung upside down. A naked man was bound head downward on this.

Below the altar steps the flagstones were decorated with a scarlet pentagram and several cabalistic figures sprayed with Day-Glo paint. A priest and priestess stood in the center of the pentagram. They wore white

hooded, floor-length robes, and their features were
hidden behind green masks.

At a signal from the priest the congregation stood.
Bright light, rose-tinted, spread slowly through the
church, sculpturing breasts, bellies and buttocks from
the gloom. Two powerful spots in back of the nave had
been activated. And now Bolan registered for the first
time the tubular steel scaffolding, the thick cables and
electric leads serving the video camera crew at the far
end of the church.

The "priest" began chanting the opening words of
the mass, his voice climbing the scale as he reached the
end of the phrase. And the celebrants responded with
manic glee. They were reading the lines, Bolan saw,
from photocopied typescripts pinned to the backs of
the chairs in front of them.

The priestess turned around, climbed the steps and
walked behind the altar. She ducked out of sight for a
moment, and then reappeared holding a wide, shallow
stoneware chalice. This would be the moment, the
warrior knew, when the camera would be preparing to
turn. Salter, Vanderlee and the others would have Sir
Simon Joliffe, in a drug-induced haze, ready to watch
the screen at the manor and go into his act.

The priest flung his arms wide. The priestess raised
the chalice above her head. The contents appeared to
be steaming. A sudden draft bent the candle flames
over and carried to the church doors a rancid stench
that almost made Bolan gag. Below the scaffolding
someone switched the gelatines coloring the two spots.

The rosy light flooding the church changed to a sickly green. The priest cried in a loud voice, "Now in the name of Choronzon, Xenoth, Marsyas and Oxymoron, I call upon you..."

Williams transferred the silenced Walther to his left hand and produced a heavy .45-caliber six-chambered revolver. He fired a single thunderous shot at the vaulted church roof and strode out from behind the curtain, shouting, "Stop this obscene blasphemy at once!"

Consternation and confusion erupted. Before the echoes of the detonation lost themselves among the pointed arches, the priestess lowered the chalice to the altar and her male confederate swung around, eyes glittering angrily behind the mask. The crowd was gaping in the direction of the doors. Some of the women covered themselves with their hands; the men looked either defiant or sheepish.

The colonel lowered his revolver, aimed carefully and shot out the spots one after the other. Swiftly he changed guns, held the silenced Walther at arm's length and blasted the video camera off its stand. "There'll be no transmission of this filth tonight," he said icily.

Over the subdued hubbub a woman's scream rang out.

"Who the devil are you?" the priest shouted. "How dare you force your way in here and start shooting—"

"'Who the *devil*' is good," Williams cut in. "That should be my line. You can call me a representative of public decency."

"This is a private party," the priestess said shrilly. "You have no right to break into it."

"I have every right," the colonel snapped. Turning to the crowd, he said, "I'm a police officer. Nobody is to leave this building until names and addresses have been taken and permission to return home granted." He plucked a whistle from the breast pocket of his shirt and blew a short blast. Half a dozen men in dark blue uniforms filed in through the vestry door and spread out around the nave. Bolan's tall, muscled bulk blocked the way to the main doors and the porch.

"You may not approve," a man in the crowd called, "but this is a private function and the law has no bloody mandate here."

"Yes," another shouted. "A party among consenting adults is—"

"Felonies and crimes committed in private are still crimes," the colonel told him.

The priestess was surreptitiously trying to smuggle the chalice back beneath the altar. Clearly she was trying to do away with something that might be used as evidence against her. He gestured to one of the policemen, who strode up to the woman and, with a grimace of total disgust, took the bowl from her. At first she struggled, and during this the altar cloth was swept aside.

Beneath the stone overhang lay the naked body of a young girl about thirteen years old. She was bound hand and foot, and there was a wide strip of adhesive tape plastered over her mouth.

"Consenting adults, eh?" Williams roared furiously. "You should be behind bars, the whole damn lot of you. And for those who think a so-called private party is a go-ahead for any kind of depravity, let me enumerate just a few of the charges you could face."

He ticked the points off on his fingers. "First of all, a church is legally a public place, even when it's unused. No function held there can conceivably be held to be private."

"The bloody place is deconsecrated," the first man called out. "So it's not properly a church anymore."

"Your mistake. St. Barnaby's has never been deconsecrated. The vicar from the next village holds a service here on one day a year—Candlemass, I think— just to keep the ordination operative. Apart from that you're guilty, individually and collectively, of sacrilege, desecration, offenses against public decency, gross obscenity, conspiracy to corrupt a minor, and possibly even procuring a minor for the purpose of prostitution."

Williams interrupted the catalog to glare toward the scaffold at the rear of the church. "And for you men, there could be additional charges concerning the creation of a pornographic or obscene document and the procurement of a minor to take part in that creation."

"This isn't a fucking *film*," one of the crewmen protested. "It's a transmission. We aren't making copies, and we don't aim to sell anything. We're hired to do a job, that's all. In any case, we hadn't even started to turn when you busted in, so where's the crime?"

"That would be for the judge to decide. Customarily if intent is proved, that's accepted as evidence of guilt." Williams turned toward the nearest policeman. "Sergeant, release that child and see that she's clothed and taken care of. Oh, and you'd better dismantle that cross abomination and release that poor fool, too."

"Very good, sir." The sergeant and another man moved toward the altar.

"There's no need to get so serious," a woman's voice from the back of the crowd complained. "Anyone'd think... I mean, Christ, can't you have a bit of fun, do a little playacting these days without the bloody police fucking it up?"

"In the circumstances, madam, I fancy you're invoking the wrong deity," Williams said coldly. "As for the police, the term you employ would more suitably be directed against the two perverts here by the desecrated altar."

He strode across and ripped the masks from the faces of the priest and priestess. As Bolan had expected, the woman was the elderly witch from Cardiff. The man, his features contorted with rage, was the one who had played the Axôngún during the fake initiation on Joliffe's island.

"Now listen to me, all of you," Williams called to the naked worshipers. "You're being fooled by these two. You've been used. Disgraceful though it is, this isn't a genuine satanist ceremony. I'm not going to go into details, but if you had swallowed that corruption—" he gestured at the chalice "—you'd have been dead within ten minutes. The stuff is, or was about to be, poisoned.''

He paused, waiting for the wave of disbelief, horror, anger, doubt to sweep through the nude ranks like wind through a cornfield. Then he continued, ''I said no details. But your deaths would have been used for a criminal purpose, part of a criminal conspiracy. I also said, and say again, you're fortunate not to be behind bars. If you aren't, it's only because your local police, who have the welfare of the community at heart, wish to spare it unwelcome publicity. Your shame is their shame. But your good behavior in the future shall be the indemnity for any leniency on our part tonight. In other words, this whole disgusting business will be hushed up, and no charges brought, provided certain stipulations are met and certain undertakings given. You will be informed of these at the local police station.'' He turned toward the priest and priestess. ''As for you two, whether or not charges of attempted murder are brought against you depends on an analysis of the filth in that bowl.''

For the second time Williams paused, chewing his lower lip. Then, in a shaking voice, he shouted, ''Now get out of here and make yourselves decent. Give your wretched names to the police and get out of my sight. People like you make me want to throw up!''

Escorted by the police, they filed through the vestry door.

BOLAN REALIZED they were being tailed as soon as they
left the yellow sodium lights piercing the fog in the village of Hexworthy.

Visibility was a little better, since a light breeze was
beginning to sweep the denser patches of mist back toward the moor, but it was still difficult to make more
than twenty-five miles per hour.

The shadow's headlights had materialized in the
mirror soon after they left St. Barnaby, but the warrior had assumed the car belonged to some local resi-
dent. It was, after all, still fairly early. Any survivors
from the mercenary guard, he reckoned, would have
left while they had the chance. They weren't being paid
to take on the British police.

But when the warrior accelerated, then slowed down,
the car behind remained exactly the same distance
away. It was a big car, Bolan thought, a Mercedes, an
Audi 100 or an executive Opel. And it was certainly
capable of much higher speeds than the souped-up
small rental he was still driving. But the country lanes
were narrow, with high, steep banks on either side, and
even if there had been room to pass, the driver would
have run into a wall of fog ahead and been forced to cut
down his speed to match the rental's, for the Executioner was rolling at the top limit conditions allowed.

The driver of the big car didn't want to pass, so Bolan tried a final maneuver. He braked very suddenly,
hauling up only on the hand brake so that the red lights
in back didn't glow to signal the loss of speed.

In the mirror the yellow lights dipped abruptly as the
car's nose plunged under heavy braking. The driver

was on the ball, all right. Even without warning, his reactions were fast enough to slow the car without gaining more than four or five yards. An ordinary driver would have closed right up, maybe even bumped the rear of Bolan's Renault.

So okay, there *was* a tail. But was the guy just checking out Bolan's destination, or was he going to play rough?

Wait and see.

The shadow made his play on a long, straight stretch of road between Dartmeet and Ashburton. The highway ran out along an embankment here, with the fields on either side drowned in a sea of mist. Visibility ahead was slightly better, but only a madman would have attempted to drive at more than fifty miles per hour. Bolan kept the needle hovering around the forty-eight mark.

Headlight reflections in the mirror grew larger and brighter. Williams swung around in the passenger seat as the roar of a powerful engine became louder. "Trouble?" he asked.

"Affirmative."

"Been there long?"

"All the way."

"I suppose it has to be—" The colonel broke off as a heavy bumper slammed into the rear of the Renault, jolting the two men against the dashboard and sending the small sedan skating across the slippery pavement. Bolan fought the wheel to bring the car back into line and poured on as much speed as he dared.

Twice more the attacker rammed the Renault with increasing force. Glass from the taillights shattered, the back seat jerked forward and the Renault slewed halfway across the road.

The car behind was an Audi Quattro, a four-wheel-drive, turbo-charged sedan whose five-cylinder engine developed two hundred horsepower. Bolan gritted his teeth and floored the gas pedal.

Skeins of mist raced toward the windshield out of the glare thrown back from the fog by the Renault's dipped lights. The front wheels were spinning on the greasy surface.

The driver of the Audi shifted down and stormed up for the fourth time. This time the impact was even harder—and it wasn't head-on, it was against the small car's nearside rear end. Tires screeched as the Renault spun clear across the road and back again as the warrior overcorrected, then regained control.

Flaring lights dazzled him. A juggernaut thundered fast toward them out of the mist. Missing the lurching sedan by inches, a large semi hauling a forty-ton refrigerator trailer swirled past with an angry blare of its horns.

Bolan cursed. Williams had wound down his window, and he leaned out and fired his Walther toward the pursuer.

The Audi's front tires were shielded, but with the last shot in the magazine, one of the headlights blinked out. The driver immediately switched on a second set and a pair of rectangular fog lights beneath the bumper. Williams grabbed a fresh clip and rammed it home.

Before he had a chance to use it, the Audi, weaving wildly now from side to side, smashed with stunning force into the small sedan. The Audi overrode the Renault's bumper and pulverized the hatchback in a shower of broken glass.

This time the thin steel panels crumpled under the blow. The whole of the mangled car frame caved in, and a sharp edge from a collapsed wheel arch sawed into the right rear tire, which burst, hurling the back of the car toward the center of the road and the nose toward the shoulder and the embankment below.

Bolan trod heavily on the pedal, grabbed the hand brake and spun the wheel. But there was nothing else he could do. The crippled Renault shot off the road, raced across a strip of grass and tipped over the edge of the embankment.

Dropping into darkness, the Executioner put everything he had into keeping the car upright on the forty-five-degree slope. Bouncing over clumps of rough grass, plowing through bushes, the Renault finally dropped a wheel into a hidden irrigation trench, tipped onto its side and began to roll.

"Cover your face!" Bolan yelled, hunching himself away from the wheel and shielding his own face with his forearms.

The car rolled over twice and came to rest with a grinding crash and an explosion of breaking glass on its left-hand side. The Executioner dragged himself from his seat and pushed open the door above his head. The engine had stalled, and the headlights were smashed, but for some reason the dome light in the roof still worked. By its dim light he saw Williams slumped against the other door. He was unconscious, but there was no blood, and his breathing and pulse were strong.

Bolan left him there for the moment and climbed out of the wreck. He unleathered his Beretta and pulled back the slide.

The Renault was lying at the edge of a cornfield. Above and beyond, a faint glow percolating through the fog showed where the Audi had pulled over at the side of the road. Above the hiss of steam, a trickle of liquid and the ticking of cooling metal, he heard the sound of voices. Two men were hurrying down the bank. One of them was O'Hara.

Bolan dropped to his hands and knees and crawled into the cornfield. When he had traveled about fifteen yards, he stopped and raised his head above the rustling stalks.

The capsized Renault was just visible in its halo of filtered light. The two men were approaching along the foot of the embankment, a flashlight beam probing the dark, stroking the ground, then fingering the wreck.

"Shit! There's only one guy inside. There should be two."

"We'll finish off this one first," O'Hara said. "The gas tank's split. The ground's soaked in the stuff. I'll put a bullet in this bastard, then we'll fire the wreck and look for the other guy if the flames are bright enough."

Bolan saw the gleam of metal as O'Hara raised a gun and aimed it at Williams's inert figure. The warrior stood. "The other guy's right here!"

O'Hara swung around with a curse; the flashlight angled Bolan's way. The beam died before it reached him. O'Hara fired blind...and wide. The Executioner lined him up—he was silhouetted against the faint glare from the dome light. Bolan had no compunction. O'Hara had been about to kill Williams in cold blood.

The Beretta coughed once. The mercenary staggered, spitting out some unintelligible curse. His hand clawed at his right shoulder. His gun arm lifted, wavered. Two more shots crashed out in the direction of Bolan's muzzle-flash.

But the warrior was six feet away, his weapon now in 3-shot mode. He squeezed off a trio of 9 mm deathbringers.

O'Hara staggered back as the first slug hit him. His arms flew up and the gun spun away. The second tore through his diaphragm, and he folded forward and dropped from sight as the third punched a hole in his face. Then Bolan heard the stumbling, rushing scurry of feet scrabbling up the bank. If the second man was armed, he must have left the gun in the Audi.

Running footsteps sounded eerily and invisibly from above when the guy gained the road. A voice called thickly through the mist, "Next time, you bastard. Just fucking wait until next time!"

It was only as a door slammed and the big car's engine roared to life that Bolan realized the voice belonged to Lem Scarff.

CHAPTER TWENTY-SEVEN

MYSTERY MILITARY MAN SHOT DEAD BY CAR
WRECK, the headline in the local paper shouted the
following morning. There was nothing about the desecration of St. Barnaby-in-Marshland.

The story, bannered on page one, reported that the
body of a man who had died of gunshot wounds had
been discovered near the burned-out shell of a rented
car at the foot of an embankment near Ashburton. The
victim, a man of about forty wearing military-style
garments with no rank insignia, was so far unidenti-
fied.

The story said that the car had been rented by an
American giving the name of Belasko. As far as the
clerk at the rental office could remember, his description didn't tally with that of the murdered man. But a
truck driver reported that one of two men who
thumbed a ride shortly after dawn did answer that description. Both men were dressed in combat fatigues
similar to those worn by the dead man.

A police statement recalled that detectives investigating another killing two weeks ago wished to interview Belasko, as they believed he might be able to assist
them.

Mack Bolan, who had himself torched the Renault after he revived Colonel Williams and helped him climb back to the road, tossed the paper aside. "I smell the heavy hand of officialdom in there someplace. Reporters assigned to murder stories usually end the piece with speculation about motive. Mettner would have it wrapped up and ready to hand to the district attorney."

"What would be his guess in this case?" Freeman asked. They were sitting by the window in her apartment. The fog had cleared, the sun was trying to break through a low overcast, and the moist streets steamed.

"Your guess is as good as his," Bolan said. "With half the police force believing Belasko is a killer, and the other half knowing he isn't, the field's wide open."

Once Williams was safely back in his hotel, Bolan had returned to Freeman's apartment. It had become for him a base of operations.

"The colonel wants me to go down to the UPI plant this afternoon," the woman told him.

Bolan carried his coffee cup to an armchair. "What for?"

"It seems the famous AX-12 reported that the big one, the so-called proof of Joliffe's connection with the deities, has been moved forward. It's tomorrow night instead of next weekend. Williams wants a rundown on the setup inside the plant."

"I reckon they moved it because they lost out on the black mass," Bolan said. "Did Phuong have any reaction on that?"

"They were furious, of course. They got out of it by telling the old man his vibrations were so powerful that the ceremony never started at all."

"No comment on O'Hara?"

"They're running in more hired help. Lem Scarff has been put in charge."

Bolan nodded. "How do you plan to make it inside UPI? It's a restricted site because of the government research."

"The colonel has fixed me official cover. The big question is what might I be up against once I'm inside."

A TWELVE-FOOT chain-link fence surrounded the plant. There was only one entrance, staffed by two guards in uniform who checked passes and shut the gates after each visitor.

The administration building was long, low and modern, set in a pattern of green lawns bright with flowers. To one side executive cars glittered in orderly rows. Behind the main building was a receding perspective of serrated roofs as workshops stretched away to the north. Inside the gates a graveled sweep encircled a flagpole, then led to a ten-story tower that rose above concrete warehouses, storerooms and recreation centers. Behind the tower was the skeleton of another that was under construction. A faint, slightly vinegary odor permeated the air.

Freeman braked the Ministry of Works vehicle outside the guards' cabin. "Mrs. Mackenzie from the ministry," she said curtly, holding the pass Williams had given her out the window. "I think your PR people are expecting me. I've come to look over your personnel arrangements."

"Oh, yes, madam," the guard replied, touching his cap. "They telephoned us from Whitehall to say you were coming. Mr. Salter will be waiting for you in reception. If you'd like to drive up to those double doors left of the flagpole, the sergeant'll park your car for you."

Rick Salter was in a petulant mood. "One simply cannot *think*," he complained, "why they sent you all the way down here when someone came to do exactly the same thing only last month."

"It's just that you're expanding," Freeman said off the top of her head. She waved her hand toward the steel skeleton behind the tower. "I guess they figured they should check out the new construction in good time."

"One did submit all the plans well in advance," Salter replied. "Oh, well, you're here now. What exactly did you want to see?"

"Ideally one would appreciate a quick look at everything." Freeman found the PR man's third-person mannerism catching. "You know we have to satisfy ourselves that recreation, rest and sanitary conditions fall within Ministry of Health norms." She repressed a smile, seeing his barely concealed irritation. They could hardly afford to risk antagonizing an official government department at this stage.

"Very well," Salter said coldly. "One is only too happy, naturally. If you would just come this way..."

Freeman saw rest rooms, recreation rooms, staff rooms, decontamination rooms and special cleansing centers for the removal of chemical waste from the skin. She inspected the first-aid unit at the side of the track where fiberglass car bodies were tested. She was paraded past innumerable benches, presses, stamping machines and molds. She walked through laboratories hissing with retorts, machine shops, and giant hangars busy with white-coated women trimming and finishing plastic consumer goods at long benches. She saw cooling towers, milling machines, looms and conveyor belts. She admired the staff tennis courts and a machine for welding plastic seams. She was given a cup of evil coffee in a canteen. And at last Salter led her across the gravel to the tower, which was what she'd come to see.

"It's our research center," Salter explained. "The new building, which will be its twin, will concentrate exclusively on guidance systems. They'll be linked by covered walkways on alternate floors."

The center was like a museum. Footsteps fell noiselessly on the padded plastic tiling. Locked showcases displayed UPI's range of everyday household products. "There are, of course, special facilities for staff in the departments dealing with clothes," Salter said as he led her past the electronic hardware and software displays on the second floor.

"Oh, yes? Why's that?"

"Well, because the poor dears do get so fatigued doing all those wearability and breathability tests."

"Breathability?"

"A nontechnical term we use—for the materials, not the wearer. You know that sheet plastic is nonporous and one perspires so dreadfully in it? Well, the woven and spun synthetics are a little dodgy, too. So, with that and the static electricity they pick up or generate when one surface rubs against another, the ease with which the material can be ventilated—or ventilates itself— becomes critical, especially when one tries to sell vast amounts to mass producers of clothes. Much of one's research, therefore, is directed toward making the stuff breathe like cotton or wool or even leather."

"So you have people wearing experimental garments made from UPI materials, doing energetic things to see how they make out?"

"And to see how they wear. You know—how fast the sleeves and pant ends fray, how quickly elbows come through, how easily a seat will split if the behind inside it is too fat. That kind of thing."

Materials Research was on the third floor. Freeman saw dozens of young women carrying out consumer tests on garments fashioned from fabrics she'd seen flowing from between huge rollers or spinning in long filaments from centrifuges. Some worked in teams, some alone and some isolated in cubicles equipped with experimental apparatus.

Taking in the geography of the building, Freeman listened with only half an ear to the PR man's sales talk. On the penthouse floor there was an observation room and Sir Simon Joliffe's private apartment. The ninth and eighth were offices, and the doors facing the elevators on the seventh and sixth were posted with signs that read Danger! Positively No Entry.

"What's the great secret in there?" Freeman asked as they took the stairs down to the fifth floor.

"Government research. You know we're working on super lightweight parts for the TASM and Stealth guidance systems, components for rocket nose cones, and so on? Well, that's where they work on them, behind those doors, trying to evolve the stuff that will supersede them. There are armed guards inside, and the shop is a restricted area. Even I'm not allowed in."

"My goodness!" she said with a straight face. Then, "How much longer has the government contract to run?"

The PR man stopped in midstride and stared back at her. "Three years," he said slowly. "But I should have thought you'd have known that. Why do you ask?"

"Er, different departments," she replied. "You must have your work cut out, explaining all this—" she waved her arm "—to press and public. And all at your fingertips with no notes!"

"One does one's poor best," Salter said, mollified. "One does have to admit, though, that one is a little bit overworked. Thankfully one has an assistant, a genuine journalist, due to start work next week."

On the floor below, medical orderlies with blood-pressure gauges and pink tubing and equipment for measuring dehydration waited by their electronic weighing machines for half a dozen women to complete what looked like some futuristic calisthenics routine. Each wore a different type of industrial protective clothing; all of them were miming some complex work rhythm at an invisible machine.

"Testing our products against similar ones made from natural fibers," Salter explained.

One woman wore a thick vulcanized material so inflexible that she could scarcely move; another was clad in a metallic blue sheath so sheer and thin that the label sewn on the back of her panties was outlined against it; a third worked in thick boots and a silver suit like an astronaut's.

"In order that one can arrive at maximum protection from radiation and so forth, and achieve minimum inconvenience through loss of fluid, sweating, cling of the material, and all that," Salter added with a wave of his hand. "We go out this way."

On the far side of the landing, beyond the bank of high-speed elevators, a heavy, paneled mahogany door was half-open. "What's in there?" Freeman asked curiously.

"Well, normally it's a lecture hall. But it's arranged at the moment for a special do of the chairman's tomorrow night. Kind of a private party. Ah, here's our elevator."

"It looks as though it were arranged for a séance," Freeman said, moving forward to peer into the big room.

Salter stared at her, one hand outstretched toward the elevator. "That's an extraordinarily acute remark for a civil servant." He walked across and closed the door.

"Even civil servants can be interested in spiritualism."

The PR man continued to stare, but said nothing. The elevator doors hissed shut. The cage sank from sight.

"It's such a typical setup," Freeman commented, "if you happen to know. People don't give lectures with the chairs arranged in that kind of circle. And all that stuff waiting on the table—cigars, brandy, bowls of flour and maize. Hardly boardroom material. I'd say, in fact, given the context, that your president or chairman or whatever he is was not only organizing a séance, but a séance for believers in the South American cult of Umbanda."

"But that's incredible!" Salter's astonishment showed on his face. He flipped back the lock of hair. "And you, if one may presume to ask, are yourself interested in Umbanda?"

"Oh, yes. I'm very interested indeed."

Thirty minutes later she stopped her vehicle by a phone booth on the outskirts of Exeter and punched out the contact number for Williams. "Meet the new mole!" she said when the connection was made. "I just got invited to the Joliffe revelation tomorrow night."

"BUT GOOD GOD," Jason Mettner said into the telephone, "why the hell didn't you tell me this before?"

"You didn't ask me, old lad."

"No, I guess not. But if Stanley Karsh is leaving his job on the *Herald* to join UPI's public relations department..."

"He is, old lad. I told you. He'll be working immediately under Rick Salter. Can you imagine a more unsavory place to be? It just shows what money can do to an otherwise blameless drunk."

"The son of a bitch never said a word. Look, Roger, how well do you know him? Karsh, I mean, not Salter."

"Middling, I suppose you could say. We sink a jar together occasionally. He's not really my cup, but he can be quite amusing and... Well, you know, there's always shoptalk."

"Do you think he'll tell Salter?"

"That the famous American crime reporter Jason Mettner has been pumping him about share transactions carried out by his new boss's company and related organizations? Well, it depends, doesn't it? How well do *you* know him?"

"Like you, but without the shoptalk."

"Then I should say it depends on how much he wants to curry favor, wouldn't you think? If he wants to get in with his new boss—and if he has no special loyalty to you—then I should say he might well mention that a well-known investigative journalist was asking a lot of questions."

"Yeah, I guess he might, at that," Mettner agreed glumly.

"No doubt about it. You didn't tell him where you were based, or give him your number?"

"Hell, no. Or... wait a minute! I didn't say where I was, but I must have given him the number, because he had to call me back with some of the information. And he did. Oh, shit!''

"Then if I were you, cock,'' Roger Cameron said cheerfully, "and bearing in mind the hints of skulduggery you've dropped, I'd pack a small bag, stub out my cigarette and catch a bus for somewhere. Fast.''

Mettner cursed himself as he hung up the receiver. If Karsh had told Salter of his interest in the financial affairs of UPI—and he probably had—then Salter would have passed it on to his fellow conspirators. And to them Jason Mettner was the name of the man who had passed himself off as Hanslip Cahill at Joliffe's house party.

Subsequently they'd found out that Mettner was the name of a blameless American newspaperman staying at the local inn, and that the impostor sought by them and the police was one Mike Belasko.

But Karsh's revelation that the real Mettner was prying into UPI affairs would provide for the first time a direct link between Belasko and Mettner himself. They'd know that the two of them were working together.

Mettner paced up and down, his mind churning. He was in Felicity Freeman's apartment again, as he had been when he dug up the financial Intel for Williams. What did this new factor imply?

That he'd be in as much danger as Belasko? Well, okay, he could ride that one out. He was often in danger, one way or another, ferreting after his exclusives.

He tapped out a cigarette and placed it between his lips. Second point. If Karsh had passed on the phone number, and they had the means of tracing the address, then this apartment, which was being used as a base, would no longer be secure.

If they had the address, they'd also know the name of the telephone subscriber. Mettner struck a match. So Freeman would be in danger, too.

Mettner paused, the flame halfway to his cigarette. Freeman was the subscriber, and she was at the UPI plant on the other side of the city.

Not knowing what a jerk he'd been, she was blithely carrying on her own impersonation at Salter's HQ. She thought she was safe because they'd never seen her before.

But if she was tied in with Mettner, and therefore with Belasko, and if they knew Belasko was staying in her apartment, and if they then connected Felicity Freeman with the unexpected "ministry visitor" in their midst, then the girl could be in deadly danger right now. And she wouldn't know it.

"Goddamn!" Mettner said agitatedly, pacing the room again.

The flame burned his fingers and he swore once more, dropping the charred match into an ashtray. He'd have to warn her, and Belasko, too, if possible. But how? How the hell could he get in touch? Williams was in London, and Belasko was out of touch altogether, somewhere in the country.

Even if Freeman was still at the plant, he couldn't call her there. Switchboards were too public. And he didn't know the cover name she was using.

He struck another match, found that the cigarette in his mouth had gone soggy, threw it away and lit a fresh one.

Deadly danger was no overstatement when it came to the UPI conspirators. They'd sent a hit man all the way to Nevada with orders to kill just because they were afraid two "government investigators" were getting too curious.

No, there was only one thing to do. He'd have to get to the plant himself and warn the woman.

As he headed for the door, three guys shouldered their way inside—a tall, bleak-faced, white-haired man with a gun in his left hand, and two hardguys.

When Mettner opened his mouth, a fist slammed into his belly. As he folded forward, gasping, a black sack was jammed down over his head and a drawstring tightened around his neck. Struggling, he felt fingers claw the cold blackness before his eyes. Arms locked around his knees; another grip tightened around his shoulders.

Choking in the rubberized, airless sack, Mettner tried desperately to lurch off balance. His captors were being carefully quiet; they couldn't afford the sounds of a fight or a heavy fall in a poorly insulated apartment building.

Fingers still groped the outside of the sack. Abruptly they tightened fiercely. Mettner heard a grunt of satisfaction as a capsule popped and a sickly stench choked his mouth and nose.

First render them helpless, Mettner thought dazedly, already framing the lead paragraph of a first-person story, and then drug them by remote control.

He heaved again . . . and dropped into the darkness, deep, deep down.

CHAPTER TWENTY-EIGHT

"The most important thing," Bolan told Colonel Williams over the telephone, "is a hang glider."

"A what?"

"A hang glider. And we need a chopper or some kind of light aircraft to lift it high enough to fly."

"A chopper?"

"The highest point on Dartmoor is nearly seventeen hundred feet," the Executioner explained, "but the slope's too gentle for a hang glider lift-off. So we have to make the height aeronautically, so to speak, rather than geographically. Okay?"

"I'm sure you know what you're doing," Williams said in a voice that implied he himself didn't.

"Next in line is a hand-held, self-powered video camera and a tough lightweight box, which should have a shoulder strap. The rest of the gear I can supply myself."

"And what about Mettner? Is he to assist you in this escapade?"

"Uncertain. I have to check with him. We have a date back at the apartment at four."

"Perhaps," the colonel said, "you might care to favor me with a brief rundown on the mechanics of this...this..."

"Escapade? Sure."

He spoke for five minutes. When he finished, Williams said, "Yes, I see. It should be most effective and most dramatic. If it works."

"I can't see why it wouldn't. I aim to go ahead, anyway."

ONCE AGAIN in Felicity Freeman's apartment, Bolan made himself a cup of coffee and paced up and down, checking over in his mind the things he had to do before darkness fell. AX-12 had reported that the mercenaries no longer attempted to patrol the whole estate. Under Lem Scarff's direction the cordon had been tightened; the guards now restricted themselves to a perimeter check, just the house and outbuildings. In those circumstances, would it be worth bringing in Mettner?

Where was the newspaperman, anyway? It was unlike him not to show on time, and it was already four-thirty.

Bolan checked his stride, cup in hand. Several small things he'd noticed without really paying attention now began to register.

An unsmoked cigarette lay beside an ashtray on the table. A full ashtray. Bolan picked up the cigarette. The tipped end was still soggy.

Frowning, he went out into the hallway. The white fleece rug was scrunched up in a corner under an occasional table. Three letters addressed to Felicity lay on the floor. Most importantly, a second cigarette—or the charred end of one—lay beside them. And a long black finger scorched into the rug showed where the cigarette had burned itself out.

Bolan hurried back to the living room. At least he could check with Williams to see if Mettner had been in contact.

He lifted the phone; the line was dead.

The signs were easy enough to read. He now had one more reason why his "escapade," as Williams called it, had to be a one hundred percent success.

THERE WAS SOME trouble maneuvering the A-frame through the helicopter's sliding hatch. Bolan was thankful Williams had insisted on one of the big Westland gunships. But at last he dropped away and spread the modified wing, catching his breath as the updraft braked the sail and he settled his body behind the control bar. The chopper clattered away toward Okehampton and the moor.

The night was warm, even at three thousand feet. Spread out below him, the dark countryside, pricked only here and there with lights, stretched away to the distant glare on the underside of a cloud bank that marked the site of the city.

There was a steady southwesterly breeze that had freshened at dusk, carrying the hang glider briskly toward Joliffe Hall. It would be no sweat locating the place—starlight on the lake would be an accurate enough pointer. The landing zone he'd chosen was the problem. A careful recon of the approach, the obstacles, the cover, none of which he knew, was vital if he was to make the target unseen. That was why he needed the height. The rolling pastureland below wouldn't create enough thermals to buoy the sail once it was below a certain point.

Bolan had spent the morning studying architects' drawings at the town planning department of city hall. The modifications to the original Tudor building had required special permission, and the Oskar Mikkonen suggestion, stored in wide, shallow drawers in the department's archives, were available for inspection.

The plans showed the warrior that the mansion's roof elevation was unchanged. In the center of the great rectangle of pitched slopes, gables and dormers was a flat space between the building's six tall hexagonal chimneys.

A later check with fire department archives confirmed that the escape regulations had been complied with. A dormer that opened onto this horizontal sector was fitted with a glass hatch, and from this a tiled gully led to the fire escape on the north side of the building.

Bolan intended to land on the flat part of the roof. Since the house was surrounded by armed men at ground level, and since there was now, according to Phuong, a magic-eye system that switched on floods all around the building if the beam was crossed, it seemed to him the logical approach.

The problems were all visual. Distance between chimneys, angle of run-in, orientation of pitched roofs—not in terms of yards and feet, which he knew, but in terms of the proportion between the sail's wingspan and the space available.

The helicopter had dropped him three miles from the estate. He reckoned he still had two to go. He could already make out the lake, a pale silver streak separating two belts of trees, with the valley a blacker brush stroke against the surrounding dark.

He approached the property downwind, making a wide circle to the south before he came in close to survey the house from above. Lights shone in one or two windows and carriage lamps illuminated each side of the main entrance, but otherwise the place was in darkness. Joliffe and the conspirators were at the plant, making last-minute arrangements for the next day's séance, according to Phuong. They weren't expected back until late.

Five hundred yards past the house he turned back into the wind, feeling the sail lift as it met the increased pressure. He planed across the building from east to west, pulling night vision goggles down over his eyes to register details. Over the lake he banked the kite and ran in crosswind to check out the hall's front elevation. Past the gate house, losing height all the time, he turned through 180 degrees and drifted back to survey the rear facade.

Faintly now he could see starlight gleam on the steep slate roofs. The flat part was a well of blackness bounded by the six brick chimneys.

Bolan wheeled once more, breaking the turn halfway to glide over the house from rear to front. He could see now, because of the disposition of the chimneys, that it would be too hazardous, trying to land along the length of the rectangle. It would be best to fly

in at right angles, although this would give him much
less space in which to touch down and come to a stop.

Altitude? One hundred fifty feet, maybe less.

Okay, he thought, time to do it. Sawing the control
bar beneath the sail's A-frame, he put the nose down
hard to swoop over the stable area in a shallow dive.
Then, pulling the bar back for a final burst of speed,
he lifted the glider over the slate roofs of the house,
turned one last time into the wind and sailed between
two chimneys, putting the wing down with the trailing
edge fluttering as he spilled out the rest of the air.

He halted only feet from the far slope of tiles,
rubber-soled combat boots soundless on the asphalt
surface. Before he slipped off the harness and disman-
tled the kite, he stood listening, every sense alert.
Nothing.

Warily he stepped out of the frame and put the metal
spars on the asphalt. The dormer with the fire escape
hatch was at the far end of the rectangle. The hatch was
in the form of a door with a push bar inside that unlocked bolts top and bottom, like the emergency exit
from a theater. There was also a padlock tonguing the
iron hatch into the door frame.

The lock posed no problem. Fifteen seconds with a
pick took care of that. The push bar was something
else. The thin, long, rigid tool he took from the camera box made it through the crack all right, but he
couldn't get enough leverage to lift the heavy bar and
displace the bolts. After almost ten minutes he gave up
and took a glass cutter with a diamond tip from the
box. A piece of putty pressed to the pane, a neat circle

engraved, a small tap with the heel of the hand . . . and
the glass disk lifted clear, allowing the Executioner to
thrust in an arm and force up the bar manually. He
opened the door and stepped inside.

He was on an attic floor, with storerooms leading off
a short hall. There were four rooms, with a steep
wooden staircase leading down to the bedrooms and
living quarters at the end of the corridor. A faint light
percolated up the stairwell from below.

Three of the rooms were filled with junk—broken
toys, trunks, old carpets, pieces of furniture. Bolan
flashed a penlight around, then got out.

The fourth room, at the top of the stairs, was locked.
He opened the door with one of his specialized instruments and went in. The thin beam showed him a professional 16 mm movie projector with soundtrack
accessories, a screen that covered one entire wall, a
floor-stand microphone and more tape editing machines.

Bolan whistled softly. Evidently this was where the
conspirators ran their doctored films once they'd been
tinkered with and spliced together in the secret rooms
below; this was where they held, as it were, the dress
rehearsal before showing the finished product to Joliffe.

He was backing out when he almost tripped over
something heavy and soft that lay across the floor. He
swung the beam downward and saw a long, narrow
package, more than six feet long, wrapped in tarpau-
lin and tied with nylon cord.

He cut the cord and unwrapped the tarp at the head end, revealing the contused, agonized features of Phuong.

Evidently he'd made one phone call too many, ventured up that wooden stairway when he should have stayed below, or given himself away too obviously for Vanderlee and Kleist to ignore the implication.

Bolan assumed the man had died not long before they'd left for the UPI plant. They'd parceled up the body and left it for disposal later.

The cause of death wasn't obvious. But Phuong had certainly been tortured first. The visible parts of his naked body were marked with burns, lacerations, weals and wounds made by hot pincers.

Had he talked before he died? Maybe not. A rubber tourniquet was still twisted around his neck, and even in death his face was contorted in some ultimate agony. For Bolan's money they'd been too eager to get at the truth, and Phuong's heart had given out under interrogation.

Creeping down to the floor below, the Executioner pondered implications. Suppose the undercover man *had* spilled all he knew? What difference would it make to Vanderlee and company? Okay, they'd have confirmation of their suspicion that someone was indeed on to their plot. Now they'd know who. But, as Williams himself had pointed out, they'd as yet done nothing that was actually illegal. There had been nothing but Phuong's word to tie them in with the St. Barnaby desecration, and now he was dead. If Joliffe was to turn over his shares to a registered charity, of which he himself was going to be the figurehead, and if he did this of his own free will and was paid the going market rate, then where was the crime? There would be no apparent coercion. And once the doctored tapes and faked séance evidence had been destroyed—as it would be as soon as the old man was convinced—it would be an impossible task to try to convince a judge and jury that undue influence had been brought to bear, especially since Joliffe himself was in more ways than one the main beneficiary.

And as for proving to a court that the aim of the entire operation was to gain control of software and hardware destined for the TASM, HOTOL and Stealth projects... Once more Bolan shook his head.

No way.

Even if such material wasn't ruled irrelevant, the lawyers might very well ask, "What operation?" Because, yet again, nothing had actually happened. It was all in the conspirators' minds. So far.

The warrior gave up on it. Better to concentrate on the means to kill the plot without calling in the law, which meant convincing Joliffe of the plotters' evil intentions rather than a judge.

And that, broadly speaking, was why Bolan was there—to prepare the ground for a counterplot that would blow Vanderlee, Kleist and the Duhamel woman wide open.

First, though, there was the problem of Jason Mettner. The discovery of Phuong was bad news and didn't bode well for the safety of the newspaperman.

Had he been kidnapped so that they could torture and interrogate him, too, to find out exactly what his connection with the Executioner was? Was it for professional reasons, to stop him from publishing what he might have found out about their plot? Or was it just to eliminate him, to get one more possible complication out of the way?

Above all, how did they know where to find him?

Whatever the answers, those questions had to be shelved for the moment. The mission, as always, came first.

It was tough, but he had to put Mettner out of his mind until he'd done what he came to do.

Lights were burning in the stairwell leading to the upper floors, and—as he'd noticed when he was planing down over the mansion's roof—illumination from the entrance hall spilled out onto the driveway. Otherwise the great house was in darkness. The servants would be asleep above the kitchen wing; the guards were all outside.

When the warrior checked out every room, he returned to the one he himself had occupied, drew the draperies and switched on the bedside lamps. He opened the insulated box containing the video camera and spread out on the bed some of the other items protected by the plastic foam lining.

Members of the "dirty tricks" brigade operated by British security services from their Mayfair headquarters in Curzon House would have recognized voice-activated bugging mechanisms, several probe microphones, a drill and bit, a couple of oscilloscopes. But there was other gear, as well, including a sensitively wired rig that was based on an idea of Bolan's own.

After he double-checked all the equipment, wired up certain components and installed switch gears in others, he repacked everything into the box in the order he intended to use it. Then he killed the bedside lights, drew back the draperies and left the room.

In the corridor outside he quietly closed the door and switched on his penlight. Then he started on the really serious work.

IT WAS A QUARTER TO TWO when the Executioner was finally satisfied that there was nothing more he could do to improve the quality of the work he had put in.

Now, alive or dead, he had to find Mettner and, if alive, rescue him and keep him under wraps until it was time to leave Joliffe Hall. If he was lucky and his plan bore fruit, it would still be many hours, long after the conspirators had gone to sleep, before he would be able to leave the house.

So where to start looking for the newspaperman?

Bolan had already checked all the bedrooms. There was no point wasting any more time there. The public rooms, the library, the den, the dining hall, the gun room, he reckoned could be safely ignored. There remained the service and storerooms off the kitchen wing, the cellars, the small ballroom and the two secret rooms in the basement.

The best bet, he thought, would be the cellars, and after that the secret rooms.

The cellars were surprisingly small for such a big house. They were vaulted, the whitewashed brick walls pierced by arched niches designed to store wine. Expensive liquor and rare vintages filled every single gap. There was no sign of Mettner, and no sign that anyone had ever been kept prisoner there.

There were more tape reels and additional cans of film in the secret rooms, but no trace of Mettner. The ballroom was empty.

He remembered the loft over Joliffe's private garage where he had himself been kept prisoner, and remembered what sucker bait Kleist had been once he was in a position to move. They might be evil, cruel and totally callous, but in action they were amateurs. Would they, he wondered, be stupid enough to use the same place twice?

They would.

He found Mettner roped to the same bed he'd been dumped on. The newspaperman was alive, but evidently heavily sedated. His breath snored through a slack mouth, his pulse was strong but alarmingly slow, his eyes were rolled upward beneath the lids.

Bolan tried slapping him awake. Zero.

He cut Mettner loose, hoisted him over one shoulder and carried him laboriously down the ladder and out into the yard. He trod softly across the cobbles, shouldered open the door that led to the vegetable garden and carried the unconscious man through. He laid him on the ground and went back for the camera box.

He was gambling now, since Mettner was so deeply drugged, on the hope that the conspirators hadn't intended to work on him until the following morning. Certainly he seemed undamaged so far. But in case they changed their minds it was vital to get him under cover before he was missed and the mercs alerted.

The safest place for this was the underground tunnel Phuong had showed him. To get there they had to traverse the vegetable garden and make the outbuildings on the far side of the wasteland beyond.

Bolan was in the garage, heading for the ladder, when he heard a floorboard creak in the loft above. He held his breath and shrank back behind the rear of a Volvo station wagon.

More creaks. As the beam of a flashlight illuminated the square opening at the top of the ladder, a harsh voice muttered, "Shit!" Then the trap blacked out and boots clattered on the ladder.

Bolan tensed. Clearly there was a checkup on the prisoner from time to time. The guy must have slipped into the rear entrance seconds after the Executioner carried Mettner out the front and into the yard.

The merc made the floor at the foot of the ladder and turned to the rear door. Bolan took half a dozen noiseless strides and leaped onto his back. The hardguy's breath was knocked from his body as his feet splayed and he pitched forward onto his face.

The mercenary fought viciously, with all his strength—a knee grinding into Bolan's kidneys, an attempted nerve hold at the top of the warrior's spine, a murderous rabbit punch.

But he was no match for the Executioner's determination. The edge of Bolan's right hand, rigid and as hard as an iron bar, slashed across the man's Adam's apple with stunning force. He didn't even feel the fingers clenched on his nape or the thumbs on either side of his windpipe that finally choked the life out of him.

Bolan scrambled to his feet. For the second time he hoisted an inert body over his shoulder and carried it through to the vegetable garden. Then he went back for the camera box. This time there was no interruption.

He transported the live Mettner and the dead merc to the outbuildings alternately, fifty yards at a time. He was carrying the newspaperman when light washed over the walls of the mansion and he heard the rustle of tires on gravel. The principals had returned from the plant. He waited, crouched behind some bushes with Mettner on the ground beside him, for the next move.

Voices. Vanderlee's. Kleist's? Cleo Duhamel's, certainly. Slater's, perhaps. No evidence one way or the other for Joliffe. Bolan presumed nevertheless that he'd be there. The upper-floor suite he occupied had been conspicuously empty.

Evidently they were all going into the main entrance on the other side of the house. Bolan could hear the car's engine idling.

Doors slammed. Vanderlee called out something, and the engine was gunned. The car circled the house and passed beneath the arch into the stable area. Through the open garden door Bolan saw a uniformed chauffeur—the same man who'd picked him up

at the railroad station—close the driver's door and
stride toward the kitchen wing.

Evidently nothing was planned in the loft above
Joliffe's garage until the following day. They hadn't
even put the car away. Mettner was to be left in care of
the mercenary guards.

That suited the warrior fine. He waited, watching the
rear of the house, until lights showed on the second and
third floor. When the upper windows went dark and
the lower remained illuminated, he nodded with satisfaction. This was exactly what he wanted.

He resumed his relay between the vegetable garden
and the outbuildings. When Mettner, the dead guard
and the camera box were all safely hidden at the beginning of the tunnel, he settled down to wait.

METTNER REGAINED consciousness one hour before
dawn. The process was gradual—a twitching of the
limbs, fingers plucking at the stuff of his jacket, fluttering eyelids and a strangled groan.

His eyes opened, scrunched up against the glare of
the flashlight, then opened again—wider this time. He
tried to sit up. "Jeez, my *head!*" And then, classi-
cally, "Where am I? What the hell am I doing here?"

"The line's been used before, but I'll fill you in,
anyway."

"My God," Mettner said when the warrior finished. "And the last thing I remember is those guys
jumping me in Felicity's hallway! So what now? We're
in some kind of secret tunnel, you say? Were you just

waiting for me to come to before hightailing it for the wide-open spaces?''

"No. I still have business up at the house. Once that's through we can go. But it won't be before dawn.''

BY THE TIME Bolan returned from his "business" at the house it was nearly four-thirty. Surprisingly there had been no alarm raised over the disappearance of the man the Executioner had killed, no sign that anyone knew Mettner was no longer shackled to the bed in the loft above the garage.

The man, Bolan reckoned, must have been on the graveyard shift, an all-night watch with no relief until daylight and nothing to do but check that the prisoner was still secure. He'd probably stepped out for a leak or a cigarette at the exact moment Bolan blew in to release the newspaperman.

So much the better. Their exit would now come as a total surprise.

Bolan motioned Mettner into the rear of a limo he'd just unlocked with one of his picks. "You know how to use a handgun?" he asked Mettner.

"More or less."

The warrior unleathered his Beretta and handed it over. "Roll down the side windows and knock out the rear once we get going," he murmured. "Slide the catch here if you want 3-shot bursts."

Bolan crouched below the wheel. The big V8 engine was still warm. Once hot-wired, it purred effortlessly, almost noiselessly, to life. Bolan eased the door shut, backed up beneath the archway, turned and slid the lever into drive. Then he fed the car gas.

The limo's automatic transmission laid down rubber and the vehicle rocketed around the side of the house toward the driveway. Gravel spun away from the wheels and showered the front steps as Bolan wrenched it past the front entry. A moment later they were barreling past the gardens and across the meadow that separated them from the belt of trees by the gates.

It was light enough now to see the driveway as a pale ribbon cleaving the darkness ahead, and to make out the shifting blurs of shadows that signified men moving among the trees.

There were shadows, too, in a cut beside the road, men racing across fields, a distorted voice calling some warning through a bullhorn. The limo was hitting sixty.

Bolan heard glass shatter as Mettner knocked out the rear window with the butt of the Beretta. Then a side window imploded, cascading granules of toughened glass into his lap. The windshield cracked and starred, and the heavy body of the limo shuddered under the assault of high-caliber slugs fired in a stream.

The Executioner brushed the glass from his knees and picked up the Desert Eagle. Bright flame flickered in the cut, from beneath the trees, from the driveway dead ahead. He hunched behind the wheel, firing three shots from the .44 Magnum as they streaked toward the mercs in the road. A triple concussion rocked the vehicle at the same time as two heavy clattering thumps shook it. Bolan had a fleeting vision of a body spun aside as limp as a rag doll, felt a sickening jolt as a rear wheel passed over a soft obstruction. Then they were past and speeding for the woods.

Mettner fired the Beretta through the broken rear window. In the rearview mirror Bolan saw a dim shape erupt from the cut and lie thrashing in the road. Bullets were streaming toward them now from beneath the trees. He swung the limo onto the grass shoulder and aimed the hood at the nearest gunners. Level with the muzzle-flashes, he steered the bouncing car with one hand and slammed three more thunderous shots into the darkness. Behind him Mettner choked another half dozen from the Beretta. A subgun blazed skyward as someone fell; a figure sprawled forward and rolled in the undergrowth as Bolan switched on the four headlights.

Only one was still working, but it was enough to reveal the iron gates two hundred yards ahead—and the two men in combat camous posted in front of them.

Fifty yards from the gates Bolan trod on the brakes. The limo snaked on the roadway, steadied, then lost way. Kicking down the transmission, he punched the gas pedal and set the big car leaping forward. Both the mercenaries were firing their MAC-10s, and sporadic shooting continued from behind.

At twenty-five yards the warrior emptied the Desert Eagle at the men. One dropped to the ground, clawing at his throat, while the other was punched against the ironwork. The car rammed the gates dead center, and they burst open.

The limo lurched through in a hail of bullets. There was a grinding of metal as both rear tires burst and rolled off the rims. The radiator grille was smashed, steam jetted from the crumpled hood, and the front fenders were telescoped back against the wheels. One hundred yards along the lane the crippled vehicle screeched slowly to a halt, scoring deep furrows into the ground.

"They won't follow us," Bolan stated. "They'd be reluctant to carry a shooting war onto the public highway, even at dawn."

"Yeah," Mettner agreed. "I guess we can make it from here on foot." He paused. From farther along the lane they heard the sudden roar of a powerful motorcycle engine. The bike took off, howling away into the distance until at last the resonant exhaust note dwindled and died.

"Five gets you ten that hotshot was riding a Harley-Davidson," Bolan said, frowning. The warrior banged open the riddled door and stepped out onto the road.

As the two men set off downhill toward the village, Bolan hefted the camera box's carrying strap over his shoulder.

"What the hell do you have in there, anyway?" Mettner asked curiously.

The Executioner patted the side of the box. "Evidence."

CHAPTER TWENTY-NINE

Felicity Freeman stared through a transparent visor at the ceiling. It wasn't an interesting ceiling, being no more than an expanse of white plaster dimly lit from below. She'd have preferred to look at something else—the rest of the room, perhaps. But since she was bound hand and foot and then roped to the top of some kind of chest, she had no choice. The antiradiation suit they must have dragged on over the simple wool dress she'd been wearing ended in a helmet that was locked around her neck. And from a metal ring in the crown of this, a cord ran tightly to the handle of the chest, preventing her from turning her head or raising it. Freeman, therefore, could only stare at the ceiling.

Around her she could hear shufflings and murmured conversation. She was still, she guessed, in the lecture hall on the fourth floor of the UPI research center where the séance was due to be held. It was at the entrance that they had jumped her.

Dressed as she imagined a minor government official interested in the occult might dress, she'd arrived at seven-thirty and asked for Rick Salter, as she'd been told. He'd come out to the car and escorted her personally to the elevator, making small talk. And then, just as they were walking into the hall, he'd stepped swiftly aside and signaled to someone behind the door. Before Freeman had realized what was going on, two women had appeared from nowhere and pinioned her arms in a paralyzing grip.

Salter had come around to face her with an unpleasant smile. "Mrs. Mackenzie, is it?" he said softly. "From the ministry! What a convenient visit. But wouldn't it have been better to have made it the Meteorological Office? Or even the Garment Manufacturers' Association?"

"I don't know what you mean. Tell these women to let me go at once."

"What I mean? Just that you'd have less chance to forget your cover name . . . Miss Freeman."

If they knew who she really was, they had to know everything. Or almost everything. "Is that supposed to be funny?" she asked.

"It depends on one's sense of humor, dear, doesn't it?" He turned to his confederates. "You better get it over with."

The taller of the two produced a flat leather case from the pocket of her jacket. "It's only good for a half hour, remember," she warned.

"That should do," Salter said, closing a forefinger and thumb over Freeman's chin and tilting her head back so that he could look into her eyes. "After that we shall see how the inquisitive Madam Mackenzie looks draped over a sacrificial altar!"

Freeman jerked her head free. "I don't think that's funny, either," she said levelly. "Sadistic sons of bitches never did amuse me much."

Salter slapped her face hard. By the time Freeman recovered from the involuntary sting of tears, the tall woman had removed a filled syringe from the leather case and increased the pressure of her free hand to bend the British agent forward. Then, as the second woman seized her hair to keep her still, the PR man reached out and rolled up her sleeve above the elbow.

Freeman was helpless. She'd break her arms if she struggled to escape the crippling holds. The upper part of her body was immobilized by the painful grip twined in her hair. Only her legs were free, and she was hinged too far forward to kick out. She lashed out behind with one foot and kicked air. Then the needle bit into her arm.

When she floated back to consciousness, she'd realized she was clothed in one of the protective suits she'd seen in the research department, presumably to conceal her identity.

Nothing had started yet, but there was a lot of movement in the lecture hall. In the limited arc of vision allowed by the visor, she could see that the place was illuminated by two low-power lamps, one crimson and the other a dark violet. Behind and above the chest was what looked like an altar covered in metalized cloth. On it were unlit candles in carved holders, cigars, and a number of bowls and glasses.

She knew the story. The cigars were a carryover from the myths of South American Indians. Witch doctors had always smoked pipes to cleanse and purify the channels through which the spirits were supposed to speak. Their modern counterparts, the mediums, used cigars. The containers would hold delicacies to appease the gods: oil from the Dende palm, manioc flour, the fiery sugarcane brandy of Brazil. Over the antiseptic odor of plastic inside the helmet, she imagined she could detect the insidious tang of incense.

The low-pitched murmur of conversation had swelled. With the increase in volume came the shuffle of feet, another scrape of chairs. The invited audience had to be filing in.

She tried to roll herself first to one side and then the other. Maybe if she could attract attention, show in some way that she was there against her will, was no part of the planned ceremony...

No way. The ropes had been tied by an expert. A cry for help then, in the hope that some of the audience at least might be outsiders, or at worst neutral? She opened her mouth to yell, but nothing happened. A crisscross of adhesive tape retained a large bath sponge that had been compressed and jammed into her mouth. Powerless to move, unable to speak, she'd just have to lie there and take what came.

But that didn't mean she was giving in. She strained every nerve to absorb every sound, every sight. You never knew when the break might come, and each item of information could be a lifesaver.

Very faintly the staccato syncopations of tribal singing manifested themselves in the background. The voices of the audience quieted, then died away. The lights dimmed.

The singing rose to a crescendo and abruptly ceased. From somewhere much nearer, just beyond her feet, a woman's voice rose alarmingly into a high-pitched incantation, mouthing words in a language Freeman couldn't identify.

With stunning unexpectedness a gong clanged loudly behind her head. Beneath the cold caress of the plastic suit her entire body seemed to tremble with its reverberations.

The lights were almost out now. Salter would have organized a lighting technician to work a rheostat.

Then, impressive against the sudden silence, another voice spoke—a woman's again, but deep and mellifluous this time, throbbing with emotion, taut with feeling. A very *professional* voice, Freeman thought.

"Tonight," the new voice intoned, "is the night of revelation. Tonight is the night of the great ones. Tonight the forces of the other side will make their choice—and from among you one will be chosen to lead. Among the followers of the right-hand path, a new force will emerge."

A shape moved into Felicity's field of vision. The speaker was standing in front of the altar. She was tall and voluptuous, her heavy breasts thrusting against the folds of a gold-threaded black robe that swathed her from neck to ankle. Freeman recognized her at once from Belasko's description.

Cleo Duhamel.

To the spirits, the woman went on, until a leader worthy of them was manifested, all men were equal. "There is neither rich nor poor, neither great nor small, neither joyful nor sorrowful. That is why you are all dressed as you are, so that all shall be seen equal.''

And after the manifestation, she continued, there was only the leader and the led, the chosen who followed the way. ''Tonight,'' the voice thrilled, ''I'm proud to be the great ones' vehicle, the channel through which their choice shall be made known.''

Duhamel moved down until she was standing beside the chest. ''But before I can make myself ready to receive the spirits who wait upon us there is a task to be accomplished. Among us tonight is one of the unfortunate ones, a follower of the left hand on whom a Mandinga, a spell, has been laid, so that the paths are closed and the spirits are unable to communicate. But the obstruction must be removed and the evil exorcized. With your help and prayers the strayed one here shall be cleansed and returned whence she came.''

For the first time Freeman realized the monologue about the unfortunate one must refer to herself. The idea gave them an excuse to have an unidentifiable figure trussed up on stage, all of which would add to the atmosphere of secrecy and ritual. But what did they intend to do? Surely they couldn't be mad enough to attempt a public murder under the pretense of exorcizing evil spirits? A theatrical stunt that would at the same time rid them of an inconvenient witness?

The woman raised her head toward the lights; there was a rapt expression on her face. Her eyes were closed, and Freeman saw with a shudder of horror that she held in both hands a slim golden stiletto with a needle-sharp point. Reflections of the crimson and violet illumination slid slowly up and down the blade as Duhamel swayed from side to side above the helpless woman.

"As a token," she said to the audience, "as a physical token of the spiritual cleansing we shall accomplish together tonight, I lay this blade upon the breast of the one who has strayed..."

Freeman heard a faint creak as the razorlike point pierced the stiff plastic of the decontamination suit and cut the material of her dress. She felt a sudden surface relaxation when it sliced through the elastic joining the two cups of her brassiere. Cool air played moistly on her bare flesh, but the weapon hadn't broken her skin.

"I call upon Xangô, Prince of Intercessors!" Duhamel cried.

"Xangô! Xangô!" the response whispered back from the unseen audience.

"Lord of the Discarnate, leader of those who intercede for us on the other side, assist us to cast out from this lost one the phalanx of the left hand! Save her from the Tutu-Maramba, the black one with the pouch, from the Homen-Marimho and Sapo-Cururu and all those who smear our faces with ghost broth in the night. Save her. Save her!"

"Save her," the voices moaned from below the stage. "Save her, save her, save her!"

Duhamel straightened and opened her eyes. She raised the stiletto to the level of her mouth, still with both hands clasped around the hilt. From behind the visor Freeman watched her stare at the rent in the plastic suit. Slowly, with her burning gaze fixed on the target, she began to bring the blade down.

Through the stifling gag the powerless woman uttered an inarticulate cry of terror and despair. Suddenly the tribal chanting burst out in a torrent of sound, and all the lights went out.

Something metallic clattered on the floor beside the chest. Freeman heard a rustle of thick material, followed by a thump. In the total darkness, breaking the silence that had fallen, a shrill laugh bubbled hysterically. Then, as the chorus of questions and exclamations broke out among the members of the audience, a woman screamed.

CHAPTER THIRTY

Pandemonium reigned in the lecture hall. Over the cries of alarm Salter and Vanderlee shouted for calm.

"Stay where you are. There's nothing to worry about!"

"It's just a temporary power cut. It'll be fixed in a minute."

Rhythmic shivers shook Freeman's body. Something sawed at the cords tethering her to the chest; a blade sliced through the rope attaching the helmet to the handle behind. Seconds later she felt the bonds shackling her ankles, knees, elbows and wrists fall away. A pair of hands lifted her shoulders, and she fell from the chest and rolled toward the altar.

Thoroughly unnerved by her experience, Freeman thought only of escape. From the guided tour she remembered there was a door in back of the stage, just behind the altar. She rose to her feet and stumbled blindly toward it, cannoning into the medium's table and upending a chair on the way. Nobody tried to stop her.

She jerked open the door and slipped through, wrenching off the helmet as she ran. The passage outside was in darkness, too.

As Freeman went to close the door again, overhead lighting drenched the hall with brilliance. Peering back through the crack, she saw a scene of total confusion.

Milling around between the chairs, some of them overturned, thirty or forty figures in brightly colored PVC decontamination suits argued and gestured, their faces invisible behind amber eyepieces set in the hoods covering their heads. In the gleaming plastic garments, slowed down a little by the stiffness of the material, they looked more like extras from a sci-fi movie than researchers into the occult. Cleo Duhamel's remark, commenting on the way they were dressed, made sense now. It was as good a way as any of making all men look equal. And as good a way as any of infiltrating the strong-arm men into a gathering without anyone noticing.

But where was the medium? What had stopped her from plunging the dagger into her defenseless victim? Lack of light shouldn't have deflected her aim, if she really meant to kill, by more more than an inch or two.

Second question—who had set Felicity free?

Number one was easy to answer. Freeman saw it at the same time as Salter and the Dutchman, the only people there in street clothes. Cleo Duhamel, hidden from most of the audience, was lying in a crumpled heap between the chest and the altar. Her arms were outflung and her dead eyes stared straight at the door. Between them was the brightly feathered tuft of a poison blowpipe dart.

Whoever sabotaged the lights must have puffed the deadly missile at the woman a millisecond before the power was cut, then picked up the stiletto intended to kill Freeman and cut her free.

The woman who had screamed when the lights went out saw the body as Vanderlee and the PR man jumped onto the stage. She screamed again. Exclamations of horror followed on all sides.

Salter and Vanderlee picked up the body and headed for the door. The audience crowded toward the stage. "Madam Duhamel has been taken ill!" Salter shouted over his shoulder. "Go back to your seats, people, please. An announcement will be made in a minute. The show—that is to say, the ceremony—will continue."

Freeman figured that it was time to go. She stopped massaging the circulation back into her limbs, straightened and started to move away from the door...and froze. She heard a stealthy sound somewhere ahead. Someone had come out of a door that led to the lighting control cabin on the far side of the stage. Freeman tiptoed forward, feeling her way along the wall of the dark corridor with outstretched hands. Soon she reached a corner, beyond which was a landing and a stairwell outlined in a faint glow from the story below.

Noiselessly she sped to the stairhead. A dark shape— a slim guy wearing a biker's leather suit—was crossing the third-floor landing heading toward the escalators. With curiosity overcoming her fear she swung herself over the rail and dropped to the lower floor.

The biker was swinging around when another dark figure stepped from a doorway and leaped at the stranger.

Freeman gasped with surprise. It was Belasko!

The warrior had the biker on the floor, pinned. The man cursed in Spanish or Portuguese, then the American said in a tight voice, "All right. Keep struggling and you break a bone. Sit up, slow and easy, while we take a look at you."

The two combatants stood slowly, and Freeman uttered another exclamation of surprise. Shaking loose a mane of thick dark hair, the biker revealed herself as a young woman.

She was large-boned and handsome in a Latin way, with big, dark eyes, a proud nose and haughty, curved lips. Her mouth was sulky, and there were tears of exasperation on her cheeks.

"So," Bolan said quietly, "the rider of the Harley-Davidson."

"What of it?" The voice was deep and vibrant.

"And the lady who killed the lights?"

"Supposing I did?"

"It follows that you killed Cleo Duhamel."

"You can't prove it."

"Not even with this?" Freeman gestured toward the elevator bank where a short blowpipe, which must have rolled away during the struggle, lay. "And I guess you killed Hanslip Cahill with the same weapon, right?"

"All right, all right. I did. I killed them both. They deserved it."

"Why?" Bolan asked.

She was crying now, tears that welled ceaselessly from her eyes and coursed down her cheeks. "I'm Emilia Carvalho," she said. "It doesn't mean anything to you? I guess not. My father was Gilberto Carvalho. He was a famous spiritist in Bahia. He died when I was four years old, and my mother and I went to live up-country. We lived among the Tehenetua Indians, and because my mother, too, was a medium we were able to help them a great deal. I learned many things from the Indians. One of them was how to use a blowpipe."

Emilia Carvalho stopped and stared out across the stairwell at the black glass cladding the shaft. Beyond the huge panes rain was lancing down into the pool of light cast by a lamp outside the administration building.

"When I was sixteen, this man Cahill came. He was pompous and rather stupid, but he had the gift. My mother fell in love with him and married him. He wasn't a bad stepfather, and things went well enough. Until this woman Duhamel appeared."

The young woman's eyes narrowed, and her expression hardened. "Quite deliberately she set out to seduce him. Not because she loved him, not even because she wanted him, but to show she could get him. He was weak, you see. They went to Rio. The only thing was, as I said, my mother did love him. And so she took her own life when he walked out on her."

"How dreadful for you," Freeman said sympathetically.

"They lived together for seven years," Emilia went on. "Then she left him, too. I'd waited for that. I wanted him to suffer. But after that they had to be punished. I swore they should pay for my mother's life with their own. And now they have, both of them."

For a moment the three people remained silent. Then there was a sudden surge of voices from the direction of the lecture hall.

"You picked up the stiletto and rescued me," Freeman said finally. "Why did you do that?"

"We were on the same side, weren't we? I'd been keeping her under observation at Joliffe Hall, watching the stupidities they faked with the old woman and those girls from London. I was waiting for my chance after I killed him at the station. I saw you at the hall. I saw this man. And when you came again with the other one, the older one with glasses, I followed you into the hall."

"So I was right," Freeman murmured. "There *was* someone there!"

"Of course there was. I've been watching you all, and wondering, for some time. The tall, thin one who smokes too much, as well."

"Cleo Duhamel was part of a conspiracy," Bolan said. "These are evil people she worked with. They plan to defraud the old man. My friends and I are trying to stop them. Will you help again?"

The young woman nodded and got to her feet.

"Shouldn't we just get the hell out?" Freeman whispered.

"Not yet," the warrior replied. "This is surprise night, and my guess is that the big shake-up should be due at any moment."

"Whatever you say, Mike. By the way, how did you get in here, anyway, with the twelve-foot fences, the guards and all that security on the gate?"

Bolan grinned. "In the trunk of your ministry Rover."

"But why didn't you tell me?"

"Our security. If you knew I was there, you might have been nervous, and however tough you are it might have showed. There's nothing as convincing in a sensitive situation as total ignorance."

Back at the far end of the unlit hallway they found the door behind the stage still ajar. On the other side of it Vanderlee was talking to Salter in a fierce whisper. "You've *got* to convince them. There's too much at stake to risk fouling it up now. The old fool has to see that film again, now, while he's still euphoric after the session back at the house. The police will have to wait. After all, they don't *know* Cleo's dead. And the longer we can stop them gossiping among themselves, the better it'll be."

"I don't know." Bolan could almost see the PR man's helpless shrug. "If it wasn't for that bloody girl! If only one knew—"

"You worry too much, Rick." Kleist suddenly spoke up. "The girl can't escape. Nor can her accomplice who killed Cleo. The guards have their orders, and the fence is already electrified. We'll track them down and deal with them later. Meanwhile, they're safe enough. They can't get out and blow the whistle on us.''

Salter sighed and turned back toward the bizarrely dressed crowd beyond the stage. Bolan watched through the crack.

''People, please,'' Salter called, clapping his hands and walking to the edge of the dais. ''Please resume your seats. You might think it awfully, well, callous, to go on with the show, so to speak, after such a spectacular collapse on the part of our star. But the doctors have been called, an ambulance is on the way, everything that can be done for Cleo is being done.''

He paused, eyeing his audience. ''As you know,'' he resumed, ''this is a very special night, a night of enormous significance to all of us, a night of positively gigantic import to one of us—the one to be chosen. And the spirits have been summoned. Will they understand if we abruptly close the contact? Would Cleo herself if she was conscious? Would she not rather urge us to continue, lest the spirits turn their backs and dismiss us as unworthy?''

Again he paused for effect. Some of the anonymous, bright figures were already sitting down. Others hesitated by their chairs. ''Now that we've gotten so far,'' Salter said in a voice vibrant with sincerity, ''let us complete our colloquy with those who have passed over. They are ready to speak. Let us listen and learn.''

Like the good PR man he was, he knew when he had them. Most of the audience was now sitting. He stopped talking, stepped off the stage and sat down himself in the front row, snapping his fingers at the back of the hall.

At once the lights dimmed and the beam from a projector shone out from a small gallery above the chairs. A rectangle of white appeared on the plain wall behind the altar. Vanderlee, with Kleist in his shiny plastic suit, stepped down and flanked Salter. There was a murmur of anticipation from the crowd.

"What you are going to see," Salter called out, "is a film shot at a private séance earlier this evening, a séance that shows without any possibility of doubt that we in this association have among us a genius of very high order, a being who can connect us psychically with no less a deity than Xangô himself!"

The projector whirred. Symbols and figures flashed backward across the rectangle on the wall. After a moment the screen went blank, then cleared to show the interior of a room—one of the Joliffe Hall bedrooms with three men and a woman sitting on easy chairs: Vanderlee, Kleist, Salter and Duhamel. Each held a glass of champagne, and all were laughing.

"What the devil . . . ?" the Dutchman shouted from the front row.

But his voice was drowned out by the voice of his screen self, spluttering over the laughter. "So tomorrow we drug Joliffe in the afternoon and prop him up for the shots where he's supposed to be in a trance . . ." Vanderlee choked, wiping his eyes with the back of one hand. "Then we doctor his aperitif before dinner— that, once he's out, is the time the film is *supposed* to be shot. Then we show the old fool the prepared footage of his so-called achievements just before we leave for the plant. Agreed?''

''I can hardly wait.'' Duhamel chuckled. ''But if only we could see the setup from behind! That shot where Rick's doubled up in the kneehole of the desk, shaking Simon from below... I nearly died laughing!''

''We've got to keep at it,'' Kleist said more seriously. ''He's got to hear dear Xangô telling him to part with the shares before the first. They say there's one born every minute. But Joliffe's gullibility is—''

''Please!'' the screen Salter urged. ''You're talking of the sucker I—''

The voice was in turn submerged by that of the real PR man. ''Turn that damn thing off!'' he yelled furiously. ''What the bloody hell's going on?''

And in the uproar that followed, as the figures on the screen shuddered and groaned to a standstill, a long, lean shape tore off its helmet and launched itself with a snarl of rage at Vanderlee. Sir Simon Joliffe was eager to lay hands on the leader of the men who would have tricked him.

In the gallery above the lecture hall, Jason Mettner smiled. Bolan's secrecy about his ''business'' within the mansion the previous night was now explained. Behind the scenes he must have switched reels on them and substituted a candid camera record he'd contrived in some way to shoot himself.

CHAPTER THIRTY-ONE

Mack Bolan charged into the lecture hall as the old man leaped from the ranks of "worshipers" in their plastic gear and sprang with a bellow of wrath at Vanderlee's throat. Freeman and the Brazilian girl followed.

Displaying an astonishing strength and agility for a man of his age, Joliffe already had the Dutchman on the floor and was windmilling at his face and chest with bony fists. A scarlet stream pumped from Vanderlee's nose.

The Executioner floored Kleist with a single powerful punch to the solar plexus that left the German doubled up and wheezing. He was looking for Lem Scarff, the tallest he reckoned of the spaceman figures milling among the overturned chairs. His Beretta was in his right hand. But even when he located the mercenaries' new leader among the blue, green and metallic silver unknowns, it was impossible to open fire. There were too many unidentifiable innocents who might get in the way.

"You take Salter," Freeman hissed to Emilia as they ran in. "I've an account of my own to settle." And as the Brazilian went for the PR man, she advanced on the shortest plastic pair in the audience, who she correctly

took for the two women who'd jumped her. The
women separated and Freeman took them one at a time
in a minor whirlwind of activity. Reaching for the first,
she seized the plastic helmet and swiveled it around so
that the visor slid to the back and the wearer was temporarily blinded. She whirled to launch a karate drop-
kick at the chin of the second, then turned back and
planted a fair left into the pit of the unsighted one's
belly. The woman folded forward with an unladylike
grunt and slumped to the floor.

Freeman glanced over her shoulder as she braced
herself to meet the attack of the other. Emilia Carvalho had Salter's arm pinned behind his back, and the
fingers of her other hand twisted into his hair. Joliffe
was still throttling Vanderlee, despite the combined
efforts of two burly men to drag him off.

But, of course, it was too good to last; the odds were
too heavy. Before Bolan could reach the mercenary
leader through the crowd, Scarff and a couple of
henchmen had backed most of the audience into a
corner to leave themselves a free field of fire. The warrior stared into the barrel of a Police Special as Scarff
growled behind his mask, "Okay, American, drop the
piece unless you want a hole in your head."

Freeman felt a hard muzzle jammed against her
spine as she sought for a dominating hold over her remaining prey, and a harsh voice grated, "Right, honey.
This is loaded and I know how to use it. Now back off
and up with the hands. *Move!*"

Warily she did as she was told. Half a dozen men
with guns, hard-eyed professionals who'd removed

their hoods, now had the whole room covered. Three more were marshaling the remains of the audience, twittering now with outrage and with fear, into a straight line. Kleist, choking, levered himself to his feet. Joliffe was bowed forward under a half nelson imposed by one of the beefier mercs. Vanderlee sat on the edge of the stage, mopping blood from his face. Bolan stood with his hands raised. He didn't look worried.

In the gallery outside the projection room Jason Mettner frowned. This wasn't quite the way it had been planned. He ducked behind the slatted rail. He had a gun—Bolan had given him the huge Desert Eagle this time—but what good would one be against a dozen pros, even if he could get a clear line on his targets?

On the floor below, Salter, in a towering rage, strode up to Freeman. "You fucking cow! You and that son of a bitch over there, Cahill, Mettner, Belasko, whatever he calls himself. Do you realize what you've done? Do you know how many months' work you just loused up, what goddamn plans you ruined for bloody ever?" He rounded on the Executioner. "How *dare* you stand there, the two of you, with your superior fucking expressions, after what you've done!"

He took a small automatic from his pocket, reversing the gun so that he held it by the barrel. "Well," he stormed, "we'll see how a touch of pistol-whipping will improve the expression on *her* face for starters." For the second time he seized Freeman by the hair to wrench back her head. He raised the weapon high in the air.

The shot came from behind the altar, a sharp crack that overlay the screech of a ricochet off the gun butt. Salter howled in pain as he snatched away his smarting fingers. The automatic spun away and clattered to the floor. The man who'd shot it out of his grasp shouldered his way past the entrance doors with a dozen Special Branch men in tow. It was Colonel Williams, and only half a minute late.

Once more there was confusion in the lecture hall.

Freeman brought up her knee before Salter had time to recover, grabbed Sir Simon Joliffe, pushed him down behind the chest and drew Emilia Carvalho behind the upset medium's table.

The Special Branch men were armed. "Very well," Williams barked. "I've got my eye in, as you see. Anyone else who wants to try does so at his own risk. Any takers?"

But as far as a shooting war was concerned, it was already a stalemate.

Vanderlee's professionals weren't so easily beaten. Dodging in among the audience they'd been strong-arming, they sidled toward the doors, keeping the police marksmen covered as they moved, shielding themselves with the hostages.

The Dutchman himself was with them, still massaging his neck, but Salter had collapsed to the floor, where he lay holding himself and moaning.

"What I thought," Williams said. "We'll just have to buck up, go in and get 'em. If nobody dare shoot, it's hand-to-hand stuff, and that's bloody well it."

In a phalanx the police moved out of the lecture hall and into the display section beyond. The mercenaries and their shields were no more than thirty feet away, moving toward a stairway at the far end of the exhibition. "Choose your man," the colonel ordered, "and try to avoid damaging the hostages. But if you have to, what the hell? The more fool they, allowing themselves to be fooled by this bullshit."

The Special Branch men fanned out purposefully.

Bolan was the first to wade in.

By the time Mettner had quit the projection room, run to the elevator bank and dashed out on the floor below, the fight was raging, leaving disaster in its wake. Struggling men, together with members of the audience attempting to get away, surged into the exhibition stands, knocking down stacks of chairs, tangling themselves in plastic hosing.

The Executioner saw the Brazilian girl trying to escape from two muscular hardguys on the far side of a car accessory stand. He wrenched open the door of a fiberglass convertible body, slid across the front seats, shoved open the other door and launched himself feetfirst at the attackers.

Williams, backing away from Vanderlee, who was clubbing him viciously with a gun butt, tripped over an outstretched leg and fell into the melee. The Dutchman, finding himself with room to spare, leaped away with a snarl and reversed the gun. Robbed at the last moment of his booty, there was murder in the man's eyes. Williams had fallen apart from the fighting group and was scrambling to his feet at the edge of the stand. He was a sitting duck. Vanderlee raised the gun.

Bolan, chopping one of the hardguys into unconsciousness, saw the danger just in time. Above him was a set of mannequins in waterproof sport clothes. Seizing the leg of a skier, he toppled the dummy over, knocking Vanderlee off balance. At the same time he reached up and swept aside the man's gun arm. Three shots plowed into the ceiling before Bolan, from his position on the floor, angled the Beretta upward and blasted a single 9 mm messenger of death into the Dutchman's chest at point-blank range.

The 158-grain hollowpoint smashed through the man's sternum, ripping apart bone, muscle and cartilage, severed the lower part of the windpipe and punched an exit wound at the base of his neck. Vanderlee was dead before he hit the floor.

The Executioner leaped up onto the blood-sprayed stand and from behind another mannequin pumped two triple bursts toward the doors of the lecture hall. Kleist, stripped now of his decontamination gear, was standing there with a MAC-10 held at waist level. There was a malevolent expression on his face, and he swayed crazily from side to side, hosing indiscriminate death into the exhibition center. A Special Branch man fell; another tripped as the heel of his boot was shot away; one of the mercenaries collapsed, cursing as he clutched a shattered leg. Bolan was unhurt, though several mannequins were riddled.

The warrior's first two bursts flew wide and high. Door panels splintered, plaster dust blossomed from the wall, jagged shards of glass shivered to the floor. Bolan's seventh shot, a single, scored.

The malevolent expression disappeared, along with the left side of Kleist's face, in a cloud of blood and bone.

A thunderous report from behind the convertible marked Mettner's entry into the fray. A plastified merc who'd been lining up a subgun on Williams was hurled backward against a ten-foot pyramid of tableware, which flew apart and rained pieces all around the body.

Police and mercenaries had been trading fire, too, on the far side of the huge exhibition hall, but now there was a temporary lull. Most of the mercenaries had been herded into a corner and were held there at gunpoint. The occult devotees were bunched at the head of the stairs, scared and wondering what hit them.

Bolan caught the agonized expression on Williams's face. "It's not your fault," he soothed, gesturing at the bodies of Kleist and Vanderlee. "They'd have killed a lot of people here. You'd never have gotten enough evidence to bring them to trial, anyway."

Williams turned to reply, then suddenly yelled, "Felicity! Watch out!"

The whole group swung around to follow his frenzied gaze. Above the doors to the lecture hall there was an observation window that must have been in the rear wall of the projection room. Framed in it were the head and shoulders of Rick Salter, his face contorted with rage. He was holding a sporting rifle, and the barrel was aimed straight at Freeman, who was standing a little apart.

A moment of frozen horror. Bolan had taken the magazine from his Beretta. Williams's gun was out of sight.

They saw a puff of smoke bloom from the muzzle of the rifle and heard the sharp crack of the shot.

Emilia Carvalho had taken in the significance of the scene, made a decision and acted on it before the others could so much as draw a breath. Launching herself across the intervening space as the rifle fired, she took the bullet intended for Felicity Freeman full in the chest and dropped lifeless at her feet.

Freeman's cry of distress was overlaid by the rattle of a bolt from above. The hate-crazed PR man was going to fire again.

Bolan was already racing for the double doors. His tactics were based on the assumption that Salter's sporting rifle would fire only two shots. Fifteen feet from the doors he halted and his hand snaked down to his right ankle. The rifle barrel vectored down to cover him.

Salter fired as the Executioner's hand flashed out and up. The warrior had pivoted as he flung the knife, and the bullet whistled past his head. The razor-sharp blade struck Salter's left arm as his hand supported the gun barrel, piercing the sleeve and slicing through the muscles of the forearm. He uttered a shrill scream of pain and rage, dropping the weapon onto the floor below. His head and shoulders disappeared from view.

Bolan ran for the stairs.

The exit from the projection room was halfway to the elevator on the main corridor. From it a trail of blood led to a narrower corridor that forked off at right angles. Bolan had slipped a fresh clip into the Beretta as he ran. With the autoloader in a two-handed combat grip he sidled to the end of the hall. Ten yards before it the bloodstains ceased. There was a door on both sides of the corridor and one at the end. Had the wounded man stanched the flow and carried on—or had he skipped into one of the side rooms?

Bolan tried the right-hand door, which opened onto an office. By the light streaming in from the corridor, he saw steel filing cabinets, desks equipped with word processors, a wall chart. The room opposite was for someone higher up on the corporate ladder—wall-to-wall carpet, a mahogany rolltop desk and a glass-topped occasional table bearing a drinks tray. And a small private stairway that spiraled to the floor above.

The warrior switched on his penlight. Beyond a leather armchair a single star-shaped splotch of red gleamed on the lowest step. He crept up into the darkness above.

The stairs led to another office, austerely modern with glass walls and modular furniture. This was the lower of the two research floors; the thin flashlight beam picked out long workbenches loaded with electronic equipment on the far side of the glass. Bolan could see a ruby laser set up, an experimental production chain transporting printed circuits. The office, he found, was part of a suite, three rooms in all. But none of them had a door opening onto the research laboratory. He frowned. The suite had to be a sort of observation post for the department head with the comfortable office below, perhaps a Ministry of Defense chief or someone connected with NATO. It would be blocked off to prevent unauthorized entry to the research floors via the spiral staircase.

So where had the fugitive PR man gone?

The warrior had noticed random blood spots on the floor, but they pointed in no particular direction. Salter must have bound the wound with something.

For personal reasons as well as the completion of his mission, Bolan was determined to get him. Salter was, in any case, too dangerous to leave at large in his present crazed mood.

In the dark he stood with every sense alert, straining to register the slightest sound, sight, smell. No light penetrated the laboratory from the sixth-floor landings, and illumination from the lamps outside the administration building far below only faintly paled the rectangles of the windows. Rain was beating heavily against the glass.

Bolan tensed. Over that steady drumming, someplace off to his right, he heard a small scraping sound. A current of moist air fanned his cheek. The noise was repeated. Something bumped softly and there was a tiny click of metal.

An open window? At this height? On a sheer-faced concrete tower with no ledges and no ornamentation?

Then he remembered the twin tower, the uncompleted second wing attached to the main building. There were no floors in place, but there was scaffolding and painters' hoists. A determined person could reach the ground that way, even on a dark, wet night.

Moving cautiously, the Executioner tracked the current of air. It came from a stationery storeroom that led off the last office at the corner of the building. The window was an aluminum-framed single pane pivoted at its center. Below it four H-section stress girders stretched across to the great bird cage of the unfinished tower.

Bolan cursed under his breath. He'd given the storeroom no more than a quick flash of the penlight when he first cased the suite. Salter must have been hiding among the cartons of supplies, waiting for a chance to use that window.

There was no sign of him on any of the girders, but it was tough identifying anything with the summer rain driving into his face. With all the personnel below in Salter's pay and no way of alerting Williams and his men, there was only one thing for the warrior to do. He swung a leg over the sill and lowered himself cautiously to the cold, wet steel of the girder.

The girder was perhaps fifty feet long, and he was a little over halfway across when the first shot rang out. He saw a bright orange flash in among the network of metal ahead, and a slug spanged off into space from the girder on his right.

Instinctively Bolan had ducked, flattening himself against the slippery steel as he continued to inch forward. Salter had dropped his rifle onto the floor of the projection room, and as far as the warrior knew, he had no handgun. If he had, he'd surely have stayed put and attempted to ambush Bolan back in the observation suite.

There remained, however, the elusive and sinister Lem Scarff.

Bolan suddenly recalled that he'd seen no tall, lean figure among the mercs rounded up by Williams's men. Had Scarff gotten out while the going was good and beaten the wounded PR man to the comparative safety of the new tower? Had they a contingency plan to meet there, where the killer's experience would help Salter escape?

That was the way it looked. But although Scarff would be able to see there was someone on the way over, he certainly couldn't see who, or precisely where. Not in the dark and in this weather. And the more he fired blind, the better. The gun belched flame again. Two more misses.

Abruptly the darkness thinned. The whole of the sixth floor behind the Executioner blazed with light. The rest of the pursuit was catching up.

It made Bolan a sitting duck, for now he'd be silhouetted against the bright rectangles of the windows. Immobilized in midair, he wouldn't have a dog's chance.

There was immediate confirmation of that. The unseen pistol ahead cracked for the fourth time, and Bolan felt the caress of the bullet as it dug a shallow furrow into his thigh.

He took the only option open to him. Swinging over the edge of the metal beam, he lowered himself to the full stretch of his arms and continued his perilous trip to the skeleton tower hand over hand. This way he could ring up no sale as a target, since he'd largely be hidden by the girder itself.

But the trip now was far more hazardous, and all Scarff had to do was wait, gun in hand, at the far end.

The wind, plucking at the cold weight of Bolan's soaked clothes, buffeted him from side to side like a pendulum. Rain ran down his neck and inside his shirt, flooding his eyes and ears. And his fingers, on which the entire muscle-tearing weight of his body depended, kept slipping on the slimy surface of the steel beam.

The beam was vibrating, a faint trembling transmitted through the tips of those fingers. Someone was walking out along the slippery steel surface. All that person had to do was to stamp on Bolan's fingers. Nobody alive could keep his grip if enough pressure and pain were applied.

Lem Scarff's voice hissed out of the darkness ahead. "Take it easy, Rick. Don't look down. Just locate the bastard's fingers and put in the boot. And if that doesn't work, smash the knuckles with your bloody hammer."

Seconds later a foot crushed heavily down on the warrior's knuckles.

"All right, you son of a bitch," Salter's malevolent voice taunted somewhere above him. "This is where you take the long drop. Goodbye, Mr. Belasko!" His foot started grinding the knuckles, mashing Bolan's hand into the steel.

Deliberately letting go again with his left hand was one of the most difficult things the Executioner did in

his life. But it was the only way to stay alive. He groped
left-handed for the butt of the Beretta, eased it from
the rig, pointed the gun upward and squeezed the trigger.

The pain in his fingers, shrieking now the length of
his arm, was so excruciating that he didn't register the
recoil which, in his precarious position, risked dislodging the remaining hand and plunging him into
oblivion. More by instinct than conscious decision, he
dropped the gun into his jacket pocket and returned his
left hand to the beam.

Hot blood spurted down over his upturned face. The
9 mm slug had penetrated the lower half of Salter's
body between the thighs, furrowed upward through the
liver, pancreas and lung and finally come to rest against
his collarbone. Salter jerked backward, was catapulted against the neighboring girder and dropped
soundlessly from sight.

Bolan continued his deadly journey, knowing that
somewhere ahead Lem Scarff would be crouched
among the ironwork, waiting for his chance to get off
a shot. The warrior came across a painter's cradle
hanging where the girder was riveted to the building's
frame. He reached for the drag rope that would raise
or lower the hoist.

The beam was shaking again. Bolan looked up and
back. Williams was edging along the foot-wide steel
pathway, followed by three Special Branch men with
drawn guns. Scarff was now somewhere on the stage
below—he could hear the guy's shoes scrape on the

metal ties. The warrior began paying out the drag rope to lower the cradle to that level.

The rough wooden contraption bumped against the new tower's outer framework as it made the fifth-floor level. Bolan heard a stifled exclamation in among the trusses that formed the core of the building. Diffused light revealed the killer's tall, pale-haired shape moving out from behind one of the main girders, and reflected off the wet barrel of a large-bore revolver as it was raised.

Crouched in the cradle, Bolan shifted his weight fast from one foot to the other, rocking the hoist from side to side in an attempt to make a tougher target against the lightened windows behind. The gun barrel followed the pendulum movement, swaying slowly like the head of a cobra about to strike.

Once, twice, the revolver spit flame, and Bolan saw, printed fleetingly against the dark by the muzzle-flashes, the intent and murderous expression twisting Scarff's face.

A bullet plucked at his sodden sleeve. The cradle dropped a sickening inch as the second nicked several strands from a supporting rope. Bolan held his own fire. The man had fired six shots now. If the gun was the Colt Python he'd used in the lecture hall, he'd now have to reload. This would give each man an even chance, since there were six shots left in the Beretta's 15-round magazine. It would also allow the Executioner time to make it from the cradle to the tower framework. More strands had already snapped under his weight. As he pushed off from the planks flooring the hoist and leaped to the nearest girder, the rope parted and one end of the cradle fell away.

Bolan dropped to his hands and knees and crawled along a wide girder. Scarff, with the pistol reloaded, appeared from behind a vertical stay in the center of the tower on a beam at right angles to Bolan's. He moved out two steps and blasted a single shot at the warrior. It was uncomfortably close, the slug flattening itself against the H-section only inches in front of him. Bolan's return shot flew wide.

Scarff drew back out of sight . . . to reappear almost at once on the far side of the vertical. He fired again, and if Bolan hadn't flattened himself, the slug would have creased him. By the time he choked out another round from the Beretta, Scarff had ducked once more out of his field of fire.

Bolan stood, moving away diagonally along a narrower beam. He dodged behind a steel pillar as the killer saw him and got off two .357-caliber skullbusters. The pillar boomed hollowly as one splatted against the curved metal; the other glanced off and ricocheted away with a shrill whine.

For a moment Bolan remained still and silent, hoping his enemy might emerge to check whether he had scored. Scarff did show, but not where the Executioner expected. He was between forty and fifty feet away. He shot once, striking sparks from the steel an inch above Bolan's head. The warrior's two-shot reply was dead accurate, but the target was fast; he'd moved one millisecond earlier.

There was one shell left in the Python's cylinder, two in the Beretta's clip. How long did it take to grab a fistful from a pocket, spill out a cylinder and feed in six? Ten seconds? Fifteen? Twenty?

It had to be long enough to allow the warrior to get within hand-to-hand combat range, because he had no spare clip with him. Put another way, it meant Bolan must be within ten seconds of his quarry before Scarff reloaded. Okay, he'd offer himself as a decoy in the hope of drawing the killer's fire. He stepped out along a girder and sacrificed a round, blasting one in Scarff's general direction.

Scarff didn't shoot.

On the stage above, Williams was shouting. A powerful flashlight beam lanced down between the trusses, carving up the night, speeding shadows, and revealing why the hit man hadn't returned Bolan's fire. He was already reloading, slamming five fresh shells into the Colt.

Bolan swore. He had only a single shot left, and at this distance nothing was certain. Against all odds and praying the flashlight would stay switched on, he ran out along the girder toward his adversary.

Crouched in a spiderweb of steel ties, Scarff was startled out of his normal cool. He half rose to his feet with the gun only partly loaded, overbalanced as one foot slipped, and fell.

He landed on his back on a ten-foot square of temporary flooring, laid across two beams on the story below. The pistol spun out of his grasp and came to rest on the far side of the planking.

Bolan was running fast now, almost in position above the square. "All right, you bastard," Scarff snarled up at him. "Come on down. Take a step nearer the hell where I'm sending you! I'm gonna break your neck, goddamn you, and throw the pieces into the—"

The Executioner leaped before Scarff could make it to the gun, crashing into the man and knocking him flat once more. The Beretta was in his right hand.

The two big men engaged at once in a desperate free-for-all as they fought for a nerve hold, a lock, the space to throw a punch. The Beretta was more a hindrance than a help—it left only one hand free to fight.

A viselike grip closed over the warrior's right wrist, steely fingers forcing the arm up over his head. As Bolan thrashed and heaved, seeking an out, the fingers crushed his hand into a fist, compressing the index over the trigger. The gun fired.

The warrior's last shot blasted skyward.

Suddenly Scarff broke free, scrambled to the edge of the platform and picked up the gun. He stood, snapped shut the cylinder and lined up the barrel eight feet from the Executioner's chest. "My pleasure, you bastard," he spit. "I hope you roast in hell."

Bolan threw the empty Beretta at him. It struck the guy in the crotch, not hard enough to hurt bad, but enough to jerk him involuntarily forward in an instinctive move to protect himself. At the same time a fierce gust of wind buffeted the gaunt structure of the

unfinished building and hurled a scatter of heavy rain-
drops into his face.

The two things together took the killer by surprise in
the moment before pressing the trigger. Maybe he
hadn't realized how near the edge he was.

Scarff uttered a hoarse curse, teetered for an instant
off balance and took one step back. He flung his arms
wide in a desperate effort to recover his balance; the
gun fell away to clatter interminably down among the
steel ties of the scaffold. For a timeless moment he
hung suspended on the edge, then, like a diver in slow
motion, he fell backward and sailed down into the dark
with a wavering cry.

"JOLIFFE'S BEING entirely cooperative," Williams told
the Executioner. "You often find that with the obsti-
nate ones, the ones who won't be told. Let them find
out on their own, and there's nothing they won't do to
even the score."

"Well, yeah, that's why we played it this way," Bolan said.

"Which means, in more specific terms?" Mettner
asked.

"Joliffe has agreed to a protocol—the defense ministry is working on the exact terms right now—provid-
ing in effect that no shares owned by the family may in
future be sold without prior approval by the authorities."

"The guys flying the B-2 will be happy to hear that,"
Bolan said. "They wouldn't be happy if they came

across their own mirror image with red stars on the wings while they were on patrol.''

Mettner grinned. "Hell hath no fury like a sucker scorned.''

Go for a hair-raising ride in

JAMES AXLER

DEATH LANDS

Dark Carnival

Trapped in an evil baron's playground, the rides are downhill and dangerous for Ryan Cawdor and his roving band of warrior-survivalists.

For one brief moment after their narrow escape, Ryan thinks they have found the peace and idyll they so desperately seek. But a dying messenger delivers a dark message....

Available in January at your favorite retail outlet, or order your copy now by sending your name, address, zip or postal code along with a check or money order for $4.99 plus 75¢ postage and handling ($1.00 in Canada), payable to Gold Eagle Books to:

In the U.S.

Gold Eagle Books
3010 Walden Avenue
P.O. Box 1325
Buffalo, NY 14269-1325

In Canada

Gold Eagle Books
P.O. Box 609
Fort Erie, Ontario
L2A 5X3

GOLD EAGLE

Please specify book title with your order.
Canadian residents add applicable federal and provincial taxes.

DL14R

The Guardian Strikes

David North

A cloud of deadly gas is about to settle, and then a madman's dreams for a perfect society will be fulfilled. Behind it all is a sinister being searching for life-giving energy. He is the last of an ancient godlike race called the Guardians, and his survival hinges on the annihilation of the Earth's population.

Standing between him and survival are two men—the former CIA counterinsurgency specialist and the swordsman from the mists of time. Once again they join forces across time to defeat the savage being determined to destroy both their worlds.

Look for THE GUARDIAN STRIKES, Book 3 of the Gold Eagle miniseries TIME WARRIORS.

Available in December at your favorite retail outlet, or order your copy now by sending your name, address, zip or postal code, along with a check or money order for $3.50 plus 75¢ postage and handling ($1.00 in Canada), payable to Gold Eagle Books to:

In the U.S.

Gold Eagle Books
3010 Walden Avenue
P.O. Box 1325
Buffalo, NY 14269-1325

In Canada

Gold Eagle Books
P.O. Box 609
Fort Erie, Ontario
L2A 5X3

Please specify book title with your order.
Canadian residents add applicable federal and provincial taxes.

TW3R

TAKE 'EM FREE
4 action-packed novels plus a mystery bonus

NO RISK
NO OBLIGATION TO BUY

SPECIAL LIMITED-TIME OFFER

Mail to: Gold Eagle Reader Service
3010 Walden Ave.,
P.O. Box 1394
Buffalo, NY 14240-1394

YEAH! Rush me 4 FREE Gold Eagle novels and my FREE mystery gift. Then send me 4 brand-new novels every other month as they come off the presses. Bill me at the low price of just $12.80* for each shipment—a saving of 15% off the suggested retail price! There is NO extra charge for postage and handling! There is no minimum number of books I must buy. I can always cancel at anytime simply by returning a shipment at your cost or by returning any shipping statement marked "cancel." Even if I never buy another book from Gold Eagle, the 4 free books and surprise gift are mine to keep forever.

164 BPM BP91

Name _____ (PLEASE PRINT)

Address _____ Apt. No. _____

City _____ State _____ Zip _____

Signature (if under 18, parent or guardian must sign)

*Terms and prices subject to change without notice. Sales tax applicable in NY. This offer is limited to one order per household and not valid to present subscribers. Offer not available in Canada.

© 1991 GOLD EAGLE   TE-A2DR

The Hatchet Force—out to strike the killing blow against a deadly enemy—the NVA.

HATCHET
BLACK MISSION

Knox Gordon

Far from the highly publicized helicopter war televised on the evening news rages the secret war. Fought in neutral Laos and Cambodia, these clandestine "black" missions are carried out by the men of the Special Forces: an elite action group specializing in guerrilla warfare tactics, ready to deploy at a moment's notice.

In the air and on the ground, behind the desks and in the jungles... the action-packed series of the Vietnam War.

Available in February at your favorite retail outlet, or order your copy now by sending your name, address, zip or postal code, along with a check or money order for $3.50 plus 75¢ postage and handling ($1.00 in Canada), payable to Gold Eagle Books to:

In the U.S.	In Canada
Gold Eagle Books	Gold Eagle Books
3010 Walden Avenue	P.O. Box 609
P.O. Box 1325	Fort Erie, Ontario
Buffalo, NY 14269-1325	L2A 5X3

Please specify book title with your order.
Canadian residents add applicable federal and provincial taxes.

GOLD EAGLE®

HAT2